MW00861150

WHERE IS ANYBODY?

Also by Simon R. Green

The Gideon Sable series

THE BEST THING YOU CAN STEAL *
A MATTER OF DEATH AND LIFE *
WHAT SONG THE SIRENS SANG *
NOT OF THIS WORLD *

The Holy Terror mysteries

THE HOLY TERROR

The Ishmael Jones mysteries

THE DARK SIDE OF THE ROAD
DEAD MAN WALKING
VERY IMPORTANT CORPSES
DEATH SHALL COME
INTO THE THINNEST OF AIR
MURDER IN THE DARK *
TILL SUDDEN DEATH DO US PART *
NIGHT TRAIN TO MURDER *
THE HOUSE ON WIDOWS HILL *
BURIED MEMORIES *
HAUNTED BY THE PAST

The Secret History series

PROPERTY OF A LADY FAIRE
FROM A DROOD TO A KILL
DR DOA
MOONBREAKER
NIGHT FALL

The Nightside series

JUST ANOTHER JUDGEMENT DAY
THE GOOD, THE BAD, AND THE UNCANNY
A HARD DAY'S KNIGHT
THE BRIDE WORE BLACK LEATHER

* *available from Severn House*

WHERE IS ANYBODY?

Simon R. Green

**SEVERN
HOUSE**

First world edition published in Great Britain and the USA in 2024
by Severn House, an imprint of Canongate Books Ltd,
14 High Street, Edinburgh EH1 1TE.

severnhouse.com

British Library Cataloguing-in-Publication Data
A CIP catalogue record for this title is available from the British Library.

ISBN-13: 978-1-4483-1165-1 (cased)
ISBN-13: 978-1-4483-1166-8 (e-book)

All Severn House titles are printed on acid-free paper.

Typeset by Palimpsest Book Production Ltd.,
Falkirk, Stirlingshire, Scotland.
Printed and bound in Great Britain by
TJ Books, Padstow, Cornwall.

Praise for the Gideon Sable novels

About the author

Simon R. Green was born in Bradford-on-Avon, Wiltshire, where he still lives. He is the *New York Times* bestselling author of more than seventy science fiction and fantasy novels, including the Nightside, Secret Histories and Ghost Finders series, the Ishmael Jones mysteries, the Gideon Sable novels and the brand-new Holy Terrors mysteries.

www.simonrgreen.co.uk

The crew is family.

After that old gang of mine split up. After the Damned, Switch It Sally and the werewolf Polly Perkins all went their separate ways. After I officially retired from the crime and caper game, and joined my partner, Annie Anybody, in just running a very special shop that bought and sold very rare items . . . I still couldn't resist going out in the night to steal things. Now and again. For old times' sake.

My name is Gideon Sable, these days. The legendary master thief, who specializes in stealing the kind of thing that can't usually be stolen – like a ghost's clothes, or a celebrity's charisma. I was never the original Gideon; he disappeared, so I stepped in and stole his identity. As far as the rest of the world is concerned, I have always been Gideon Sable. I made it my mission to steal from people who deserved to be punished – for justice, or revenge, or a chance to make myself exceedingly rich. I don't have a crew to back me up any more, but still I sneak out on my own. For the thrill of the game and the joy of the con, and because stealing things no one else can is what I live for.

ONE

Phone a Friend

It all started with Annie Anybody.

We were working late in the shop. Just checking what was on the shelves and writing it down on clipboards. Because computer inventories tend to have nervous breakdowns when faced with the kind of things we offer. Stocktaking is one of those dreary but necessary tasks that have to be done to keep a shop running. Of course, it would probably help if the stock stayed where we put it, but it had never been that kind of shop.

'OK, that's it,' I said finally. 'I am ready to throw stock out the front door, rather than count it.'

Annie sighed and shook her head. She was wearing a white T-shirt over blue jeans, no makeup, and her blonde hair was a buzzcut. Her way of saying she was just being Annie and not any of the other personas in her head.

'There's still a lot to do, Gideon.'

'It can wait,' I said, tossing my clipboard over one shoulder.

'Are you in a hurry to be somewhere?' said Annie.

'No,' I said.

She shrugged. 'I have to check the secure rooms out back, and then I'll call it a night too.'

I nodded. We inherited the very private rooms from Old Harry when we took over the shop. Rooms with such powerful shields that not even Heaven and Hell could overhear what was said in them.

'I have to pop out for a while before I go home,' I said casually. 'I think I know where I can pick up some more of those long-distance scrying glasses.'

She gave me a hard look. 'You paid far too much for that last set.'

'They're worth every penny when it comes to spying on people from a distance.'

'If you're a voyeur,' said Annie.

'Well,' I said, 'that goes without saying.'

Annie stretched languorously and then looked round the shop, with its shelves and display cases packed full of weird and wonderful items. The lucky yeti's foot, photos of cities that never existed and two feathers from the phoenix's wing, forever burning in their fireproof container. Annie smiled reflectively.

'We've come a long way, haven't we?'

I had to smile too. 'Ever since I stole that pookah's paw from that bad guy businessman, Sir Norman Powell, and set us on the road to who and what we are.'

'Do you ever regret any of it?' said Annie.

'No,' I said, just a little surprised. 'Do you?'

'No,' she said.

I watched her disappear into the forest of standing shelves that seemed to fall away forever. The moment she was out of sight, I got ready to leave the shop. I checked my pockets, to make sure I had all the necessary tools of my trade, and then paused, to see how I looked in the tall standing mirror that rolled obligingly forward out of the shadows. I was dressed in my usual black and white, because style is something other people do, and because it helps me to not stand out in a crowd. And I have to say, despite all the stresses and strains of my time in the thieving game, I remained in reasonably good shape and handsome enough to run most cons. I nodded approvingly at my reflection, but it just folded its arms and scowled at me disapprovingly. I sighed quietly.

'Sidney . . . Please don't mess with my image.'

'You're going out again,' the mirror said accusingly. 'On your own. Without Annie. I can't keep telling her you're working on the accounts.'

'You don't have to tell her anything.'

'I'm no good at dissembling!' Sidney said loudly. 'I go into full panic mode if she gives me a hard look. Oh, go on then. Never mind that I'll be stuck here on my own, worrying my heart out. Don't stay out too late, and don't be afraid to call for help if you need it!'

'I do not need another mother,' I said sternly.

Sidney sniffed. 'You need something.'

I took one last quick look around the shop before I left, to make sure the more lively items were behaving themselves and wouldn't pose a problem while I was out. A long line of wee-winged fairies plugged into light sockets glowed brightly as they sang a merry tune in their high-pitched voices. They seemed cheerful enough, for current junkies. Two small clockwork Battling Demons™ were sitting on the countertop, sipping cups of steaming brimstone as they swapped gossip over who was doing who in infernal circles. And the nineteenth-century chess-playing automaton sat quietly in its corner, playing patience with a pack of Tarot cards and cheating itself into an existential crisis.

I slipped on my special sunglasses that allowed me to see hidden things, so I could check my defences and protections. I smiled approvingly at the concealed man-traps that could hold anything they gripped until time ran out, and the unseen hanging chains with their vicious hooks that could rip the soul right out of an intruder and imprison it in an astral cage until I felt like doing something about it. No one steals from me and gets away with it, if only because that would be just too damned ironic. I nodded to the stuffed grizzly bear by the front door.

'Watch the ranch while I'm gone, Yogi.'

The bear growled an acknowledgement.

I stepped out of the shop and into the street, where faded amber streetlights laboured to produce islands of illumination in the curling mists. I closed and locked the front door, and breathed deeply of the misty morning air. It was still some hours short of dawn, but the night seemed full of anticipation and promise, for those ready to grab an opportunity with both hands and make it their own. I looked carefully up and down the street, but no one was out and about. I straightened my back and strode off into the night, my fingertips tingling at the thought of getting hold of someone else's valuables and making them my own. Someone who deserved it, of course. Every crime has a victim, so I always make sure that whoever I go after has done something really bad and deserves everything I do to them.

It wasn't far to my destination, because nothing is ever far in

the warren of winding streets that make up the dark heart of Old
Soho. The world beneath the world, the underworld of crime,
where it's always wolf eat wolf, and the devil take the unprepared.

One of the side benefits of running a shop like mine is that
when people venture in to buy, they often can't resist the opportunity to gossip. All the latest speculation on who's making a
name for themselves on the scene, who's reappeared after being
gone for years and who's offering the kind of things some people
would sell their soul, or someone else's, to get their hands on.
So when a regular customer leaned in close and lowered his
voice, eager to spill the beans about the latest exhibition at the
Babel Project, I paid attention.

The Babel Project was part museum, part celebration, and one
of the most acclaimed collections of communication technology
in the hidden world. Every kind of telephone, radio and two tin
cans connected by superstrings that you can think of. And people
have come up with some very strange ideas when it comes to
passing the word over a distance. The owner and manager of the
Babel Project liked to boast that if you didn't see it in his collection, it must be an urban legend.

Entrance to each new exhibition was strictly by invitation only.
In fact, you couldn't even find where it was located without the
proper invitation card to open your eyes to its presence.
Fortunately, I had such a card, and for once I didn't have to steal
it. I swapped it for something my regular customer wanted even
more: an extremely rare edition of *Alice's Adventures Underground*
by Lewis Carroll. The only version with an answer to that most
famous of unanswered riddles: Why is a raven like a writing
desk?

Having read the answer, I was pretty sure the book was a fake
and a forgery. But the new owner seemed perfectly satisfied, and
I became the proud possessor of an invitation card to the Babel
Project's latest exhibition. And that was where I was headed,
with larceny and retribution in mind. I swaggered through the
narrow streets, radiating confidence and potential violence in
equal measures. You have to walk like a predator if you don't
want to be prey. At this ungodly hour of the morning, in the
shadow-wreathed streets of Old Soho, the night people come out
to play, and they take pride in never playing nicely.

The old dark magic still lingered in Old Soho: danger and temptation, charm and sin . . . All of it available at knock-down prices if you knew where to look. And if you didn't, there was always some helpful soul ready to step out of an alleyway and steer you in the right direction. For a percentage. There's always plenty of trouble to get into, in the narrow streets of Old Soho.

As I neared the corrupt heart of the ancient maze, the pavements became increasingly crowded with familiar faces. Harlequins and Columbines, with blood dripping from their pointed teeth; chancers and good-time girls making the scene, flashing their confident grins so no one would notice what big teeth they had; and bright-eyed twilight souls moving endlessly from one party to the next. Dancing on bleeding feet, smiling till it hurt, for fear that if they stopped, they'd never be able to start again. It's not easy being a free-spirited fun-seeker in Old Soho.

An aristocratic vampire lady wrapped in black leathers, dangling chains and a studded choker led a well-respected businessman along on a leash. A gaggle of ghosts drifted in and out of each other as they celebrated their death days with memories of old wine from empty bottles. And all kinds of musicians, singers and strippers hurried from one ill-paid engagement to the next, making the night last as long as they could so they could squeeze one last chance of employment out of it.

That's life in Old Soho. Where magic is real, if a little shop-soiled, and the sinning is easy.

I finally arrived at a narrow side street standing just off the main drag, tucked away from casual view. My sunglasses dipped my gaze below the surface of the world to reveal that the devil's carnival of dubious attractions and members-only night clubs were, in fact, protected by all manner of pitfalls for the unwary, shining brightly on the night like a technicolour assault course. I could also make out a few fading spirits of the recently deceased, moaning plaintively as they tried to figure out what hit them.

Monsters disguised as victims waited patiently for someone dumb enough to try to take advantage of them. Giggling fiends lurked in alley mouths, looking for really rough trade. And over-sized night-club bouncers waited hopefully for someone to start something. A raucous crowd of succubi hung around the entrance to a gentleman's establishment, giving the unholy come-on to punters with more money than sense. If they could see the ladies of the early morning the way I did, those punters would run a mile. Lust demons may be aristocracy in Hell, but beneath their practised glamours lay a terrible truth.

At first glance, the Babel Project could have passed for just another storefront, with its peeling paint and shabby woodwork, lurking in plain sight like a predator in the tall grass. Behind the smeared and fly-specked glass of the only window stood a large framed photograph of an old-time two-part telephone. Not much to look at, unless you knew what it was. My fingertips tingled so hard they ached, as I studied the infamous Dead Line. Because I know all there is to know about things worth stealing.

While Alexander Graham Bell was responsible for the first working telephone, he wasn't that interested in creating a form of mass communication. Like many of his generation, Bell was obsessed with finding a way to make contact with the afterlife. He wanted a telephone that would let him talk to the dead. The result was the Dead Line.

Bell only made one call on his new telephone. He never told anyone what he heard, but in every photo of the man in later life, everyone remarked how his eyes looked lost and haunted. Perhaps because he knew what was waiting for him. Putting a photo of the Dead Line in the window was like dropping bloody bait into the water to attract sharks. A promise of wonders and marvels, and all the colours of darkness.

The Babel Project wouldn't be opening its doors for several hours yet. The owner and manager, Mister Particular – so called because he was very particular about the kind of people he did business with – was out of town. Rumour had it that the infamous Tiresias telephone had finally surfaced, after decades of being little more than a rumour. A telephone that could let you talk to the love of your life you haven't met yet.

So I had a brief opportunity to get in and out of the Babel Project without being spotted. And do the dirty on Mister Particular, who'd been known to order the deaths of people who wouldn't sell him what he wanted. I was really looking forward to hitting him where it would hurt the most: by stealing one of his most prized exhibits. I headed for the front door, with avarice burning brightly in my heart.

The Babel Project's hidden protections were nothing out of the ordinary. A concealed trapdoor in front of the door, just waiting to collapse under my weight and drop me out of this world and into somewhere far more unfriendly. Supernatural landmines, ready to transform me into something that would make a hellspawn puke. And an invisible cage hanging in mid-air, containing one really pissed-off attack demon.

It snarled silently as I drew nearer, and thrust one of its many-jointed arms through the bars. Vicious claws strained to reach me. Dark and twisted and bristling with spiky fur, the demon reminded me of those horrible bird-eating spiders, only the size of a man and with the malevolence dialled up to eleven. I couldn't get to the front door without putting myself in reach of the demon's claws, so I got out my skeleton key that could unlock anything. I aimed it at the invisible chain supporting the demon's cage and unlocked the spell connecting the chain to the cage. The cage dropped out of the air, hit the hidden trapdoor and just kept on going, disappearing out of this world forever.

I always enjoy this part of the dance. Matching my thief's wits against whoever designed the target's protections. Stepping around the trapdoor was easy, thanks to my sunglasses, and the lock on the front door just threw its hands in the air and gave up when it saw the skeleton key coming. I pushed open the door with a flourish and strolled right in.

Sometimes I wonder why they don't just put everything valuable out on the pavement in a black plastic bin liner, for me to carry away.

I stood very still in the deserted foyer and studied everything with great interest. Framed photographs lined the walls, portraying famous phones, historical triumphs in communication and a few items that had to be forcibly removed from the history pages because they were just too disturbing. One photo showed a flayed human face pinned to a board that supposedly would allow you to talk to the spirits of those not yet born. Some said it was the face of Alexander Graham Bell.

I thought wistfully of all the easy ways I could have robbed this place when I still had my crew. Lex Talon, the Damned – armoured by Heaven and Hell, courtesy of the halos he'd cut from the heads of two angels he'd murdered. Switch It Sally – that dark-skinned sophisticated beauty with the cut-glass finishing-school accent I knew for a fact she wasn't entitled to, who could swap one item for another of equal size without anyone noticing. Polly Perkins – Indian werewolf, exotic dancer and the best tracker in the business. And, of course, my own beloved Annie Anybody, who could fool anyone into thinking she was anybody. With a crew like that, I could have cleaned this place out and disappeared before the security guards even had a chance to suspect something had happened.

I told myself that doing the job on my own made it more of a challenge, and therefore more fun, but I was having a hard time convincing myself.

I took out my special compass that always points to what I need, and followed the needle through a series of empty corridors. I stepped over or ducked under the traditional invisible beams ready to sound an alarm if broken, and got down on my hands and knees to crawl past certain portraits on the walls, whose eyes watched endlessly for unauthorized visitors. And, of course, there were more attack demons in their unseen cages, straining at their chains as I dodged all the triggers that would have released them.

I didn't mock the demons as I passed them by. Those things have no sense of humour, and very long memories.

I finally reached the door to the display room: a massive slab of solid oak stained a murky crimson by more soaked-in human blood than I was comfortable thinking about. Cabalistic signs had been carved deep into the wood, generating layer upon layer of defensive measures, some of which I recognized as being quite staggeringly nasty. The kind that could travel back in time to wipe out all your previous generations. You have to study up on that kind of thing in my line of work, but no one says you have to enjoy it.

I produced my skeleton key and felt some of the invisible protections wince as they contemplated their inevitable undoing. I pushed the key steadily forwards, unlocking each layer of protection in turn. It took a while to get to the door itself, at which point the lock just said to hell with it, and the heavy door swung smoothly back. I stepped into the display room, locked the door behind me and grinned happily as I took in the treasures laid out before me.

In an ideal world, I would have backed up a truck to the front door, loaded everything in with a shovel and departed like a conquering hero. But professional thieves know better than to get greedy. If I did clean out the place, Mister Particular would make such a fuss in the underworld markets that I'd have a really hard time shifting the stuff for anything like its proper value.

But if I took just one small item, it could be ages before anyone even noticed it was missing.

I threaded my way carefully between the exhibits, treading softly and touching nothing. I had no doubt each and every one was primed to set off an alarm if disturbed. Under normal circumstances, someone like me would never have been admitted; the display room was only open to genuine collectors and connoisseurs. And, of course, nothing here was ever for sale; Mister Particular only agreed to show off his collection so he could lord it over his fellow enthusiasts. For him and his kind, the joy lay in being able to say, *I have this, and you don't.*

The various items had been set out on pedestals and velvet cushions, inside glass cabinets and, in the more extreme cases, chained to iron anvils. To keep them from escaping, or attacking the guests. Phones in all sizes and designs, from sleek seventies trimphones to mobile phones that could go roaming in places that weren't even supposed to exist. I paused before something with so many dimensions it hurt my eyes just to look at it. Future comm tech that fell off the back of a timeslip.

And then I stopped in my tracks, as the phone Alexander Graham Bell had created to speak to the departed suddenly started ringing. Its tone sounded like a funeral bell. A quick glance through my sunglasses confirmed that all the defences around this particular phone had shut themselves down, so I picked up the receiver before the ringing could attract attention. I knew all kinds of people who were dead, but I wasn't sure I wanted to talk to any of them. Still, whoever it was had gone to a lot of trouble to make this call happen, so it must be important.

'Hello?' I said, in a determinedly non-committal way.

'Hello, Gideon,' said a familiar voice. 'How's reality treating you?'

'Johnny?' I said. 'Johnny Wilde, the infamous Wild Card? How did you know to find me here?'

He just laughed.

'Are you dead?' I said carefully.

There was a pause as he thought about that. 'Hard to say. More like I'm in between.'

I knew better than to ask, *In between what?* 'I am rather busy, at the moment . . .'

'I know,' said Johnny. 'I just wanted to remind you . . . In the end, it's always all about Annie.'

The line went dead. I carefully replaced the receiver, and the defences snapped back into place. I honestly didn't know what to think. All my wheels were spinning and getting nowhere. The Wild Card slipped between the curtains of the world and disappeared backstage long ago. Why would he reach out to me now? And what did Annie have to do with anything? I made a mental note to discuss that with her later and then pushed the thought to one side. I had work to do.

Finally, I came to a halt before a very ordinary-looking mobile phone, set on a plush black velvet cushion. The sign said simply, *The Doppelganger Device.* One of a kind, highly collectable, extremely valuable . . . And on top of all that, I could see a lot of potential in a phone that would let you talk to yourself.

I learned of its existence while attending a haunted house clearance sale. *Everything must go, because it won't leave us alone.* Every room was stuffed with strange and interesting pieces, and I spent a happy hour drifting from room to room and browsing at a respectful distance, until I happened to bump into an old colleague: Bad Bill Barnacle. A man so secretive he made sure even his cover name was completely unbelievable. We got chatting, discussing the ones that got away and others we had to shake off, before the conversation turned to items we'd heard about but never actually seen. And that was when Bad Bill mentioned the Doppelganger Device. And once he'd explained what it could do, I knew I had to have it.

I reached into my jacket pocket and brought out a phone that looked just like the one in front of me. I'd mocked it up in my private workshop from an old photo of the original, courtesy of Bad Bill, but the end result was good enough that no one would realize it wasn't the real thing until it was far too late. Unfortunately, I couldn't just switch one phone for the other. The moment the Device's weight came off the pad, every alarm in the place would go crazy.

I sighed briefly. It was at times like this that I missed having Switch It Sally around. She could be an absolute pain in the backside, but she was never less than the complete professional. She could have swapped one phone for the other so swiftly the pad wouldn't even have noticed.

Fortunately, I had a few tricks of my own.

I took out my special ballpoint pen and hit the button. Time crashed to a halt. The light in the room darkened as it slid down the scale into infra-red, and the crimson-tinged air became thick as treacle. The silence was absolute, in a way that always made me feel Something was listening. I held on to the deep breath I'd taken before I activated the pen, because there was no air to breathe between the tick and tock of the world's clock, put away the pen and lifted the Doppelganger Device off its velvet pad. The defences didn't react because they didn't know anything was happening. I had to fight the inertia of the stilled world just to get the phone moving, and the moment the Device was free of the pad, I pressed the fake down hard into the waiting indentation. Then I stepped back and hit the button on the pen again, and Time crashed back into motion.

I breathed deeply, keeping my gaze fixed on the velvet pad, just in case it could tell the difference. But everything seemed still and quiet. I relaxed a little and hefted the Doppelganger Device in my hand. And that was when the black velvet pad spat out the fake phone and every alarm in the place went out of its mind.

Bells and sirens screamed their heads off, as I stuffed the time pen and the Doppelganger Device into my pockets and glared around me. Every phone in the place was ringing at once, like a bunch of spiteful birds. I didn't even bother looking at the door. Whole new levels of security would have kicked in by now, making sure nothing could unlock it from this side. And I didn't look for another way out because I already knew there wasn't one. I was trapped, caught red-handed and guilty as hell.

Heavy footsteps approached the other side of the door. It seemed there were some guards on duty, after all. No doubt heavily armed and under orders to shoot first and ask questions afterwards. A fist banged loudly on the other side of the door.

'Whoever is in there, drop all your weapons, kneel down and put your hands on top of your head! You will not be harmed if you follow instructions!'

Yeah, right. They'd kill me whatever I did, just so Mister Particular could set an example to anyone even thinking about breaking into his place.

'Stand back!' I yelled. 'I have a soul gun!'

I had no idea what such a thing might be, but it sounded impressive enough to make any sensible guard pause. My first thought was to let them open the door, hit the button on my pen, squeeze past the guards while Time was stopped and then make a run for it. But if the guards were too closely packed, I'd never make my way through all of them before I ran out of breath and had to hit the pen again. And even if I could force my way through, it would slow me down so much that when I did drop back into Time, I'd still be in range of the guards' guns.

All these thoughts flashed through my mind in a moment before I pushed them to one side. I don't do panic, because I am always the man with the plan.

I smiled at the Doppelganger Device and dialled a number at random. It only rang for a few moments before my own voice answered.

'If you're calling me, either you're in trouble or you're going to be.'

'It's me,' I said.

'Of course it is,' said my voice. 'Who else would be using this phone?'

'I need help,' I said. 'Really very urgently and right now.'

The voice sighed resignedly. 'All right. You'd better come through.'

The door behind me crashed open and armed men spilled into the display room, but I'd already hit the hash key on the Device. A dimensional gateway appeared before me, and I plunged into the swirling vortex. I didn't know where I was going, and I didn't care. Whatever was waiting had to be better than what Mister Particular's guards had planned. The howl of the vortex filled my head and then suddenly cut off. Because I was standing in the middle of a very upmarket party.

The room was the size of a town hall, with pale-veined marble pillars and detailed friezes on the walls depicting the Greek gods getting up to what they did best with style and enthusiasm and no regard for propriety. A massive fountain pumped out water with such force and volume it generated its own rainbows. Balloons floated overhead, bumping against the ceiling and occasionally getting into savage butting contests as they established superiority. And everywhere I looked, rich and important collectors drifted back and forth, chattering loudly. It was the Babel Project, but aimed at a much better class of person.

The crowd milled happily back and forth, showing off their smart suits and elegant gowns. I admired the vivid splashes of colour, eccentric cuts and styles, and a surprising number of tattoos and piercings on open display. The high and mighty knocked back the free champagne and helped themselves to expensive nibbles from silver trays presented to them by waitresses wearing nothing but wisps of gossamer silk – and expressions that quietly suggested they weren't being paid enough to put up with this. There was a general air of our betters at their play, and I felt like robbing every single one of them blind, just on a general principle.

This was another Babel Project, in a different world, and standing right in front of me was another me. He'd dyed his hair silver-grey, and he was wearing a splendid pair of brass pince-nez, but his face was much the same. Though I liked to think I didn't smirk quite that openly. He was wearing a dazzling white tuxedo with raised gold trimmings, and a scarlet sash plunged across his chest from shoulder to waist. I'd never looked that good in my life. So I just nodded casually, and we both put away our Doppelganger Devices.

'How did you get yours?' I said.

'The same way you did, I expect,' said the other me. 'From someone who didn't see me coming. So . . . what brings you to my neck of the woods?'

'A number of very upset security guards,' I said. 'If it's OK with you, I thought I'd hang out here long enough for the trail to go cold.' I nodded at the elegant throng circulating cheerfully around us. 'Nice party. But not, I would have thought, my natural element or yours. Are you here under your own name?'

'Perish the thought,' he said. 'I'm working.'

'Is your crew here too?'

He looked at me a little askance. 'I always work on my own. I don't like sharing. Now, please, lose the sunglasses. Too many people here might recognize what they're for.'

It was a measure of how shaken I was by recent events that I needed him to remind me of that. I removed the sunglasses in an entirely casual and unhurried way, and slipped them into an inside pocket. I gestured at the other me's immaculate white tuxedo.

'Who are you supposed to be, precisely?'

He didn't exactly preen, but he looked as if he wanted to. 'Currently, I am Lord Peter Triskellion. The real Lord is a total recluse. No one's seen him in public for years, so no one remembers what he looks like. So if I say I'm him, I am him.'

He broke off as a tall and slender elf lady drifted out of the crowd to join us, moving so gracefully her elegantly shod feet barely made contact with the floor. She was wrapped in an ankle-length gown of shimmering silver, and her inhumanly long fingers sparkled with bejewelled rings. Her face had a harsh and almost brutal beauty, topped with pointed ears and a huge puffball of silver hair. She nodded languorously to Lord Peter and addressed him in a rich, sultry voice that reeked of bedrooms they had in common.

'Darling,' she said. 'I thought I told you to never darken my door again. Unless you felt you absolutely had to.'

'I am Lord Peter Triskellion,' he said, just a bit pointedly. 'And not any legendary master thief you might have mistaken me for.'

'Oh, how daring, darling,' the elf lady murmured. She let her fingertips drift down the front of his jacket. 'And I thought you came here looking for me. My bed has been so empty without you to savage me in the nights.'

'Then you probably shouldn't have tried to stick a knife in

my back the last time we were together,' Lord Peter said equably.

She laughed softly, a sweetly poisonous sound that raised all the hackles on the back of my neck. 'Happy times . . .'

'What brings you here, Evadne?' said Lord Peter. 'I never knew you to be interested in any kind of technology, never mind telephones.'

'But I do like to meet people,' said the elf lady. 'Especially when I'm feeling a bit peckish.'

She turned her sultry eyes on me, in a way that suggested she would have liked to double-take if she hadn't been so busy being languid. The tip of a pointed tongue emerged briefly, to caress her thin lips.

'Peter, darling,' she said, without looking at him, 'do you know you appear to be in two places at the same time?'

'It's my new party piece,' Lord Peter said smoothly.

The elf lady nodded slowly. 'Two of you. My dear, the possibilities . . .'

She waved goodbye to both of us with a flutter of her elongated fingers and drifted back into the crowd in search of someone else to call *darling*.

'Elves,' said Lord Peter.

I nodded. Elves would always do what they would do, whatever world you were in.

Another celebrated individual appeared out of the crowd and headed our way, and I tensed because I knew that face from my world. Dominic Knight – gentleman adventurer, avenger of wrongs and general down-bringer of the ungodly – smiled easily at Lord Peter and me. Apparently, entirely unconcerned that there were two of us. Lord Peter and I both nodded companionably back at him, because it was hard not to. Suave, debonair and effortlessly sophisticated, Dominic Knight dominated any setting he deigned to attend just by being there. Almost offensively handsome, with jet-black hair and ice-blue eyes, his easy smile made it clear he knew he was always going to be the better man in any room, but was prepared to overlook it.

And his outfit . . . There had never been such a tuxedo. Dark as the night, devilishly stylish and topped with a blood-red bow tie that was tied just badly enough to show he'd taken the trouble to do it himself. His shoes had been polished to within an inch of their life, and his diamond cufflinks blazed like stars.

'Love the new look . . . Peter,' he murmured. 'Don't worry, it's none of my business if you're passing yourself off as someone else. Though I feel I should point out that if this is you, who's this standing at your side?'

'I'm him,' I said. 'Just not from around here.'

Dominic nodded understandingly. 'Of course. I thought I detected the echoes from a dimensional transfer.'

Lord Peter and I didn't even glance at each other. We just accepted he could do that because he was Dominic Knight. I only like to think of myself as legendary. He really was.

'Are you part of Mister Particular's security?' said Lord Peter, quite casually.

'Perish the thought,' said Dominic. 'Can't stand the man. One of these days he'll cross the line and I will catch him at it, and then I'll bring him down and bury him. No matter how well connected he thinks he is. But as far as the pair of you are concerned . . . As long as I don't actually see anything untoward going on right in front of me, I doubt I'll feel the need to get involved.'

'Awfully good of you,' drawled Lord Peter.

Dominic smiled. 'I thought so.'

He drained the last of the champagne from his glass and disappeared back into the crowd. Several waitresses came rushing forward to offer him another glass. The elf lady Evadne called out, 'Darling!' and Dominic smiled and went to meet her. Proving just how brave he really was.

The last time I saw my world's Dominic Knight, he'd been dying from a bullet in the back that was at least partly my fault. But it's not easy to apologize to someone for accidentally getting them killed when they're standing right in front of you. Just one of the many reasons why I detest dimensional travelling. I turned to Lord Peter and did my best to sound as though I was merely making conversation.

'Why are you here? And why as this Lord Peter?'

He raised an eyebrow. 'You don't have him, in your reality? Let's just say he's done more than enough to justify being taken advantage of. I stole his invitation to this little do when he visited my shop in search of powdered unicorn horn. For when absolutely everything else has failed you . . . I sold him the contents of my dustpan in a pretty box, for a suitably exorbitant price. I have to say I was surprised to see the old recluse out and about; I thought the miserable scrote died years ago. Only the need for something so hard to get would have lured him into the open. But he couldn't resist boasting about being invited to Mister Particular's latest, and I just happened to have a contract to acquire a particular item from the exhibition. So I lifted the invitation card from Lord Peter's pocket while he was distracted by my stuffed dancing bear.'

'Where is the real Triskellion?' I said.

Lord Peter grinned. 'Groaning on his bed of pain in a very private hospital, after taking what he thought was powdered unicorn's horn.'

I accepted a glass of champagne from a passing waitress and sipped it thoughtfully. Lord Peter still hadn't said exactly what it was he was there for, and I found that just a tad worrying. If he couldn't tell me, who could he trust? I took a moment to check out the milling crowd. No one had reacted to my appearing out of nowhere, thanks to the concealment glamour built into my Doppelganger Device, but the more time I spent here, the more likely it was someone would recognize my face. Lord Peter had his disguise, but I was on open display. So, when in doubt, keep busy. I flashed Lord Peter my most charming smile.

'Can I be of any assistance?'

'As soon as an opportunity presents itself.'

'You don't have a plan?' I said.

'I prefer to think on my feet,' said Lord Peter, just a bit coldly. 'And then disappear with my prize before anyone notices there aren't quite as many exhibits as there used to be.'

And that was when an oversized flunky in an ill-fitting frock coat raised his voice to address the assembled company. Everyone took their own sweet time breaking off their conversations and turning to look in his direction, to make it clear they were far more important than any mere servant. But they still turned to look, because everyone wanted to hear about Mister Particular's latest acquisitions. The flunky waited patiently until he was sure all eyes were upon him, and then waited just a bit longer, to put the crowd in its place.

'Ladies and gentlemen, and others, the door to Mister Particular's inner vault will be opening shortly. Please have your invitation cards ready for inspection.' He paused again, to enlarge on the drama of the moment and stretch out his brief moment of authority. 'Mister Particular has asked me to remind you that while all of his new collection is there to be observed and admired, no one is to touch anything if they like having hands. And, of course, any attempt at illegal behaviour will be met with drastic counter-measures.'

The assembled guests just glanced at each other, as if to say, *What else?* I looked at Lord Peter, who was smiling easily. I recognized the smile, because it was exactly how I felt when a caper was about to get underway. Full speed ahead, damn the torpedoes and devil take the mark who doesn't see it coming in time. And then my smile disappeared as a large airport-style body-scanner appeared out of nowhere, right in front of the great steel door that led to the inner vault. I studied them both carefully. I had not been expecting the extra complication of a body-scanner, because in my world the Babel Project didn't have an inner vault.

This promised to be even more interesting than I'd anticipated. It made me wish I'd brought a large sack with me to bear the swag away, because when the mark is asking for it this badly, they deserve to have it given to them good and hard. And that was when a dozen armed guards appeared out of nowhere, arranged on either side of the scanner's arch. The whole crowd was suddenly much more quiet and attentive. I glanced quickly at Lord Peter, and was relieved to see his smile was still firmly in place.

'The scanner has been set to detect all unauthorized high-tech and magical items,' said the flunky. 'Including body implants and mystical auras. Please do not attempt to enter the inner vault if you suspect you may not qualify, because a refusal may lead to sudden violence.' He smiled at the audience, some of whom were stirring uneasily. 'If anyone wishes to return to the foyer and restrict themselves to admiring those items already on display, they are, of course, welcome to do so. No inferences or accusations will be made.'

A number of guests left the room with quiet dignity. The guards stood very still, guns at the ready. A few of the more confident souls in the crowd were already lining up before the body-scanner, smiling and chattering cheerfully to make it clear they had nothing to hide. The first to enter the scanner's arch was the elf lady Evadne, and immediately every alarm went off at once. The guards started to raise their guns and then quickly thought better of it when Evadne turned her sultry eyes on them. She smiled slowly.

'Sorry, darlings. Just a few intimate piercings, from the Unseeli Court. Who wants to see?'

She started to hike up her gown, and the flunky gestured urgently for two guards to escort her to a side room. Evadne looked as though she was enjoying the prospect. The guards looked worried. I leaned in close to Lord Peter.

'Did you know about the scanner?'

'Of course,' he said quietly. 'But I could use a distraction, to help clear the way. Any ideas?'

'Always,' I said. I studied the queue before the scanner. 'Anyone there you really don't like?'

'I feel spoilt for choice,' Lord Peter murmured. 'But the worst of the bunch would have to be the large gentleman at the back: Sir Jocelyn Stuart.'

A large, fleshy type in a frankly shabby suit, Sir Jocelyn had a flushed face and greedy eyes. He looked like a shark intent on sneaking into a paddling pool.

'He should have been locked in a cage and thrown off a cliff long ago,' said Lord Peter. 'But he has connections.'

'Then you wouldn't object to my dropping him right in it?' I said.

'Go for it.'

I moved forward to join the queue and placed myself directly behind Sir Jocelyn, who didn't take his eyes off the steel door. Which made it easy for me to quietly drop a little something into his jacket pocket. I always carry a portable door with me: a small black blob that when slapped against a wall immediately transforms itself into a guaranteed escape route. I didn't want to give it up, but I needed everything else more. And the blob should prove sufficiently hard to explain to the guards.

Sir Jocelyn entered the scanning arch with a confidence bordering on arrogance, which made his shocked expression all the more satisfying when the alarms hit the roof again. The flunky gestured to the guards, two of whom quickly closed in and hustled Sir Jocelyn away. He struggled futilely, shouting, 'Don't you know who I am?' which I've always found somewhat redundant. The guards didn't seem particularly bothered, and he was soon gone. The discovery of a well-known burglar's tool in Sir Jocelyn's pocket should keep them occupied for a while. And now there were four fewer guards to deal with. I looked to Lord Peter, as he produced a very familiar-looking ballpoint pen.

I just had time to take in a deep breath and clap a hand on Lord Peter's shoulder, to link myself to him, and then he hit the button and Time slammed to a halt. The whole room became saturated with infrared light, and the crowd froze in place like so many elegant statues. Lord Peter and I moved quickly past the waiting queue and through the body-scanner. The alarms didn't go off because as far as the machine was concerned, we weren't there. By the time we got to the steel door, I already had my skeleton key out, and I had the door open in a moment. It still took both me and Lord Peter to heave the steel door open against the world's stubborn inertia, but we were soon inside the inner vault, forcing the door shut behind us. I locked it again with a flourish, and Lord Peter set Time back in motion. We grinned at each other.

'We have the best toys, don't we?' Lord Peter said happily.

'The best tools of the trade,' I said.

We turned to consider the contents of the inner vault, like pirates who'd just uncovered a new treasure trove. The steel-walled room was packed with assorted birds in cages, glowering at us with cold, malevolent eyes.

'Excuse me,' I said, with what, under the circumstances, I considered to be great restraint. '*Birds?*'

'All part of the history of communication,' Lord Peter said grandly. 'Mister Particular has one of everything here – from genetically modified parrots who can memorize entire speeches, to dodos who can psychically imprint important maps and documents in their meat.' He grinned at me. 'You didn't really think they were killed because they tasted so good, did you?' He wandered around the vault, peering interestedly at one cage after another. 'See that miniature pterodactyl, hanging upside down from the top of its cage? It can memorize everything it sees from on high and then display it on a wall of your choosing.'

'OK,' I said. 'What is *that*?'

Something with wide membranous wings wrapped around its body like a leathery cloak was slamming its horned head against its cage with enough force to bend the bars. It paused as it sensed our eyes upon it, and shot us a malevolent glare before returning to its task with increased ferocity. The cage began to bump forward with the force of every blow.

'Warp raven,' said Lord Peter. 'Let's hope we're finished and out of here before it breaks loose.'

'Dangerous?'

'Like you wouldn't believe. It can be trained to carry messages and is highly prized because it can destroy anything that gets in its way. Unfortunately, it resents being forced to do anything, and it bears grudges. It could kill and eat everything in the Babel Project and still have room for dessert.'

'Does Mister Particular know that?'

'I'm sure someone must have mentioned it to him.' Lord Peter looked happily round the vault. 'Every bird in this vault would sell for more money than you could spend in a year. No wonder Mister Particular was so keen to show them off.'

'A wild bird in a cage sets all Heaven in a rage,' I quoted.

He looked at me. 'Don't get sentimental. We have work to do.'

'I don't normally deal in living things.'

'Then it's high time you started.'

Lord Peter moved quickly along the rows of cages, peering this way and that, and finally stopped before a small black bird with ragged feathers. It cocked its head on one side and addressed him in a harsh voice.

'Who do you think you're looking at, you little punk? You get too close and I'll have your eye out and stick it in a martini. I am not a commodity! And what the hell are you wearing? You look like an ice cream that's gone off.'

'Are you sure this is the one you want?' I said solemnly.

Lord Peter picked up the cage and gave it a good shake. 'Behave yourself, bird – and keep the noise down until we're out of here.'

The bird clung to its perch and glared balefully at him. 'You give me a concussion and I'll sue! Don't let the feathers fool you; I can afford real lawyers!'.

Lord Peter looked at me. 'Don't feel sorry for him. This is a rescue mission. I have a buyer waiting who'll pay serious money to get this little troublemaker back.' He peered in at the bird. 'That's right: you're going home, you horrible object. Though what Wotan wants with you is beyond me . . .'

The bird hopped eagerly back and forth on its perch. 'I knew that one-eyed gallows god couldn't cope without me!'

Lord Peter nodded easily to me. 'That's it. Job done. Feel free to help yourself to anything that looks expensive.'

'I'll pass,' I said.

He shrugged. 'Then our business is concluded. It's been . . . interesting.'

He fished a small flat box out of a pocket with his free hand, hit the red button on top and disappeared.

I stood there for a moment, blinking at the space where he'd been. My other self had just abandoned me in a high-security vault full of treasures acquired by one of the most dangerous and vindictive collectors in living memory, with a whole bunch of armed guards outside the only exit. The birds looked at me in a *What did you expect?* kind of way, and I was honestly lost for an answer. Lord Peter could have teleported me out with him, but he'd chosen to leave me behind so I could take the blame for his theft. What were the worlds coming to when you couldn't even trust yourself?

I indulged myself with some really foul language but had to stop when most of the birds joined in. Some added comments of their own. I took a deep breath and looked quickly around the vault. If I'd still had my portable door, I could have just slapped it on the rear wall and walked right out of here, but that option was gone. I moved over to the steel door and thrust my skeleton key into the lock, giving it the special extra half-turn that would keep the door locked no matter what anyone outside did. That should buy me some time.

But even as I thought that, the entire steel door vanished, replaced by something far more ordinary. One of the smarter guards had used the portable door they'd found on Sir Jocelyn.

And I couldn't use my key on the portable door because they don't come with locks. Why should they? They're not real doors. There was no other way out. That was the point of a secret vault. But as my gaze swept over the rows of birds in cages, a new idea came to me. The door behind me started to move, but I was already turning my skeleton key in mid-air, and every door on every cage sprang open. I pointed at the main exit.

'There! That's your way out. And your chance for revenge!'

I'd barely finished speaking before the air was filled with a dark storm of flapping wings. The escaping birds buffeted me back and forth as they shot out of the open door, and there was a sudden outbreak of screams outside as the birds went full Hitchcock on everyone in sight.

I took out my Doppelganger Device and smiled happily. My other self hadn't thought this through. I dialled my own number and hit the hash key, and the swirling vortex appeared in front of me. I strode into the dimensional gateway and immediately appeared in a gloomy back street. Because the Babel Project in my world didn't have an extra vault. I slipped the phone into my pocket and strolled off into the night.

When I finally got back to my shop, the front door was half open. I stopped and carefully considered the situation from a cautious distance. I was sure I'd locked that door before I left, because I never made mistakes when it came to security. And I never left the door half open, even when I was in the shop. Could someone have burgled the place in my absence? It didn't seem likely.

I put on my sunglasses to see if my defences had been triggered and was shocked to discover they'd all been shut down. My shop, and all the marvellous things it contained, had been left unprotected. I moved quickly over to the front door and pushed it all the way open. It slammed against the inner wall with a deafening crash, but there was no response. I strode inside, doing my best to appear large and threatening.

There was no one in the shop. All my stock was still where it should be, apparently undisturbed. The wee-winged current junkies cried out to me happily, as though nothing out of the ordinary had occurred. I turned to the stuffed grizzly bear standing guard by the front door.

'What happened here?'

'Nothing happened,' growled the bear. 'Damn! Have I been dozing again? I hate it when I miss things.'

'Someone got in while I was out!' I said loudly.

The bear shook its head firmly. 'No unauthorized people have entered the shop. I would definitely have noticed that. You know I would.'

'What about Annie?' I said.

'She was here a minute ago,' said the bear.

I raised my voice and called her name, but there was no answer. And then, finally, I noticed the envelope left lying in plain sight on the countertop. I moved quickly over. The envelope was addressed to me, in unfamiliar handwriting. I opened it slowly, because there was no way this was going to be good news.

I have taken Annie Anybody, said the letter. *She is perfectly safe, for now. Don't look for her. You won't find her. If you ever want to see her again, you must find and steal Time's Arrow. I will exchange Annie for the Arrow. You have forty-eight hours, starting from dawn this morning. Once you have the Arrow, I will contact you again with further instructions.*

It wasn't signed.

I frowned hard. I knew about Time's Arrow. I was probably the only thief who even had a chance of stealing it. Some things are so well guarded that they aren't a challenge – just certain death and destruction.

I slipped the letter back into the envelope and tucked it away in an inside pocket. I'd check it for clues later but didn't expect to find any. This whole affair had the smell of professionals at work.

The odds were that the kidnapper would kill Annie whatever happened, to ensure her silence. But they must know I'd never hand over the Arrow without proof she was still alive. Just the thought of her, alone and in danger, was enough to drive me insane, but I clamped down hard on my emotions. I couldn't save Annie if I lost my grip.

But . . . given what Time's Arrow was, and where it was, this wasn't something I could do on my own. I was going to have to put my crew back together.

TWO

Hell on Earth

S tanding alone in my shop, surrounded by familiar items
that no longer comforted, lacking the only thing that really
mattered, I stood very still for a long time. Thinking hard,
considering my options, getting nowhere. The man with the plan
had been caught off guard, and now I had no choice but to dance
to someone else's tune. It was very quiet in the shop, as though
everything was holding its breath to see what I would do. I
thought about tools of the trade, strange and unusual weapons,
plans within plans, tricks and stratagems and double-crosses. And
in the end, I did what I should have done in the first place. I
raised my voice and addressed the shadows.

'Sidney! Front and centre!'

The tall standing mirror came rolling forward into the light.
'All right, all right, I'm here! And don't shout at me! I'm delicate!'

I managed a small smile. 'Since when?'

'Just because you're a mirror, everyone takes advantage,'
Sidney muttered sulkily. 'What do you want? I was watching my
soaps.'

'Annie has been kidnapped,' I said.

'That's not possible!' Sidney said immediately. 'No unauthorized person has entered this shop since you left. I'd know. You
know I would.'

'My unknown enemy put a lot of thought into this,' I said.
'But that just means I have to do what I always do: out-think
them, run rings around them and make sure they never see my
end game coming.'

'What do you need me to do, boss?' said the mirror.

'First, check out my home,' I said. 'Just in case Annie is there.
If she isn't, run a general search until you find her.'

'On it, boss.'

The mirror planted itself in front of me. I had a brief glimpse of my reflection, looking more strained and upset than I was comfortable seeing, and then I was replaced by a series of images showing every room in my house, all of them empty, followed by places Annie and I had always been fond of. Familiar streets, out-of-the-way settings, magical gardens . . . But no sign of Annie anywhere. The images were flashing by so quickly now that they barely registered, and the mirror started to shake and shudder from the strain of its pursuit. The last few images dissolved into bursts of light and colour, and the whole glass turned cloudy and opaque.

'I'm sorry, boss,' said Sidney. 'I can't find her anywhere. Whoever took Annie must be seriously powerful to be able to hide her from my all-seeing gaze. Do you have any idea who it might be?'

'I'm struggling to put a name in the frame,' I said. 'It could be someone I robbed, someone I did wrong or someone I walked over to get where I am. Or perhaps someone decided that since I don't have a crew any more, I must be vulnerable and an easy target . . . But, then, why take Annie? Why not come after me?'

'How much are they asking for her return?' said Sidney, careful to keep his voice entirely businesslike. 'Can you raise it?'

'They don't want money,' I said. 'They want Time's Arrow.'

Sidney whistled respectfully, which is a disturbing sound for a mirror to make.

'Of course,' he said. 'Only a legendary master thief could hope to get their hands on something like that. But . . . how did the kidnapper get to Annie in the first place? Doesn't matter whether she's at home or at the shop, she's always surrounded by serious protections. You saw to that.'

'Because I always knew the day might come when someone would go after her, to get at me,' I said steadily. 'Annie can usually look after herself, no matter who she's being . . . But some of the enemies I've made wouldn't be stopped by anything usual. The shop's defences weren't just down; they'd been turned off.'

'How is that even possible?' the mirror said sharply. 'Only you and Annie know the pass codes.'

'I know!' I said. 'None of this makes any sense!'

'Maybe . . . someone wanted to make it clear just how powerful they are,' Sidney said slowly. 'So you'd know better than to try to mess with them, and just concentrate on going after Time's Arrow.'

'That sounds like someone who knows me,' I said.

'Throw me some unusual suspects,' said Sidney. 'I'll find them.'

I thought about it. 'What about that enchanting cat burglar, the Feline Noir?'

'She's on the run,' Sidney said immediately. 'Nearly got caught burgling the Vatican, again. Left a whoopie cushion on the Pope's throne and stole Pope Joan's autobiography from the Vatican's Secret Library. I don't know where she gets the grudge from; it's not like she's religious. Either way, she's got enough worries on her plate to keep her from going after you. And why would she want to target Annie anyway? Oh, wait a minute . . . Didn't the two of you have a thing, some time back?'

'That was ages ago,' I said firmly. 'Long before Annie came back into my life. How about Danny the Dip? Best hands-on thief in the business. He could steal someone's clothes while they were walking along in them, and the victim wouldn't even notice till things got a bit draughty.'

'Danny is currently working for British Security,' said Sidney. 'They've been using him to acquire certain important items from foreign agents convinced no one would dare rob them in broad daylight. Danny is by all accounts very successful in his new role, extremely well paid and in danger of becoming respectable.'

'Why would Danny want to work for British Security?' I said.

'I don't think he was given a choice in the matter.'

'Hard-Hearted Hannah?' I said. 'The most seductive confidence trickster in the business? She could steal a man's heart, his wallet and his hopes for the future – and make him love every minute of it. I was always surprised she never made more of herself.'

'She retired,' said Sidney. 'So she could marry Long Tall Maggie. It can happen to the best of us.' The mirror sighed reflectively. 'They sent me a link, so I could watch the ceremony. It was very romantic. I always cry at weddings . . .'

'Remind me to send them a toaster,' I said. 'How do you know all this stuff, Sidney? Have you been reading those trashy gossip magazines again?'

'One of us has to keep up with what's going on,' the mirror said haughtily. 'And I'll have you know, some of the writing in those magazines is top-notch. And let me remind you, since any mirror is every mirror where I'm concerned, I can see out of any of them. Which means there's not much that gets by me.'

'But you still can't find Annie,' I said.

'No,' said Sidney. 'Sorry, boss.'

It bothered me that he couldn't find her. I would have bet on Sidney against the world, though, of course, I could never tell him that. He was hard enough to work with as it was.

'Maybe someone wants to take the Gideon Sable identity away from you?' said Sidney. 'The way you stole it from the original.'

I looked at him sharply. 'Could the original Gideon have escaped from wherever he's been all this time, to steal his old life back?'

'No,' Sidney said immediately. 'I have all kinds of alarms in place, to warn if he ever shows up again.'

I nodded slowly. 'None of those people are smart enough to have planned something like this. It has to be someone new. Someone from outside the fields we know.'

'Then how do they know you?'

I looked at the mirror. 'Everyone's heard about me.'

'Of course,' said Sidney. 'What's the plan, boss?'

'For now, play the kidnapper's game. Until I'm in a position to turn the tables on him.'

'I have always admired your optimism, boss,' said the mirror. 'Can I just politely enquire: what the hell is Time's Arrow? I mean, yes, I've heard of it; everyone has. But what does it do?'

'Time's Arrow allows you to travel back down your own timeline and remake all the bad decisions of your life. Every wrong path that made you what you are today, instead of the person you intended to be. History itself would change, so you had always been the person you thought you should be.'

Sidney hummed thoughtfully, which was another disturbing sound for a mirror to make.

'So this is someone who wants to use Time's Arrow, not just

sell it on. Who would hate their life so much that they'd risk unravelling history just to change it?'

'Someone very driven,' I said. 'And ready to sacrifice anyone else to get what they want.'

'Where is this appalling object, right now?' said Sidney. 'Do you need me to locate it for you?'

'I already know where it is,' I said. 'I always knew where all the really valuable things are. Time's Arrow is one of the prize exhibits at the Midnight Museum, right here in Old Soho.'

'OK . . .' said Sidney. 'We are now officially in serious trouble. I have heard of the Midnight Museum, and not in a good way.' He paused for a moment. 'Though I have to say, even allowing for all the incredible levels of security and protection, and the fact that people like us are never going to be welcome there . . . I have always wanted to take a look around that place. They say the Midnight Museum has wonders and marvels beyond the dreams of thieves like us . . . But then, you never take me anywhere!'

'There's a reason for that,' I said.

'I know how to behave!' the mirror said loudly. 'I can make polite conversation without swearing!'

'But you do tend to stand out,' I said. 'And besides, there's always the chance the Museum would try to seize you, so they could put you on display.'

'Of course,' said Sidney. 'I wasn't thinking. You're quite right. Where would I be, without you to look after me?'

'I hate to think,' I said. 'Let's start with the basics. The Midnight Museum is a very exclusive repository for some of the rarest and most extraordinary items in the world. Down the years, I have put a lot of thought into how best to sneak in and get out again with one of the exhibits . . . Because if I could pull off a heist like that, people would never stop talking about it.'

'And the Members of the Midnight Club would never stop coming after you,' said Sidney.

'Oh, I wouldn't keep it,' I said. 'I'd post the item straight back to them the next day. First-class, signed for. I'd just want everyone to know I could do it.'

'You're weird,' said Sidney. 'Still, Time's Arrow . . . Would you ever consider using it yourself? To rewrite your own life? I mean, you've endured some pretty hard knocks in your time . . .'

'But I ended up with Annie,' I said. 'Which is all I ever wanted. I would never do anything to risk that.'

'And I thought I was the romantic one,' said Sidney. 'You'll be asking to borrow my Doctor and Nurse novels next. But you can bet the kidnapper knows you feel that way. That's why he can trust you to steal Time's Arrow and not keep it for yourself. But that means he didn't just target you for your legendary thieving skills. It must be someone who knows all about you! Someone you know has betrayed you!'

'I can't think about that right now,' I said. 'The first step . . . is to find a way into the Midnight Museum.'

'That's a hell of a first step,' said Sidney. 'You can count the number of people who've got past those protections on the fingers of either of the hands I don't have.'

'But once I have Time's Arrow,' I said, 'I can move on to the second step. Negotiating with the kidnapper from a position of strength. I can threaten to destroy the Arrow if any harm comes to Annie.'

'That's a dangerous game to play,' Sidney said carefully.

'I know.'

'Do you have the beginnings of a plan?'

'I'm working on it.'

'How do people normally get inside the extremely well-guarded Midnight Museum?' said Sidney.

'You can only gain access by becoming a Member of the Midnight Club,' I said. 'And the only way to do that is to donate an item worthy to be accepted as an exhibit in the Museum.'

'So you need to steal something really special, in order to steal something even more special,' said Sidney. 'Your life is beyond weird, Gideon. But come on . . . this shop is packed with really good stuff. There must be something here they'd want.'

'Nothing good enough for the Midnight Museum,' I said. 'They're only interested in the exceedingly rare, the worryingly strange and the utterly unique.'

'Like what?' said Sidney.

'Knuckle bones from the hand of the leper Jesus healed, used by Roman soldiers to gamble for the Christ's robe,' I said. 'The Resurrection Ruby, formed out of a drop of fossilized blood from the Wandering Jew. Alexander the Great's sword, which cut the Gordian Knot. The magically assisted arrow that pierced King Harold's eye at the Battle of Hastings. And these are just the ones I'm sure about. There are all kinds of rumours about what the Museum has.'

'Then you need to offer the Club something so good they absolutely have to have it,' said Sidney. 'Something so incredibly amazing their teeth will ache all winter if they let it get away.'

'To do that,' I said, 'I have to put that old gang of mine back together. And since I haven't had an e-mail, a phone call or even a sudden premonition about any of them in some time . . .'

'But you used to be so close,' said Sidney.

'The Damned was determined to do as much good as he could before his time ran out and he got dragged down to Hell,' I said. 'To him, that meant killing as many bad guys as possible. And since Sally had given up trying to save him, she went with him. They chose a path I couldn't follow, so all I could do was wave them goodbye.'

'Didn't you try to talk them out of it?'

'I stopped talking to them when they stopped listening to me. Then Polly Perkins decided she needed to prove her worth as an adventurer in her own right. Which meant striking out on her own, without any backup.'

'OK . . . What about previous members of your crew?' said Sidney.

'The Ghost is still happily possessing Fredric Hammer's body and doing good deeds with the man's ill-gotten gains,' I said. 'I wouldn't feel right, imposing on his second chance at life. And the infamous Wild Card disappeared long ago.'

'Good,' said Sidney. 'Just thinking about that man sends shivers up the spine I haven't got any more.'

I remembered Johnny Wilde phoning me at the Babel Project to tell me *It's always all about Annie.* Had he been trying to warn me about the kidnapping? Then why couldn't he have been more straightforward . . . I had to smile. Because he was the Wild Card, and his mind didn't work that way. I nodded briskly to the standing mirror.

'Find my crew, Sidney. Start with the Damned and Switch It Sally.'

'You do know that if people like that don't want to be found, they won't be found,' the mirror said carefully.

'I have faith in you Sidney,' I said. 'And so would Annie.'

'You always did know how to fight dirty,' said Sidney. 'OK, let's go fishing! You supply the bait and I'll bring the dynamite!'

The mirror flashed up a series of views and locations from all over the world. Some so far off the beaten track that only seasoned travellers in the hidden world would even have heard of them. The Bureau of Forgotten Sorrows. The Elven Tea Room. The Lamentable Orchard and the Nightmare Church. There were sudden glimpses of awful things pressing up against the other side of the mirror, come and gone in a moment. The mirror's wooden frame began to creak and warp.

'I'm getting close,' said Sidney. 'Something's fighting me . . .'

'Keep trying,' I said.

'Always,' said Sidney. 'Hold it, hold it . . . There! I've got Lex . . . and Sally! They are currently investigating an isolated villa deep in the south of France, with defences that would have the soul right out of most burglars if they lost concentration even for a moment. But not good enough to keep me out! I am Sidney; hear me roar! All I have to do now is lock on to a mirror inside the villa, and all its shields won't mean a thing.'

'Be careful the security guards don't detect your presence,' I said.

'Please,' said Sidney. 'Remember who you're talking to.'

'Sorry,' I said. 'What can you tell me about this villa?'

'Scanning, scanning . . . Got it! Oooh . . . we are talking old-school Satanists. A whole bunch of really rich and powerful people, who believe they owe everything they have to their worshipping the Devil and making sacrifices to him.'

'Human sacrifices?' I said.

'Which part of "They worship the Devil" are you having trouble following? Blood and horror come as standard.'

'Do they have a suitably ominous name for themselves?'

'Lords of the Inferno.' The mirror sniffed loudly. 'Sounds more like a goth rock band to me.'

'Never heard of them,' I said.

'I think that's the idea, boss. Though if I mentioned some of the names involved, you'd probably know them. All convinced no one can touch them because they're protected by the Powers of Darkness. If you listen to rumour, which I always do, these people spend their getaway weekends up to their ears in abduction, torture and ritual murder.'

'Can you sense any actual dark forces at work?'

'I am a talking mirror who can spy on people from afar,' said Sidney. 'I don't know anything about that sort of thing, and I don't want to.'

'The Damned wouldn't be targeting these people unless he was convinced they were the real deal,' I said. 'How many of these Devil worshippers are present in the villa, right now?'

'All of them! This is their big gathering of the year, when they rededicate themselves to their Infernal Master. Which is presumably why Lex chose this particular night to break in. Though, given the size of the group, and what looks like a whole army of heavily armed soldiers surrounding the villa, and the possibility of Dark Powers at work . . . I have to wonder if Lex and Sally might just be out of their depth, for once.'

'Send me in,' I said.

'Sometimes I wonder if you understand a word I'm saying,' said Sidney. 'What makes you think you'd last ten minutes against the Lords of the Inferno and all their forces?'

'I can out-think them,' I said. 'They can't be that bright, or they wouldn't have made a deal with the Devil in the first place. There is a whole branch of literature dedicated to making it clear that never works out well.'

'I suppose you know what you're doing,' said Sidney. 'Actually, I don't, but I just want this conversation to stop.'

'Send me in,' I said.

The image in the mirror showed a massive white structure, proud and palatial, with pillars and porticos, gargoyles on the guttering and heavy wooden shutters covering all the windows. The sprawling grounds surrounding the villa were packed full of ancient statues in the classical style and a great many mercenary soldiers in anonymous black uniforms. The view in the mirror moved in closer, until it seemed to be right there in the grounds with the soldiers. I half expected them to look round, to see who was peering over their shoulders.

'I need to be inside the villa, Sidney,' I said.

'I'm trying! The layers of protection get stronger and nastier and more likely to eat you alive the closer you get. I'm looking for a mirror somewhere inside that I can sneak you in through . . . Yes! Got one!'

Sidney showed me a long, narrow corridor, with rich carpeting, gloomy portraits and some seriously valuable antique furnishings and fittings. Most of the lights had been turned off, so that everything was draped in shadows, presumably to add to the general ambience.

'I'm not seeing Lex or Sally,' I said.

'This is as close as I can get you, boss. They're not far off.'

'Then I'm going in.'

'Hold on there, buckaroo!' said Sidney. 'Don't you want to tool up first and fill your pockets with some serious weapons? You're going to be facing practising Satanists, armed soldiers and possible outbreaks of the Dark Arts. I wouldn't go in there without a depleted-uranium chainsaw in each hand.'

I was momentarily distracted. 'Do we have something like that in stock?'

'If we don't, we should seriously consider getting some in,' the mirror said firmly. 'Just for occasions like this. If Lex and Sally weren't already in there, I'd say nuke the place from orbit, just to be sure.'

'You know I prefer not to use weapons,' I said.

'I think you should think carefully about making an exception in this case.'

'Send me in,' I said.

'The door's open,' said Sidney.

I stepped into the mirror. And just like that, I was somewhere else. I looked quickly up and down the corridor, to make sure I had the place to myself, and then slipped on my sunglasses . . . But there didn't seem to be any magical defences. Perhaps the villa's owners thought they didn't need any, given the strength of their shields and the armed battalion in the grounds.

The corridor was so gloomy I had to put my sunglasses away, or I wouldn't have been able to see anything. What little illumination there was came from the occasional black wax candle grasped in a stuffed human hand. Dribbles of melted wax suggested the candles hadn't been lit long. The shadows lurking in the corridor were very dark and very deep. They looked as if they could hold anything – anything at all. The air smelt of sulphur, spilled blood and sour milk: the smell of Hell.

I patted my pockets, to assure myself all the tools of my trade were ready to go, but before I could set off down the corridor, I became distracted by a very unpleasant set-up on a side table. Seven severed cats' heads had been set in a circle and mounted on spikes. Carefully positioned to cover every direction, the cats' eyes moved to follow my every movement. I'd seen illustrations of something like this in a really old book on ceremonial magic. It was a basic surveillance spell. Eyes that never slept because they couldn't. Unnecessarily cruel, but that was probably the point. And I thought, *I am not having this . . .*I took out my skeleton key, pointed it at the cats' heads and turned it in mid-air, unlocking the spell. The cats' eyes closed slowly, and I thought I glimpsed something that might have been gratitude. I looked quickly around, in case I'd attracted something's attention, but everything seemed still and quiet. The Lords of the Inferno probably considered themselves so powerful that they didn't have to worry about minor problems like burglars. Let them keep on thinking that, while I stole the high ground right out from under their feet. I put away my key and followed the corridor until suddenly it branched off in half a dozen different directions.

'Take the first on the left,' Sidney murmured suddenly in my ear.

I didn't quite jump out of my skin. 'I didn't know you could do that.'

'Lots of things you don't know about me.'

'How are you still in contact?'

He sniffed loudly in my ear. 'I'd like to see the barriers that could keep me out. Besides . . . I lost Annie because I wasn't paying attention. I'm not losing you as well.'

'Thanks, Sidney.'

'Oh dear God, we're not having a moment, are we? You know I don't do sentiment. Get your head back in the game and turn left, before something nasty bursts out of the woodwork.'

'You think that's a possibility?'

'Don't you? I'm not even in the villa and it's still putting my nerves on edge.'

I took the turn and kept going. 'How long until I reach Lex and Sally?'

'You're almost there. I dropped you off as close as I could manage, considering I was simultaneously having to fight off a dozen different attack spells. You're lucky you got in here with all your important bits still attached.'

'And you didn't think to mention this before because . . .?'

'You know I don't like to boast.'

'Yes, you do,' I said. 'It's what you do best.'

'You have no idea what I do best,' the mirror said smugly. 'Just as well; it would only freak you out. You do know I'm only making conversation because I'm feeling extremely nervous?'

'Can you see what Lex and Sally are up to?'

'No,' said Sidney. 'And that's starting to worry me. The security in this villa is like a Russian doll; no matter how many layers I slip past, there's always more. And they all have teeth. Hold it! There are people coming your way.'

I stopped and peered quickly up and down the corridor.

'I'm not seeing anyone.'

'They're in the next corridor! Scanning, scanning . . . There's a hidden alcove, behind those hanging curtains to your left. Get your arse out of sight, now!'

I slipped between the curtains and pulled them together. The alcove held a single shelf supporting a vase of black roses, that dug painfully into my back. I watched carefully through a narrow gap in the curtains, as several figures in dark robes went striding past. Their cowls were all pulled well forward to hide their faces.

'They can't have any real magic abilities,' said Sidney. 'Or they'd have known you were there.'

'You could have given me a little more warning,' I said.

'I'm doing the best I can! Just focusing my gaze inside the villa is giving me a headache in the head I haven't got.'

'Is it safe to come out yet?'

'Yes! Why are you still hanging around?'

I emerged from behind the curtains and set off again.

'Robes and cowls,' I said. 'All very traditional.'

'They've probably just been reading too much Dennis Wheatley.'

'That man knew what he was talking about,' I said.

'There are rumours,' Sidney said darkly.

'And you believe all of them.'

'It keeps life interesting. Now, pay attention; you're getting close. Take the second right and tread carefully; you're about to run out of carpeting.'

I moved silently across the bare wooden floorboards, planting each foot with precision. There were standing skeletons with shattered bones held together with copper wire. I held my breath as I walked past them, but none of the skulls moved to follow me. An old-fashioned grandfather clock had a transparent cover, to show off the human organs that made it work. The heart was still beating, and the lungs filled and emptied. And someone had covered a side table with a pile of severed feet. Pink ribbons had been tied in neat bows around the big toes.

'Don't ask,' said Sidney. 'You really don't want to know.'

'Are you sure you're not picking up any dark forces?' I said quietly.

'You're lucky I can keep track of you! The villa's protections are ganging up on me to force me out.'

'The moment you think you're in real danger, get the hell out,' I said.

'I won't leave you,' said the mirror. 'You're walking into Hell itself, and you're going to need a guide. Check out the protections ahead.'

I quickly put my sunglasses back on and stopped dead as I saw the shattered remains of supernatural snares and magical traps flapping in the air like glowing ribbons. Someone had walked right through them, as though they were nothing.

'The Damned was here,' I said.

'Keep your eyes open,' said Sidney. 'He might have missed something.'

I walked slowly forward, carefully avoiding the twitching ends of sundered defences, stirred to a last vestige of awareness by my presence. Through my sunglasses, I could see the supernatural venom still dripping from the rags and tatters of a defence system that would have sent anyone screaming down to Hell if they hadn't already been Damned. I peered quickly about me.

'Are you sure this is the best route, Sidney? Only I'm having to duck and dodge like no one's business.'

'It's only because the Damned bulldozed through these protections that you're getting anywhere!' said Sidney. 'Don't nag!'

'Wouldn't dream of it,' I said.

'You're not fooling anyone but yourself,' said Sidney.

I finally came to a high-up gallery over a great open hall, and there were Lex Talon and Switch It Sally, crouching behind a wooden bannister as they looked down on what was happening below. I took off my sunglasses and looked down into the hall. It was packed with rows of kneeling Satanists, all of them wrapped in their dark robes and cowls, staring rapturously at something I couldn't see at the far end of the hall. I moved quickly forward to join Lex and Sally, and the Damned raised his voice without turning his head.

'Hello, Gideon. I had a feeling you'd be joining us.'

Sally looked round sharply, and for a moment I thought she was going to whoop loudly and shout out a greeting. I made frantic hushing gestures, and she grinned broadly. I knelt beside her, and she hugged me so hard I thought I was never going to breathe again. She finally let go, planted a big kiss on my cheek and smiled dazzlingly.

'Darling, it's been such a while! What have you been up to?'

'Stealing from the rich and keeping it,' I said. 'I'm more concerned with what you're up to.'

'The usual,' said the Damned. 'Death and destruction, and getting my hands bloody as I put an end to evil men.'

'He hasn't changed,' Sally said fondly. She glanced back the way I'd come. 'How did you get in here?'

'Sidney helped,' I said.

'Tell her I said hi!' Sidney shouted in my ear.

'Will you please keep the volume down!' I said. 'I'm working!'

'Is that Sidney?' said Sally. 'Tell him I said hi!'

'Everyone, keep the noise down,' said Lex, still staring out over the hall. 'The Lords of the Inferno might be a bit distracted at the moment, but they're not deaf.'

I took a moment to look Lex and Sally over, realizing for the first time how much I'd missed them.

Lex Talon was a huge, brutal figure, with broad shoulders and a barrel chest. His face was as harsh and grim as ever, with cold,

cold eyes. He was wearing a simple black catsuit, complete with black leather gloves, which did surprise me a little. Lex didn't usually do subtle. He tended more towards just walking into the lion's den and kicking the big cats around. Two bracelets glowed sullenly on his wrists, holding Heaven and Hell within.

Sally was tall, aristocratic and drop-dead gorgeous, with very dark skin and dyed blonde hair in a bowl cut. Her smile was never less than dazzling, and her eyes sparkled with mischief, because for Switch It Sally the whole world and everything in it was only there for her to play with. She was also wearing a smart black catsuit, but it looked good on her.

Lex had to know I was looking at him, but still he didn't turn his head.

'Save the reunion for later,' he said flatly. 'Time is not on our side. It's not just the number of Devil worshippers, or the magical defences, or the soldiers outside that bother me. The Lords of the Inferno are planning something really bad, and we need to stop it before it starts.'

'Do you like the new outfits?' Sally said brightly, cutting in the moment Lex stopped talking. 'You wouldn't believe the trouble I had talking him into it. In the end, I had to tell him it made him look dramatic.'

'You do too,' I said generously.

She smiled happily. 'Darling, I knew you'd understand.'

I loved the way she still brimmed over with confidence, even though she was deep in the house of her enemies and heavily outnumbered. It probably helped that she had the Damned at her side. I would have bet on the Damned against any number of armies.

'I know why you're here, Gideon,' said Lex, pressing his face against the bannisters for a better look at what was happening below. 'As soon as my work here is done, we'll help you find Annie.'

'Lex,' I said, 'is there some reason why you won't look at me?'

He finally turned his head, and his face was as harsh and implacable as I remembered.

'I had to go away. I didn't want you to see what I was becoming. I didn't want to see you being ashamed of me.'

'That was never going to happen,' I said. 'We're crew. And the crew is family.'

I put a hand on his shoulder. It felt like trying to squeeze a cliff face, but after a moment, he nodded slowly. Sally bobbed up and down with excitement.

'Yay! The winning team is back together!'

'Can we please remember the noise levels?' said Lex. 'I don't want the Satanists to know we're here until I'm ready to deal with them.'

'Hold it,' said Sally, frowning at me suddenly. 'What was that about finding Annie?'

I knew she'd catch up eventually.

'She's been kidnapped,' I said. 'I came here to ask for your help in getting her back safely.'

Sally glared at Lex. 'You knew about this? When were you going to tell me?'

'The angel Ethel told me it was going to happen,' said Lex. 'And I wasn't sure Gideon would want our help. We did walk out on him.'

'Idiot,' Sally said fondly. 'Honestly, what can you do with the man?' She punched Lex in the shoulder, but he didn't seem to notice.

'For the moment, let's concentrate on what's happening here,' I said diplomatically. 'Lex, are these Satanists the real thing?'

'They act like they are,' he said. 'You should see the local police reports.'

I had to raise an eyebrow at that. 'Hold everything and put it in reverse. You have police contacts now?'

Lex actually smiled briefly. 'You taught me that acquiring good information is key to getting things done. Satanists are like serial killers; they go through predictable stages on their way to becoming all that they shouldn't be. The Lords of the Inferno have escalated, from kidnappings and sexual assault to torture and ritual murder. And they always get away with it because they have friends in high places. The few times the local police tried to take these people down, they were instructed to back off.'

I looked to Sally, and she nodded quickly. 'We passed some recently dug graves in the grounds on our way in. Some of them looked really small.'

'My contacts warned me that the Lords of the Inferno were planning something big,' said Lex. 'Something terrible enough that no one would ever dare trouble them again. If they're planning what I think they are, they deserve everything I'm going to do to them.'

'But what if they're just wannabes?' I said. 'Rich freaks, playing at being Devil worshippers?'

'My halos know evil,' Lex said heavily. 'Hell is here, in this villa, just waiting to be let loose on the world. And I will kill everyone in this place before I let that happen. It's important to send a message.'

'Who to?' I said.

'Every other Satanist group,' said Lex. 'They can play dress up and run their stupid rituals, and have all the group sex they want, and I won't give a damn. But the moment they cross the line, I'll be there waiting for them. To show them what Hell on Earth really is. And smile, as they scream.'

I looked at Sally. 'And you're ready to go along with this?'

She shrugged quickly. 'A good wife should take an interest in her husband's work.'

Two black-clad soldiers suddenly appeared at the end of the gallery. Going by the expressions on their faces, they weren't expecting to see us. They started to raise their guns, but before Lex or I could do anything, both soldiers collapsed dead on the floor. I turned to Sally.

'What did you just do?'

'I swapped their heart valves,' she said calmly.

'I never thought of you as a cold-blooded killer,' I said.

'We are what the world makes us, darling.'

I looked to Lex, but he had nothing to say.

'The Damned has dedicated himself to the path of death and destruction,' said Sally. 'And I go where he goes.'

I was still looking at Lex. 'What happened to your hopes for absolution through acts of penance?'

'After everything I've done, I think it's a bit late for that,' said the Damned. 'Forgiveness is no longer an option. If it ever was.'

Sally put a hand on his arm and squeezed it, smiling fondly. 'He threw away every hope he had when he killed all those

people to save me when I was kidnapped. Everything he is now
is because of me. How could I not stand by him?'

'Death and destruction isn't you, Sally,' I said.

'It is now.' She met my gaze unflinchingly. 'I knew what Lex
was when I married him.'

I started to say something, but she talked right over me.

'Tell me about Annie being kidnapped . . .'

I filled Lex and Sally in on the details. They looked at each
other.

'Professional job,' said Lex.

'I thought so,' I said.

'Why do people keep coming after us?' said Sally, just a bit
plaintively. 'Why can't they just leave us alone?'

'Because we're the good guys,' said Lex. 'And no good deed
goes unpunished.'

I couldn't tell whether Lex was joking or not. Sally looked at
him firmly.

'We have to help Gideon save Annie. He helped you when I
was taken.'

'I hadn't forgotten,' said Lex. He nodded briefly to me. 'As
soon as I'm finished here, my time is yours. For old times' sake.
And because I have missed being part of the crew.'

'It would be nice to get back to some old-fashioned thieving,'
said Sally. 'After spending all this time hip-deep in blood and
slaughter.'

Lex turned to her. 'I thought you were enjoying yourself?'

'Not really my thing, darling,' Sally said lightly. 'I was just
being supportive.'

Lex looked at her reproachfully. 'You never said.'

'You were busy.'

Lex nodded and looked back into the hall, where the Devil
worshippers were swaying back and forth on their knees in their
version of religious ecstasy.

'I can't let this go, Gideon,' he said flatly. 'These are awful
people, getting ready to do something really awful. I have to stop
them, or what's left of my life is meaningless.'

'But you don't have to kill them all,' I said carefully.
'Remember what I taught you, Lex. The best way to hurt rich
and entitled reptiles like these is to take away the things they care

about most. The Lords of the Inferno believe their worshipping the Devil has made them special. Take that away, and what are they? Just a bunch of self-deluding thrill-junkies. Destroy their devilish reputation, make them look like common criminals, and the people they rely on for protection will throw them to the wolves, rather than put themselves at risk. Let the police have the Lords of the Inferno. The best lawyers in the world couldn't keep these creeps from getting everything that's coming to them, because the evidence of what they've done is still buried in the grounds. Putting them on trial will make sure the truth comes out and give some closure to the victims' families. Let these pampered scumbags rot in prison for the rest of their lives; that will be Hell on Earth, for them.'

Lex nodded slowly. 'How do we bring them down? Do you have a plan?'

'I always have a plan,' I said.

Actually, I was still thinking on my feet. I peered through the bannisters. The Lords of the Inferno were prostrating themselves before an old stone statue, set in the place of honour on a raised dais. It was human, but with shaggy legs and cloven hooves, and curling horns thrusting up from its brow. The Goat of Mendes: manifestation of the Prince of Darkness in the world of men. The statue wasn't that impressive, and I was having a hard time seeing what the Devil worshippers saw in it, until a great Voice boomed suddenly from the unmoving mouth.

'Be welcome, my children! Worship me and serve me in all things, and I will raise you above all others!'

And just like that, I knew what was going on.

'Sidney?' I said. 'Sidney!'

'All right, I'm here – no need to shout!' said the mirror. 'What do you want?'

'How clearly can you see what's going on in this villa?'

'I can see everything you can and a lot more besides. While you've been catching up on old times, I've been having a good look round. You would not believe what some of these dirty bastards have been getting up to in the back bedrooms. I'm not easily shocked, but trust me when I say they'll never get those stains out of the sheets.'

'Never mind that now,' I said. 'Take a look at the statue at the end of the hall. How is it talking?'

'Concealed speakers inside the head,' Sidney said briskly. 'I've already located a small communications centre, not far from you. There's no mirror inside the room, so I can't be sure what's going on, but I'd bet good money that someone in there is responsible for the big spooky voice.'

'And when were you going to tell me this?'

'I just did,' said Sidney.

I thought about saying several things, but I didn't. There's never any point in getting mad at Sidney; it's just the way he is. I looked down into the hall again and concentrated on what the Voice in the statue was saying.

'Leave this place, and go down the road to the village. Drag the people out of their houses and into the streets, and slaughter the men, women and children like the animals they are. Open their steaming insides to the chill night air and fill the streets with blood and screams. This sacrifice will make you worthy in my sight, and I will bestow upon you power such as you have never dreamed of. I will make you gods, and all shall bow down before you. Glory in the carnage you make, and defy the powers of the world to do anything about it. You are the Devil's children, and the world and all that's in it shall be yours, for you to do with as you wish.'

I looked to Lex. 'You were right. A mass killing, to stamp their name on the world. Sidney! I need directions to that comm centre.'

'No problem!' said Sidney. 'Go shut that bastard down. He's giving us disembodied voices a bad name.'

I turned to Lex and Sally. 'Hold your positions. I won't be long. I have a plan.'

'Of course you do, darling,' said Sally.

I followed Sidney's murmured directions, and a few corridors later, I was standing outside a locked door. I pressed my ear against the wood and could just make out the statue's Voice, still busy whipping up his followers' passions. A quick flourish with my supernatural key, and I eased the door open and peered inside. There was just the one man, sitting at his ease before a microphone, watching the hall on the monitor screen. No robe and cowl for him; just a black T-shirt and some distressed jeans. He had a rich, deep actor's voice, effortlessly commanding and charismatic, like any good con man.

I eased forward. On the screen, the Lords of the Inferno were rising to their feet and embracing each other, laughing happily in anticipation of the slaughter to come. I moved in behind the statue's Voice and overturned his chair, spilling him on to the floor. And then I kicked him hard in the ribs. He curled into a ball, gasping for air. I don't like to think of myself as a violent man, but sometimes you just know being reasonable isn't going to get you anywhere.

I grabbed the man with both hands and pulled him up on to his knees, and only then realized that I knew him. I hauled him on to his feet and thrust my face into his.

'Norman Grant?' I said. 'What is a small-time con artist like you doing here? How did you end up as the Voice of Satan?'

'Just lucky, I guess,' he said, smiling nervously. 'Hello, Gideon. Not so small-time now, am I? What are you doing here?'

'Putting an end to this,' I said.

He shrugged. 'I'm finished with these idiots anyway.' He glanced at the monitor screen and grinned broadly. 'I lucked into this gig when the original leader hired me to be the Voice of the Goat of Mendes. He wasn't a believer; he was just in it for the sex and the power. But I saw a way to make some serious money out of this operation. So I used the statue's Voice to denounce him to his followers, and they swarmed all over him and tore him to pieces! I told them to put their money into secret accounts I'd organized, and they never even argued! After that, I just got curious to see what I could get away with. What new extreme thing I could get them to do. They really thought the Devil was talking to them through a battered old statue . . .'

'I just heard you order them to commit mass murder,' I said.

'I'm only telling them to do what they had in mind anyway,' said Norman. 'And while they're busy in the village, I can make off with all their money, disappear to somewhere sunny and live the good life.'

'How many innocent people will die, to pay for that?' I said.

'You can't make an omelette,' said Norman. 'Come on, Gideon; there's enough money in this for both of us . . .'

I slammed my knee into his groin, and he sank to the floor again. I stood over him for a moment, breathing hard, and then made myself move away. I spoke into the microphone, and my voice came booming out of the statue. The Devil worshippers froze where they were as they realized its Voice had changed.

'You've been fooled by a con man,' I said. 'You don't have a deal with the Devil, and you never did. I see from the control panel before me that the con man recorded his instructions and your eagerness to carry them out. So I think I'll just send these files to the police and let them deal with you. I'm sure they'll find enough evidence buried in your grounds to make the charges stick.'

I shut down the mike, and it was only the work of a few moments to transfer the files. On the monitor screen, the Lords of the Inferno screamed and howled and clutched at each other as they realized they weren't special after all.

I got Norman on his feet, threw him out of the communications room and sent him staggering through the corridors. He kept trying to talk to me, but I wasn't listening. When we got back to the gallery, he took in the dead soldiers and the Damned, and all the colour dropped out of his face. He swallowed hard.

'You don't want to kill me, Mr Talon. I'm only a simple criminal.'

'I know,' said Lex. 'But sometimes you have to take out the trash.'

He took hold of Norman with both hands, lifted the con man effortlessly over his head and then called down to the panicked crowd.

'I am the Damned!' Lex said loudly. 'And this cheap crook was the Voice you've been listening to!'

He threw the screaming man into the hall below. The crowd scattered, and Norman's scream broke off abruptly as he hit the floor hard. The Lords of the Inferno broke and ran, fighting each other in their desperation to escape through the only exit.

I nodded to Lex and Sally. 'The police are on their way.'

'You were right, Gideon,' said Lex. 'Breaking their spirit was very satisfying.'

'Sidney?' I said. 'Beam us home.'

'Ah,' the mirror said quietly in my ear. 'Bit of a problem there.'

I shook my head. 'That really wasn't what I wanted to hear right now, Sidney.'

'I can't transport you from inside the villa! You might have broken the Satanists, but their shields are still in place. Sneaking you in was hard enough; getting three of you out is beyond me. You'll have to go out into the grounds, so I can get to you.'

'Into the grounds,' I said. 'Where an army of heavily armed soldiers is waiting to greet us.'

'Well,' said Sidney. 'Every plan has its drawbacks.'

'If I'm following this one-sided conversation correctly,' said Lex. 'We're going to have to fight our way out, through an army of professional soldiers?' He smiled slowly. 'You're so good to me, Gideon.'

Sally shook her head. 'Testosterone. It's such a curse.'

Down in the great hall, it all seemed very empty now the Lords of the Inferno were gone. Crumpled robes had been left lying in piles on the floor, as though their owners thought they could discard their old identities and blame their crimes on them. I stopped before the statue on its raised dais. It looked even less impressive, up close. Until it slowly turned its jagged stone head to look at me. The air was suddenly filled with the stench of spilled blood and sour milk. I fell back, and Lex stepped forward to put himself between Sally and the new threat. The statue stretched unhurriedly and then casually crossed one shaggy stone leg over the other. The eyes in the jagged face glowed redly, like banked coals, and the stone lips stretched in an unpleasant smile as the statue nodded familiarly to Lex.

'You have always been such a disappointment to me.'

'Glad to hear it,' said Lex. 'Am I supposed to believe you're the Devil?'

'If you like,' said the statue.

'We just robbed you of your followers,' said Lex. 'Made them a joke in the eyes of the world.'

The statue shrugged easily. 'There are always more.'

'Sidney?' I said quietly. 'Is this real? Can you tell?'

'There's no one left in the villa to run the con,' the mirror said in my ear. 'And I don't know how you'd pull this off anyway. So I'm going to say yes, this is real, and I am crapping myself. I didn't even know I could do that.'

'Hello, Sidney!' the statue said cheerfully. 'Catch you later!'

'What are you doing here?' said Lex. 'Why manifest now?'

The statue looked at him thoughtfully. 'You've been making a real difference just lately, Lex. I think it's time for you to come home. Where you belong.'

Sally immediately put herself beside Lex. 'You can't have him! He's mine!'

The stone head turned to stare at her. 'He was mine long before he was yours, darling.'

'You'll have to go through me to get to him,' said Sally.

'But you're mine too,' said the statue. 'Didn't you know? Those who support a sin are just as guilty as those who commit it. No excuses, no bargains and no time off for good behaviour.'

I moved forward to stand on Lex's other side. 'The Devil always lies.'

The statue nodded to me. 'Except when a truth can hurt you more.'

'There is always time to repent and make atonement,' I said steadily. 'Lex and Sally are going to help me, because they're my friends, and because it's the right thing to do. Things like that will put them beyond your reach forever.'

'Don't you just hate loopholes?' said the statue. 'I suppose I'll just have to take all of you now . . .'

And then the statue broke off as the ghosts of seven dead cats appeared out of nowhere to form a circle around Lex and Sally and me. A few nodded to me, and I thought I recognized familiar eyes. The statue sighed.

'There's always something. Another time, then.'

'I'll never let you take my friends,' I said.

The statue laughed softly. 'A challenge? Very well, then . . . The best games are always those played for mortal stakes. And the devil take the hindmost . . .'

The red glare in its eyes faded away, and suddenly the statue was just a statue again. The ghost cats faded away and were gone.

Lex stepped forward and punched the statue's head right off.

'See you soon,' he said.

Out in the grounds, I could hear approaching police sirens and the Lords of the Inferno crying out miserably as they ran for their lives. The soldiers were running to take up defensive positions, and it quickly became clear that when the police arrived, the soldiers would have them seriously out-gunned.

The officer in charge caught sight of Lex and Sally and me, and seemed to understand at once that we were the cause of his present troubles.

'Stand where you are!' he shouted. 'Or you're dead meat!'

'Well, that's not very nice, darling,' said Sally.

'I'll take care of this,' said Lex.

The halos at his wrists glowed dazzlingly, and the armour of Heaven and Hell surged over Lex in a moment, enveloping him from head to foot. The armour didn't so much cover Lex as replace him: a greater thing overwriting a lesser. The darkness that made up his left side wasn't simply the complete absence of light; it had a terrible presence all its own. Like the dark at the end of the universe, after all the stars have gone out. His right side blazed like the sun come down to Earth: light without end or limits. His featureless armoured face had no eyes, but he could still see his enemies. He was the Damned, the power of Heaven and Hell manifest in the world.

Soldiers everywhere cried out and fell back, as the armour's presence beat on the air like the flapping of great wings. Give the officer his due; he didn't retreat a single step. He drew a pistol and aimed it at Sally.

'Stay away from me! Or your woman gets it!'

Sally smiled at him cheerfully. 'Hello, darling! I am Switch It Sally and I have just swapped all the bullets in your gun for some wooden plugs I always carry with me, for occasions just like this. Teach you to threaten an unarmed woman.'

The officer pulled the trigger and nothing happened. He screamed for his men to open fire. I grabbed Sally, and we both hit the ground, burying our faces in the neatly cropped grass. Bullets ricocheted away from the Damned's armour, to chip and shatter statues all around him. Sally and I kept our heads down and tried to make ourselves very small.

The roar of massed gunfire was painfully loud at close quarters, but the guns soon exhausted themselves against the Damned's armour. The officer kept shouting orders, but no one was listening to him. The soldiers started to back away, as the Damned strode forward, the weight of his armour driving his feet deep into the lawn.

He broke into a lumbering run, all strength and purpose but no grace, and he was in and among the soldiers before they had time to react. He raged through the armed men, striking them down with his armoured hands and trampling their broken bodies underfoot. He tore off limbs and heads, and punched in chests and faces. The officer shouldn't have threatened Sally. That made it personal.

The Damned left a trail of the dead and the dying behind him, and didn't look back once. He stormed through the grounds, picking up soldiers and throwing them down so hard they never got up again. The last few turned to run, throwing their guns aside. The Damned picked up classical statues and threw them like missiles, crushing the soldiers in mid-step.

He left the officer till last. The man looked around at his dead men and then walked straight at the Damned, who stayed where he was, and waited. The officer produced an automatic pistol, thrust it into the Damned's armoured face and opened fire at point-blank range. The Damned just stood there and let him do it. The officer kept firing till he ran out of ammunition; the gun did no damage at all. The Damned didn't even flinch. The officer threw his weapon away and swore disgustedly.

'I surrender. I know when I'm out-gunned.'

'I don't take prisoners,' said Lex,

'What kind of man are you?' said the officer.

'Damned.'

'Been there, done that,' said the officer. 'You killed my men, you bastard.'

'The people you worked for here murdered innocents,' said the Damned. 'And they were getting ready to kill a great many more. By protecting them, you helped make all of that possible. Which makes you just as guilty as them.'

'We're professional soldiers!' said the officer. 'Just doing our job!'

'Same here,' said the Damned. 'See you in Hell.'

He punched the officer in the face with such force that his armoured fist burst out of the back of the man's skull. The Damned shook the dead man free in a flurry of blood, let the crumpled body fall to the ground and then looked unhurriedly round him. Once he was sure he hadn't missed anybody, the armour disappeared back into the bracelets, and Lex was just a man again. Sally scrambled to her feet and rushed forward to hug him tightly. I took my time getting up. It had been a long day. The grounds were so littered with bodies that it looked like a battlefield. The grass was churned up and soaked with blood, and the broken statues looked like so many more bodies. Sally looked at me.

'Are we really going to let those Devil worshippers run away?'

'If you listen carefully, you can hear the police arresting them,' I said. 'With malice aforethought, from the sound of it. They must have been frustrated, not being allowed to go after people they knew were incredibly guilty. The evidence I just sent them should be more than enough to make sure none of the Lords of the Inferno escape justice.' I nodded to Lex. 'Why be merciful and kill them when it's so much more satisfying to destroy them?'

'You're starting to sound like me,' said Lex. 'That's not a road you want to start down, Gideon.'

'I know,' I said. 'Sidney? Can we go home now, please?'

'Leave it to me, boss.'

The standing mirror appeared in the grounds before us. I led the way into the reflection, and just like that we were somewhere else.

THREE

Hunting Party

I led Lex and Sally out of the mirror and back into my shop. Sidney greeted their arrival with a series of loud retching noises.

'Is it really too much to ask for you people to remember to clean your shoes first? What have you been stepping in?'

'I suppose it's good to be back,' said Lex. 'Nice to know nothing has changed.'

The wee-winged fairies plugged into the electric light sockets took one look at the Damned, stopping singing just long enough to scream shrilly in chorus and then popped out of existence like so many glowing soap bubbles. A whole series of items quietly disappeared from my shelves, some so quickly that they left collapsing vacuums behind. The stuffed bear standing by the door bowed its head respectfully to Lex, while Sally spun round in circles, beaming all over her face and clapping her hands delightedly.

'This is just so sweet! They remember you, Lex!'

'He does make an impression,' I said.

Sally went bouncing round the room, happily picking things up and putting them down again in the wrong place.

'And it used to be so peaceful here . . .' sighed Sidney.

Sally shot the standing mirror her most dazzling smile. 'Go ahead, nag me about my lifestyle choices, Sidney. You know you want to. Make me nostalgic for the good old days!'

Sidney growled under the breath he didn't have. 'It's at a time like this I wish I'd become a plumber like my mother wanted. Always good money in plumbing.'

Sally laughed, wrapped her arms around the mirror in a big hug and planted a resounding kiss on his glass, leaving a lipstick imprint that quickly faded away.

'It's good to be back!' said Sally. 'Group hug!'

'Let's not,' said Lex.

Sally shook her head at me. 'What can you do with that man . . . that doesn't involve serious levels of discipline and industrial-strength medication?'

'Later,' said Lex.

Sally bounced up to him and pinched his cheek. 'You're still my big old teddy bear.'

Despite everything, I had to smile. 'You see the world very differently from the rest of us, Sally.'

'How long has Annie been missing?' said Lex.

'She disappeared somewhen in the early hours of this morning,' I said. 'I'm pretty sure it happened here.'

'And you didn't notice?' said Sally.

'I was out,' I said.

Lex raised an eyebrow. 'Off stealing something special? Could someone have attracted your attention to that particular item, to make sure you wouldn't be around when they came for Annie?'

I started to say no and then thought about it. I hadn't told anyone I was interested in the Doppelganger Device, but I couldn't seem to remember quite when I first decided I was going to steal it. Could someone have deliberately pointed me at the Device?

'There was nothing here to indicate any violence,' I said finally. 'Nothing to show Annie fought back, which isn't like her.'

'Is her trail still warm?' said Lex.

'If there was a trail, I'd be following it,' I said. 'There's nothing. Which means we're dealing with a professional.'

'Good,' said Lex. 'You know where you are with a pro. It's the amateurs you have to worry about.'

'What can we do to help, Gideon?' said Sally.

'I need my crew,' I said. 'Including Polly. If anyone can follow a trail that isn't there, I'd bet good money on her werewolf instincts. Do you know where she is?'

Sally carefully didn't look at Lex. 'Polly was determined to start bringing down bad guys all on her own. I did try to talk her out of it, on the grounds that the last time she went solo, it didn't work out too well, but she insisted she was ready. So Lex and I let her go. That's what parents do.'

'She's had some successes,' said Lex. 'She took down the King of Sin. And the Giggling Ghoul.'

I nodded. 'I heard they'd disappeared from the scene.'

'Polly didn't kill them!' Sally said quickly. 'Just burned down their businesses, terrorized their clientele, persuaded the bad guys it was time for them to retire.' She smiled fondly. 'Polly always said the best way to stay on top of being a werewolf was not to think like a wolf.' She stopped and frowned. 'But she always made a point of checking in regularly, to let us know how she was. And do a little discreet boasting. But we haven't heard from her in over a week.'

'Anyone else, we might have worried,' said Lex. 'But she is a werewolf, after all.'

'She's never been quiet this long,' said Sally.

'No,' said Lex. 'She hasn't.'

I turned to the standing mirror. 'Find her, Sidney.'

'On it, boss.'

A series of images shot across the standing mirror, come and gone almost too quickly to make an impression.

'So!' Sally said brightly. 'How's business, Gideon?'

'It's interesting work,' I said.

Lex picked up on my tone. 'But not satisfying?'

'I do miss the thrill of the old days,' I said. 'That's why I was out on the steal when they came for Annie. If I'd been here . . .'

'They would only have chosen another time,' said Lex. 'Do you have any suspects in mind?'

'No one stands out,' I said. 'There aren't any real threats left from our bad old days.'

'Of course not,' said Lex. 'I killed them all. I never did see the point in leaving enemies behind to bear a grudge. And most of them needed killing anyway.'

Sally did her best to lighten the mood. 'You mustn't worry about Annie, Gideon. She can look after herself.'

'Prepare to be astounded!' Sidney said loudly. 'Feel free to applaud wildly and scatter pressed flowers at my feet, for I have located Polly Perkins! And you're not going to believe where she is . . .'

The mirror showed us a silver-grey beach, with great waves lapping against it, overlooked by a dark and brooding jungle, under a night sky full of stars in unfamiliar constellations.

'She's on holiday?' said Sally.

'Given where she is, that strikes me as unlikely,' said Sidney.

'You're looking at Bounty Island. A tiny speck in the South Pacific, way off all the trade routes, and completely untroubled by tourists, explorers or bird-watchers. Because, as far as the rest of the world is concerned, this island doesn't exist. The current owner has gone to great pains to ensure it doesn't appear on any map.'

'Who owns it?' I said.

'Brace yourself for a blast from the past,' Sidney said grandly. 'The lord of this little island paradise is Alan DeChance, his own bad self.'

Lex and Sally frowned and looked to me. I did my best to keep the disquiet out of my voice.

'DeChance is an old-school villain – and seriously dangerous. His reputation runs to several volumes, and the index alone would turn your hair white. If Polly is on that island, she is in a world of trouble and way out of her depth.'

'Didn't DeChance run illegal safaris in various African states?' said Lex. 'So people with more money than sense could pay over the odds for a chance to shoot endangered species?'

'That's him,' I said. 'Played the Great White Hunter role for all it was worth.'

'I remember the man now,' said Lex. 'He specialized in tracking down the last example of a particular species, so his client could take the credit for making it extinct. DeChance . . . He disappeared, just as I started to take an interest in him.' He smiled briefly. 'Perhaps he was afraid I was hunting him.'

Sally patted him lightly on the arm. 'Not everything is about you, dear.' She turned to me. 'So what is DeChance up to on this tiny little island?'

'Sidney?' I said. 'Dazzle us with your world of gossip.'

'Oh, sure, now you need me to know something, you're ready to acknowledge my extensive store of dubious information,' sniffed the mirror. 'And, of course, you're quite right. I know things even the fates have overlooked. DeChance has spent the last few years quietly tracking down and collecting strange and unusual creatures, from the darkest corners of the hidden world.

Everything from the rare to the unlikely, the magical and the mystical. The most dangerous beasties in the bestiary. Everything that ever threatened humanity's peace of mind is now locked up in DeChance's private menagerie on Bounty Island. He sets them loose, one at a time, so that extremely well-paying clients can pursue them through his jungle in the name of sport.' Sidney paused for a moment, humming tunelessly. 'You know . . . it is possible Polly was lured to Bounty Island, just so DeChance could capture her and make her the prey in his next hunt.'

'That bastard piece of shit has our little girl?' said Sally. 'We have to do something!'

'We will,' I said. 'And DeChance really isn't going to like it. Sidney, get us to Bounty Island, right now.'

'And that's where we run head first into a problem of epic proportions,' said Sidney. 'I can't get anywhere near it. DeChance's shields are too strong. Hardly surprising, I suppose, considering all the supernatural strangeness he has to keep locked up. That distant view of the beach is as close as I can get. I've never seen protections this strong. I hate to think how many rare specimens he must have sacrificed to power shields like these. I can almost see the ghosts holding them up.'

'How does DeChance invite people on to the island for these private hunting parties?' said Sally.

'You got me,' said Sidney. 'He doesn't advertise in any of the magazines I subscribe to. It's all word of mouth and personal recommendations.'

'What kind of creatures are we talking about?' said Lex. 'And if they're that dangerous, how does DeChance control them?'

'Now we're in my territory,' I said. 'And my extensive knowledge of items worth stealing. Somehow, DeChance got his hands on the Mandrake Medallion. Originally created by the great Victorian explorer and adventurer, Sir Mandeville Mandrake, to give him control over all the wild things in the world. As long as they were in close range. Not so he could kill them, but because he wanted to live among them. He'd become disenchanted with human civilization and sought peace among the beasts of the jungle.'

'Would I be right in guessing his little piece of Heaven on Earth didn't work out too well?' said Sally.

'He lost the Medallion,' I said. 'Or had it stolen. And when he tried to live among his beastly friends anyway, they killed and ate him. There's a moral in there somewhere, but I can't be bothered to dig it out. The point is, DeChance can use the Medallion to control anything wild, no matter how powerful it is, and then chase it through the jungle with his hunting parties.'

'But why would he want Polly?' said Sally. 'She's just a werewolf!'

I looked at her steadily. 'He may have wanted to demonstrate what happens to people who go after him. The moment she came within range of the Medallion, Polly would have fallen under its influence, and DeChance could put a silver collar on her.'

Lex scowled at the standing mirror. 'Sidney, are you sure you can't get us anywhere near this island?'

'The shields extend for miles in all directions,' said Sidney. 'How's your swimming?'

'If DeChance did lure Polly to him,' I said, 'you can be sure he did his research on her first. Which means he knows about us. He'd want to make sure we couldn't come to the rescue.'

'I'll keep trying,' said Sidney. 'Any wall will break if you hit it hard enough and long enough.'

'We don't have time,' I said. 'Odds are the hunt has already started, and Polly is running for her life.'

'We taught Polly everything there is to know about how to bring down bad guys,' said Lex. 'Anyone who tries to hurt her is going to end up as bite-sized chunks.'

'That would normally be the way to bet,' I said carefully. 'But DeChance has been running these hunts for some time. He'll have learned how to stack the odds in his favour. I don't doubt Polly will lead the hunt a good chase, but as long as DeChance has the Mandrake Medallion, Polly's head will be going home as someone's trophy. Unless we can sneak on to the island in time to change the odds.'

Lex looked at me. 'Do you have something in mind?'

'I have an item on my back shelves that might do the job.'

'Hold your horses and phone the knackers' yard,' said Sidney. 'Are you telling me you've got something that will get you into a place even I can't crack? How long have you been holding out on me? I tell you everything!'

'No, you don't,' I said.

'I tell you everything you need to know. And if what you've got is that good, why didn't you use it to get access to the Devil worshippers, instead of leaving me to work my fingers to the bone banging my head against the villa's protections? And yes, I do know that was a mixed metaphor and there was no need for all of you to think it so loudly.'

'I have a piece of future technology that fell off the back of a timeslip,' I said. 'A teleport bracelet from the twenty-third century. Unfortunately, it didn't come with any operating instructions. The people I brought in to appraise it were very firm that if I got even one part of the set-up procedures wrong, there was a very real risk I would arrive with important bits of me missing. They ran all kinds of tests and diagnostics to make the bracelet ready for use, but given how keen they were to get their payment in advance before I tested it, I decided to just leave it on the shelf.'

'Can you make it work?' Sally said bluntly.

'I have to,' I said. 'Polly needs me. Sidney, take a look at shelf one seventy-two, security box twenty-three, and bring it here.'

'I am not your servant!' Sidney said loudly. 'I'm only doing this because I want to help Polly too.'

'And because you're dying to see what a teleport bracelet looks like.'

'Yes, well that too, obviously.'

A gleaming steel box shot out of the mirror and skidded across the floor. I picked it up, opened the lid and looked inside.

'Hello . . .' I said. 'How long has that cat been dead? Only joking . . .'

I took out a chunky steel bracelet studded with coloured buttons and any number of flashing lights. I held it up so everyone could get a good look, and though Lex and Sally didn't actually make *Oooh!* and *Aaah!* noises, they looked as if they wanted to.

'This should get me past DeChance's shields,' I said. 'Because it was designed to sneak past security measures that haven't even been invented yet.'

Lex put out his hand. 'Give me the bracelet. Polly is my daughter.'

'Our daughter,' said Sally. 'If you're going, so am I.'

I held on to the bracelet. 'I'm the one who always has a plan. You can guard the shop while I'm gone.'

'Are you sure about this, Gideon?' said Sally. 'You're a thief, not an adventurer.'

'Polly is part of the crew,' I said. 'That makes her my daughter too, in every way that matters.'

I snapped the bracelet around my wrist, and immediately a whole bunch of new and interesting lights chased each other round the bracelet. I would have felt a lot safer if I'd had some idea what that meant. I carefully pushed what I'd been told were the right buttons.

'Gideon . . .' said Sidney. 'Once you're on the island, if you need help, call me. And I will move Heaven and Earth to find a way to you.'

'Of course you will,' I said.

I took a deep breath and hit the last button. The bracelet produced a deep and ominous humming noise. I raised it to my mouth and spoke very distinctly.

'Destination: Bounty Island, in the South Pacific. Time: now. Activate: all shields and security protections. Teleport!'

The world dropped out from under my feet. I was falling forever into a void I could sense but not see. I just had time to think, *What did I do wrong?* and then I was standing on the silver-sanded beach.

I quickly checked myself over, to make sure every part of me had arrived safely, and let out my breath in a relieved sigh. I looked up and down the deserted beach. The slow lapping of the incoming waves leant the scene a feeling of peace and calm. But even though it was night, the heat was still so intense it made my exposed skin smart. A cool breeze gusted in from the ocean, but it didn't even take the edge off. I was already soaked in sweat.

I took off the teleport bracelet, slowly and very carefully, and slipped it into an inside pocket. Partly because I didn't want anyone on the island to know I had it, but mostly because I didn't want to risk banging the buttons against something.

'Sidney?' I said quietly. 'I made it.'

There was no response.

I moved quickly across the beach, loose sand shifting treach-
erously under my feet as I headed for the jungle. The moment I
crossed the boundary, the huge trees shut out most of the moonlight, and I had to stand and wait until my eyes adjusted to the
gloom. Shafts of shimmering light dropped down through breaks
in the canopy, pushing back the dark. The massive trees were
packed tightly together, as though to repel intruders, but there
was a single narrow trail. Just beaten-down earth, cut in a straight
line, its sides trimmed with almost military precision so that not
a branch or twig or leaf protruded to block the traveller's way.
The trail was so narrow that two men could walk it side by side,
but only as long as they kept their shoulders pressed together. I
took in how closely the trees were set together, and opted for
the path, even though doing something that obvious made me
feel as though I'd just pinned a target on myself.

I was pleasantly surprised at the lack of insect life. Having
watched my share of David Attenborough documentaries, I'd
been expecting flies, mosquitos and every other kind of angry
buzzing thing. But either they didn't come out once it was dark
or DeChance had shot them all. Even as I thought that, a spider
the size of a small dog went scuttling across the trail ahead of
me, and I was halfway up the nearest tree before I calmed down.

The jungle was full of sound and fury, a deafening bedlam
that rose and fell on every side. As though every living thing
was attacking, humping or eating each other, possibly simultaneously. I kept moving along the path, hoping that if I ignored
them, they'd offer me the same courtesy. I got out my compass,
and the needle pointed straight ahead, hopefully towards
DeChance's base of operations. I wasn't quite sure what I was
going to do when I got there, but I had no doubt something
would suggest itself.

Dim shapes moved among the trees, forcing their way through
curtains of hanging vines and twitching liana, but I had no idea
what they might be. Perhaps DeChance and his hunters had taught
the local wildlife to keep their distance and mind their manners.
Something moved in the shadows beside the trail, slipping
between the trees with almost supernatural grace and ease, always
matching its pace to mine. It never made any move to emerge
on to the trail, for which I was quietly grateful. I kept my hand

near my time pen. If anything big and unpleasant did make a pass at me, I was ready to stop Time and run for my life. It's good to have a plan.

I tried to take my mind off my silent companion by studying the trees surrounding me. They were unlike any I'd ever seen before. Wide as well as tall, their long, drooping branches were weighed down by heavy greenery. The trunks were gnarled and twisted like old men's faces, and as the moonlight came and went, it bestowed a kind of animation, as though the faces were turning to watch me pass. Like predators only pretending to be trees, so they could lure me in and do something unpleasant. I kept to the centre of the trail, putting as much distance as possible between me and the jungle.

A sudden flash of colour caught my eye, as a huge parrot dropped out of nowhere to perch on a branch. Its plumage was so bright it was almost psychedelic, and it looked big enough to carry off most small mammals. The bird studied me with beady, suspicious eyes as I moved on. I just hoped it wasn't part of DeChance's security network.

Sweat ran down my face and dripped off my chin, and I had to keep brushing it out of my eyes. My clothes were soaked, and not just from the heat. The constant pressure of unseen eyes was wearing me down. And then the great trees suddenly fell back to reveal a moonlit clearing with a house right in the middle. I stayed in the shadows at the edge of the clearing and studied the house carefully. A squat bungalow, with bamboo walls and a flat roof, it seemed to lurk in the shimmering moonlight, like a big dog suspicious of strangers. No windows and no sign of a door. And no way to tell whether anyone was at home.

This had to be DeChance's house, given that the only trail in the jungle led straight to it. Why weren't there any guards? I slipped on my sunglasses, but there wasn't a single defensive shield or hidden guardian. I put the sunglasses away. Perhaps everyone was out, hunting Polly.

My hands clenched into fists that ached to hit someone. I made myself breathe slowly and steadily. I couldn't help Polly if I lost control. First rule of the thief: concentrate on the problem in front of you. And right now, that meant getting inside the house, so I could figure out what was going on. I moved into the clearing, one step at a time. I felt very exposed without trees or shadows to hide me, and the moonlight was as bright as a theatre spotlight. And then I looked round sharply as I heard footsteps heading my way. It seemed the guards had finally showed up.

I took in a deep breath and hit the button on my pen. The moonlight was suddenly soaked with the blood-red light of infra-red, and the guards' footsteps cut off as a great silence descended on the world. I forced my way through air thick as treacle and set off round the opposite side of the house to the guards. The bamboo walls seemed to just go on and on, without a break. I had to find an entrance before I ran out of air. I was seriously considering punching a hole through the bamboo wall when I finally stumbled across a very ordinary-looking door.

I didn't have time to check for defences; I just unlocked the door with my skeleton key and barged straight in. I forced the door shut, hit the pen again and breathed deeply, leaning against the door for support. Two sets of footsteps passed by on the other side. I hadn't realized the guards were that close. I stood very still, concentrating on the footsteps as they moved on round the house, and then pushed myself away from the door and looked around.

All the lights were off: a good indication that everyone was out. A single electric lamp had been left glowing on top of the coffee table. A light to come home to, so DeChance wouldn't have to walk into darkness? We all have our own special fears.

In my mind's eye, I saw Polly in her wolf form, racing through the jungle, plunging through the trees and hanging vines, while DeChance and his hunters moved steadily, remorselessly, after her. Carrying guns with silver bullets, and something to cut the wolf's head off afterwards, so they could take it home as a trophy. And I hated them all so hard I could taste it.

I took the lamp from the table and held it up to spread some light across the room. Comfortable chairs, big enough to sink into, colourful rugs on the floor, bookcases and some very striking examples of primitive art. A well-stocked bar and a really big television. I didn't hear any air-conditioning, but the room felt refreshingly cool. I moved quickly round the room, taking in everything and touching nothing.

The door on the other side of the room opened on to DeChance's trophy room. Everywhere I looked, stuffed and mounted heads stared back at me. Glass eyes glistened as I held up the lamp, and yellowed teeth snarled in grimacing mouths. A unicorn, a gryphon, a basilisk, a roc, a gorgon and an on-leaper. Most of them so dangerous I felt a little relieved they were dead. But I still felt bad that so many amazing creatures had been killed in the name of sport. You kill monsters because you have to, to save innocents from harm, not to make yourself feel good. I turned slowly in the middle of the room, and the moving lamplight leant an illusion of life to the staring eyes, as though I was being judged and condemned by a jury of the dead. I didn't even want to count how many heads there were, but I had to wonder just how long DeChance had been running his hunts.

The next door was solid steel, with a computer lock. I showed it my skeleton key, and the lock threw up its electronic hands and surrendered. The door swung back, and just like that, I was inside DeChance's private menagerie.

Bright lights snapped on automatically, an illumination so harsh and unrelenting it left no room for shadows. I took a moment to be relieved the house had no windows, so the guards wouldn't know there was an intruder, and then I set the lamp on the floor and studied the cages set out before me.

They came in all shapes and sizes, with thick steel bars and heavy locks, but only a handful were occupied. The nearest contained a dragon no bigger than a large dog. It lay curled up with its snout on its paws, wrapped in mottled wings. Two thin plumes of smoke rose from its nostrils, but the dragon didn't even stir as I passed by.

Something vaguely human, with bottle-green scales and large clawed hands, which looked as though it might have emerged from a Black Lagoon in a really bad mood, glowered at me with unblinking goggle eyes. An overhead sprinkler kept the creature moist. The eyes showed no signs of intelligence, but when I moved in for a closer look, a clawed hand shot between the bars and nearly took my face off. I gave the creature a disappointed look and moved on.

The next cage held something roughly humanoid but with the face of a death's head moth. It sat slumped at the back of its cage, staring at the furry hands in its fuzzy lap. Its coat boasted a complex pattern of black-and-white stripes, and the hands and feet had stubby claws. Its gossamer wings hung limply from its shoulders, deliberately broken. Perhaps it had tried to escape. The fuzzy head came up, and the death's head moth looked at me sadly with glowing silver eyes. I nodded and moved on.

A tall, slender figure stood stiffly upright behind the next set of bars. Its long, grey robe hid all the details of what it contained, and the cowl showed nothing but darkness. For all its human shape, it stood inhumanly still – more like a statue than a living thing. My skin crawled. Whatever this thing was, it wasn't from around here, and I couldn't help feeling we were all a lot better off for this particular creature being locked up.

I had been thinking about letting everything go free, just on general principles, but the figure in the grey robes made me think again. And then a warm and pleasant voice addressed me, from further back.

'There's no use trying to understand the Grey Presence, dear boy. It doesn't talk, doesn't move . . . Doesn't do anything really. I think it's sulking.'

I gave the Grey Presence plenty of room and moved on, until I was standing before a large manticore, held in a cage only just big enough to contain it. A manticore has the body of a lion, an eagle's wings and a scorpion's tale. I had to wonder what its parents saw in each other. Though it can get very foggy on the moors. The flat face had human attributes, and its eyes were calm and knowing. There was power and threat in the creature, but also grace and warmth. Presumably, a creature with that complicated a shape had to have room in it for many qualities.

There was dried blood on the floor of the cage and more on the bars.

'Yes,' said the manticore. 'My cage is too small. There isn't room to spread my wings or even turn around without hurting myself. That's deliberate, to leave me stiff and uncomfortable and unable to rest, so that when they finally let me out of here, I'll be too angry to do anything but run and fight . . . And so weakened that when the hunters finally catch up with me, I won't be able to put up much of a struggle. Because this is sport, after all. Fair play need not apply. Which is why your little werewolf friend is in so much trouble.

'And no, I can't read your mind. Though I would say that, wouldn't I? Are you going to let me out, or are you still thinking about it?'

'Maybe later,' I said. 'After I've done what I came here to do.'

'You're here to kill DeChance,' said the manticore. 'Best of luck, old thing; I'm sure we'd all feel so much happier. We might even throw a party, with hats and streamers and things.'

'Where is DeChance?' I said. 'Right now?'

'Leading a party through the jungle. Hunting the young were-wolf woman, who arrived on this island with the laudable intention of making DeChance pay for a lifetime of sins. She thought her werewolf form would give her the advantage, but she hadn't reckoned on the Mandrake Medallion. Ah, you've heard of it. Good, that saves on the exposition.

'Your friend spent some time here with us, in her own under-sized cage, screaming with pain where the silver collar touched her, and howling with rage at being confined. She dashed herself against the cage again and again, but even her wolf strength couldn't break these bars. DeChance let her out an hour ago, suitably cowed by the Medallion, of course.

'He always tells his victims there's a boat moored and waiting on the far side of the jungle, and that if they can get to it before the hunters can get to them, they're free to go. But it's a lie. Just another small cruelty, to make the victim so crazy with rage at the deception that they'll charge right at the waiting guns.

'But your little wolf friend seemed bright enough not to do the obvious thing. I can see her now: running silently through the jungle, hiding in the shadows . . . Looking for a chance to take out the hunters, one by one. She can't win, not against silver bullets and the Medallion . . . But she should be able to do for some of them before the others kill her.'

'You like to talk, don't you?' I said.

The manticore did its best to shrug in the space available. 'There's not much else to do here, and others are such poor company. If you want to save your little friend, you'd better get moving. Follow the path at the rear of the house; it'll take you straight to the hunting party.'

'How many are there?'

'Four men, two women – and DeChance, of course. Each and every one in a killing mood, with ammunition to spare. They haven't caught up with the werewolf yet, but they must be getting close. Whoever makes the kill gets to take the wolf's head back with them, as a trophy. To prove to their fellow executives what big strong heroes they are. Probably put the head on display in the boardroom, to keep the underlings in their place. Unless, of course, a werewolf turns back into a human after she dies. I admit to a complete lack of knowledge on such matters. Still, the trophy is what these people have paid an obscene amount of money to acquire. Though you'd be amazed how many of them can't actually take the killing shot when the prey's right in front of them. They can destroy thousands of lives with a casual outsourcing, but they can't pull the trigger when it matters. Now, will you please get the hell out of here? Before it's too late.'

'I will free you all,' I said. 'When I return.'

'If you return,' said the manticore.

I made my way back to the steel door, opened it and then stopped to look at the locked cages. All the creatures were staring at me, even the Grey Presence. I took out my skeleton key, pointed it at the cages and turned the key on the air. There was a stubborn resistance as unseen security protocols fought back, but I just piled on the pressure until all the locks on all the cages snapped open.

'That's it,' I said. 'What happens now is up to you. Have a nice day.'

The manticore was already squeezing out of his cage, spreading his wings and flexing his curved scorpion sting.

'Happy trails, dear boy.'

The Grey Presence was outside its cage, though I never saw it move. The cowl started to turn in my direction. I slammed the door shut on it and hurried back through the house.

I opened the front door a crack and listened carefully. Not far away, two guards were talking quietly. One grousing about the endless heat, while the other grunted acknowledgements. I didn't have time to come up with a good plan, not with the creatures behind me and Polly and the hunting party up ahead. So I just hit the button on my time pen, forced the door open and slipped past the two guards while they were frozen in place. I started across the open clearing and only then spotted a group of motion-less figures emerging from the jungle path. Some days, things wouldn't go right if you paid them. I hurried round the side of the house until I found the trail at the rear and then bolted into the jungle for as long as the last of my air would carry me.

I finally hit the pen again, stumbled to a halt and leaned on the nearest tree, fighting for breath. My holiday trip to an island paradise was taking a lot out of me. The oppressive heat envel-oped me like a sweaty blanket. The jungle was as dark and noisy as ever, but this time I found it comforting, because the constant bedlam helped to hide my presence. It should also keep DeChance and his hunting party from knowing I was coming after them.

I forced myself away from the tree and moved on down the trail. *Hang on, Polly. I'm on my way.* I took out my compass, and the needle pointed unwaveringly ahead. A sudden fusillade of shots rang out, and the whole jungle fell silent. I stood very still. There was no scream and no sound of a body falling to the ground. A few more shots rang out, but they sounded tentative, and the echoes quickly died away. The prey had evaded the hunters.

The jungle uproar started up again. I padded quickly along the moonlit trail until I saw a group of people up ahead. They were standing close together, apparently convinced there was safety in numbers, and arguing loudly over whose fault it was that the wolf got away. I moved off the trail and into the trees, slipping carefully past curtains of hanging vines and lianas. The hunters were so busy blaming each other that they had no idea I was closing in on them. Sweat dripped off my face, but my heart was cold. I hadn't decided yet what I was going to do, but I was sure something suitably unpleasant would occur to me.

I stood very still, just another dark shape in the jungle gloom, close enough to make out the individuals in the group. I had no trouble recognizing DeChance. A tall, rangy figure, dressed as a traditional Great White Hunter. A white linen suit with razor-sharp creases, a fedora hat with a tiger-skin band, and a wide leather belt bearing two knives heavy enough to cut anything's head off. He carried his rifle at the ready, with the ease of long experience.

DeChance was older than I expected, with thinning grey hair and a pencil moustache. His face was deeply lined, probably more from exposure to the elements than age. He was the only one watching the jungle, and his gaze was calm and focused. He was smiling slightly, but there was no humour in it.

His clients stood awkwardly around in well-tailored tropical suits already heavily wrinkled and stained with sweat. They looked like so many extras in a low-budget movie. They might have been something big in the boardroom, but in the jungle, they were out of their depth, and they knew it. They all carried rifles like DeChance's, but none of them looked as if they knew how to use them. They were tired and frustrated, and starting to wonder whether this had ever been a good idea. But they still had that look in their eyes, an eagerness for the hunt and a taste for blood and suffering.

'You never said this would go on for so long!' one of the businessmen shouted at DeChance. 'We came for the kill, not the chase!'

'You can't pay for a kill,' said DeChance, his voice calm and assured. 'You have to earn it.'

Another of the businessmen sniffed loudly. 'You made things far more difficult than they needed to be. You should have slowed the wolf down with silver shackles, to give us more of an advantage.'

DeChance laughed in the man's face. He was the only one there who looked as though he belonged in the jungle, and he lorded it over his clients like a rock star with his entourage.

'The wolf has to run free or there's no sport in it. It's all about pitting your skills against hers. You paid for the joy of the hunt and the thrill of the chase, and this is all part of the experience. Now, stop whining and check your weapons. I doubt very much that what you shot at was the wolf, but she must have discovered by now that there is no getaway boat, so you can expect her to turn up any time soon, with blood and horror on her mind. Emotions strong enough to overwhelm her good sense and send her straight into your waiting guns. So keep your eyes and ears open! She could leap out of the shadows, rip out your throats and be gone in a moment. And as long as she stays out of range of the Mandrake Medallion, I won't be able to do a damn thing about it.'

The businesspeople looked suitably impressed and crowded closer together, like cattle in a pen that can tell there's a storm coming. They peered into the jungle, straining their eyes against the shadows. One of the men looked right at me and didn't see a thing. One of the businesswomen suddenly raised her rifle and fired off a shot.

'Stop wasting ammunition!' DeChance snapped. 'That was just the local wildlife. The wolf won't be so obvious.'

The woman who'd fired flushed angrily but lowered her rifle. I eased forward, any small noise I made covered by the jungle din, until I was standing right at the edge of the trail. So close I could have reached out and touched any of them. And still they had no idea I was there. Even DeChance, the Great White Hunter himself, was too busy sneering at his clients to notice.

I hit the button on my time pen and froze them all in place. I stepped out on to the trail, grabbed the nearest businessman and hauled his stiff and unresponsive body back into the trees. I got as far as I could on one breath and then dumped the man on the ground. I restarted Time, and he opened his mouth to scream. I kicked him hard, burying my boot in his gut. All the breath went out of him, and he collapsed, curling miserably around his pain.

Back on the trail, the other members of the hunting party were crying out in shock and horror, because one of them had apparently just disappeared into thin air.

I looked at the wretched figure lying at my feet. He and his fellow hunters were planning to kill Polly. So to hell with them. I crouched down beside the man, and he flinched away.

'Why are you doing this?' he said. 'Don't you know who I am?'

'I don't care,' I said. And something in my voice kept him from saying anything else.

I had been thinking about killing the man and leaving his body for the others to find. But now . . . He just looked too pathetic. I didn't need to kill him, to send a message. I stopped Time again, picked up the businessman and hauled him back to the trail. Either he was getting heavier or the day was taking its toll on me. At the edge of the trail, I restarted Time and kicked him out on to the path. He appeared suddenly from the shadows, crying out and

flailing his arms, and one of the other businessmen shot him in
the face. The body crashed to the ground and didn't move. And
I couldn't find it in my heart to feel the least bit sorry for him.

The shooter sat down suddenly on the trail and hugged his
rifle to him, shaking in disbelief. The others stood very still,
shocked into silence. Only DeChance stared into the shadows,
looking to see where the dead man had come from.

'How could he just vanish and then reappear so suddenly?'
one of the businesswomen said loudly.

'It wasn't the wolf,' said DeChance. 'No claw or teeth marks
on the body. It would appear . . . we're not alone. Someone else
has joined the game.'

The hunters raised their guns and stared around them. I stood
very still, and none of them saw me. DeChance kicked the man
sitting down.

'Get up. The rules have changed. Someone out there thinks
he's hunting us.'

'Who?' said the man, as he scrambled awkwardly to his feet.
'How could anyone have landed on this island without your
security people knowing?'

'Good question,' said DeChance. 'I may have to fire a whole
bunch of people once this is over.'

'Call your guards,' said the man, 'Get them out here to protect
us.'

'And spoil the fun?' said DeChance. For the first time, he had
a real smile on his face. 'This just adds to the challenge.'

'Are you insane?' one of the businesswomen said loudly. 'We
could die out here! Call your guards!'

'Grow a spine,' said DeChance. 'If any of you need the guards
that badly, you can follow the trail back to the house. But I'm
not going with you. Not while there's hunting to be done. And
really . . . how far do you think you'd get on your own?'

The hunters looked at the trail and then at the jungle, and
didn't move.

'First sensible decision you've made,' said DeChance. 'Let's
go.'

'Where?' said the businesswoman.

'Anywhere,' said DeChance. 'Standing around like this just
makes us a better target.'

'What are we going to do?' said the man who'd killed his fellow hunter.

'Forget the wolf, for now,' said DeChance. 'We need to figure out who's after us and how best to deal with them. They don't have a gun or they would have used it, so we still have the advantage. Once we've killed them, we can get back to the wolf, and one of you can earn your trophy.'

'This isn't what we paid you for,' said one of the businessmen.

DeChance smiled. 'Think of it as a bonus.'

He set off down the trail, his rifle at the ready, and the hunting party went after him.

They didn't look back once at the body on the trail.

I moved silently along with them, just another shadow in the jungle. I thought about using the time pen again and abducting another hunter, but I didn't. DeChance might recognize what was happening. You don't get many second chances with an old-school villain like DeChance, because they really have been there, done it all and remembered where they'd buried the bodies.

Besides, I'd been using the time pen a lot, and that was bad. When I inherited it from the original Gideon Sable, via his safe deposit box, the pen came with a warning. *Don't use it too often. They're watching.* I had no idea who *They* might be, and I didn't want to find out the hard way.

I started to move a branch out of my way and only realized at the last moment there was a snake wrapped around it. At least a dozen feet long and as thick around as a man's arm, the snake studied me with cool indifference, its forked tongue flicking out to taste the air. I was pretty sure it was a constrictor, and that gave me an idea. I chose my moment carefully and then grabbed the snake behind the head. I'm not sure which of us was more surprised that move actually worked. I pulled steadily, and the snake reluctantly unwound itself from the branch. The sheer weight of the long body almost pulled it from my hand, but I dragged the snake over to the edge of the trail and then used all my strength to throw it at the hunting party.

The snake sailed ungainly through the air and landed on one of the businessmen. It immediately curled around his body and squeezed with everything it had. The man couldn't even find the breath to cry out. Blood spurted from his mouth, eyes and ears. The other hunters cried out and scattered, but DeChance stood his ground. He glared into the jungle, rifle raised. I stood very still. DeChance turned away, aimed his rifle casually and shot the snake in the head. The whole length of its body convulsed, and both snake and businessman fell dead on the trail. The remaining hunters stared wildly about them, making all kinds of unhappy noises. DeChance shouted at them until they shut up, and then fixed them with a cold glare.

'The man is dead,' said DeChance. 'You're not. But you might be if you keep standing around here. So move.'

By accident or design, his rifle had moved to cover the hunters. They looked at each other and set off down the trail again. Just two men and two women now, and DeChance. I kept up with them easily enough as they hurried along the trail, but I was so busy concentrating on them I didn't see the really large monkey until it reared up right in front of me. Big and hairy, furious red eyes, bared teeth. And my first thought was: *What is something like that doing on a small island in the South Pacific?* Followed by: *They can be really dangerous when they're upset.* I hit the button on my pen, grabbed the frozen monkey, hauled it over to the edge of the jungle, restarted Time and kicked it out on to the trail.

All the hunters screamed as a large and furious monkey appeared out of nowhere, and the monkey screamed even louder as it attacked them. The two businessmen didn't even have time to raise their guns before the monkey tore them to pieces. Blood flew everywhere. The two businesswomen fell back, forgetting for the moment that they had guns. DeChance didn't. He shot the monkey in the back and waited for it to fall, and when it didn't because it was too intent on tearing the two dead bodies apart, he shot it twice more. The monkey stopped what it was doing and sat down suddenly, like a child who'd just run out of energy. It made a low, puzzled hooting sound and then fell backwards and lay still.

I felt sorry for the monkey. It hadn't asked to be made part of someone else's war. But having seen what it did to the two hunters, I was just glad it didn't have a chance to do the same thing to me.

One of the businesswomen screamed furiously at DeChance. 'This hunt is over! This is not what we signed up for! Take us back to the house and the guards, so they can protect us from this madness!'

'You really think we'd get that far?' said DeChance. He sounded calm, almost amused.

'What the hell else can we do?' shouted the other business-woman.

'I would suggest the two of you stand back to back,' said DeChance. 'So whatever's out there can't catch you by surprise. Feel free to shoot anything that moves that isn't us. I'll call the guards to come here.'

The businesswomen moved quickly into position, covering both sides of the trail with their rifles. They were both breathing hard, but their hands were surprisingly steady. It was obvious to me that DeChance was setting them up as bait, hoping to lure the mystery attacker into targeting the women while he watched the jungle. He had a radio at his belt, but he wasn't even reaching for it. I had a sudden feeling I wasn't alone. I turned my head slowly, and there was a werewolf crouching beside me. Tall and lithely muscular, with a shaggy wolf's head, a lean, mean power-house covered in thick black fur, Polly's eyes gleamed golden in the gloom. I hadn't even heard her approach.

I just had time to nod to her, and then Polly launched herself on to the trail. She ducked under the first businesswoman's gun and slammed into her with a lowered shoulder. The force of the blow sent both businesswomen crashing to the ground. Polly was upon them in a moment, slashing at them with her claws. Blood gushed on the night air, and both hunters died so quickly that they never even got a shot off. Polly crouched over the two bodies, grinning unpleasantly at DeChance.

He slowly brought his rifle to bear on her, but she stayed where she was, out of range of the Mandrake Medallion, deliberately risking her life to hold DeChance's attention – and give me time to do something. I hit the button on my pen and moved out on to the trail. Polly and DeChance were frozen in place, their eyes locked in the endless stare of hunter and hunted. I moved in behind DeChance and drew back a fist. I only had time for one blow, and it would have to kill the man, or he'd kill both of us.

I restarted Time, and DeChance spun round to face me, his rifle
trained on my face.

'Don't move!' he said loudly, as much to Polly as to me. He
nodded easily at me. 'I knew someone had to be playing games
with Time. Is that Gideon Sable's time pen? We worked together
a few times, and I still remember what it felt like. Drop the pen,
or I'll drop you. And her.'

I smiled easily back at DeChance and tucked the pen into my
jacket pocket. 'Don't want to risk damaging it. Who knows what
might happen?'

'So you're the current Gideon Sable,' said DeChance, still
covering me with his gun. 'What are you even doing here? There's
nothing on my island you'd want to steal.'

'Polly is part of my crew,' I said. 'And you can't have her.'

He shook his head slowly. 'Sentiment will be the death of
you.'

DeChance stepped carefully backwards until he could cover
Polly and me at the same time. The werewolf was still crouched
over her kills, grinning widely to show off the blood dripping
from her fangs.

'Don't be bashful, wolf,' said DeChance. 'Come on over here
and join me. Let the Mandrake Medallion put you under its spell
so I can make you kill your friend.'

Polly growled. A low animal sound, full of all the dark savagery
of the jungle. She didn't move.

'Do as you're told, little wolf,' said DeChance. 'Or I'll gut-
shoot your friend, and you can listen to him scream.' He sounded
entirely calm and relaxed. The professional hunter at his work.
'Not a bad ending to the hunt. Two legends for the price of one.
You shouldn't have come here on your own, Gideon.'

I smiled back at him. 'What makes you think I did?'

I nodded at the shadows beside him, and from out of the jungle
stepped the manticore, the death's head moth, and the Grey
Presence. DeChance fell back several steps, swinging his rifle
round to cover them. I gestured urgently at Polly to hold her
ground and then smiled at the new arrivals.

'I knew you'd follow me.'

'Of course you did,' said the manticore. 'You're the man with
the plan.'

'I still have the Mandrake Medallion,' DeChance said loudly. 'You know what that does to you.'

'Doesn't do a damned thing for me,' I said.

I hit the button on my pen, walked over to DeChance and took the Medallion from around his neck. I then moved back out of his reach and restarted Time. DeChance stared at me, with the pen in one hand and the Medallion in the other, and for the first time I saw fear in his eyes.

'You fool,' he said. 'They'll kill us all.'

'I don't think so,' I said. 'You're the one who imprisoned them; I'm the one who set them free. It's all about the kindness of strangers.' I nodded to the manticore. 'He's all yours. And once you're done with him, so is this island. Have fun with it. And happy hunting.'

The manticore smiled at DeChance. 'Run.'

DeChance raised his rifle. The Grey Presence gestured lightly, and the gun turned to dust in DeChance's hands. He turned abruptly and ran off down the trail. And the manticore, the death's head moth and the Grey Presence went after him.

The werewolf padded over to me and turned into Polly Perkins. More than six feet tall, with really long black hair, the young Indian woman was drop-dead gorgeous and entirely naked. Her dark skin was covered in sweat, and her eyes were exhausted, but she still had a smile for me. I took off my jacket and draped it round her shoulders.

'Thanks for coming after me,' said Polly.

'That's what family is for,' I said.

I took out the teleport bracelet and snapped it into place around my wrist. The twenty-third century technology made happy busy sounds as it powered up. I took Polly's hand in mine.

'Let's go home.'

FOUR

When That Old Gang of Mine Gets Together

P olly and I appeared just a few yards short of my shop's front door. Pretty good navigation, considering the bracelet did all the heavy lifting. A quick glance around confirmed we had the street to ourselves. It was still early in the morning, and Polly shivered inside my jacket as the sweltering heat of Bounty Island was replaced by the chill of Old Soho.

'Let's get you inside,' I said. 'And into some fresh clothes.'

Polly nodded tiredly. 'A cup of tea would be nice.'

'I think we can manage that,' I said. 'Milk with three sugars, right?'

She smiled briefly. 'You remembered.'

I put my arm across her shoulders and escorted her over to the shop. I pushed open the front door, and the stuffed grizzly bear reared up before us, all claws and snarling fangs. I stared at him coldly.

'Very nice, Yogi. A bit late, and aimed at entirely the wrong person, but I appreciate the effort.'

The bear dropped back into his usual stance and wouldn't look at me.

'And don't sulk!' I said sternly. 'You sulk louder than anyone I've ever met!'

Polly sneezed violently, almost pulling herself out of my grip. Lex and Sally came rushing forward, and I handed Polly over to them. They hugged her tightly, saying her name again and again, and she clung to them like a drowning woman going down for the last time. Sidney the standing mirror blasted triumphal music out of his glass. I found a chair and sat down heavily. It had been a long day, and it wasn't even close to being over. I would have been hard-pressed to name one part of me that wasn't aching or complaining, but it did warm my heart to see Polly back in the arms of her parents. Lex and Sally finally let her go and stepped back to look her over critically. Lex pulled my jacket close around Polly, like a father tucking his child into bed, and Sally glared at me.

'What took you so long? And why is my daughter in such a state? I haven't smelt this much sweat since I crashed a football team's changing room.'

'I don't think I'll ask,' said Lex.

'I was there to steal the trophy!'

'Of course you were.'

I didn't need to check my clothes to know I stank like the back end of a horse that had just crossed the finishing line. I levered myself out of my chair and on to my feet, swaying just a little.

'Things got a bit out of hand on Bounty Island,' I said.

'Being hunted?' said Lex.

'Being hunters,' I said.

Lex nodded approvingly to Polly. 'That's my girl.'

I gestured to the rear of the shop. 'There are hot showers out the back, Polly, and you should be able to find something you can wear in Annie's wardrobe.'

Sally hustled Polly towards the back. 'We need to find you some clothes you can still keep on, while you're being a wolf.'

'When I'm a wolf, I don't want clothes,' said Polly. 'And afterwards, it's not like I'm shy. I work as an exotic dancer, remember? If my heaving, naked body isn't inflaming an entire night-club dance floor with raging lust, I'm not doing my job.'

'I swear I used to be the interesting one in this family,' said Sally. 'Come along, dear.'

They disappeared out the back, with Sally still chattering cheerfully away. Lex nodded to me.

'Thank you for bringing my little girl back.'

'Any time,' I said.

'Any problems with the teleport bracelet?'

'It did what it was supposed to,' I said. 'But I still don't trust it. Far too many ways for it to go wrong.'

'Like arriving somewhere and finding it had turned you inside out?' said Lex.

I looked at him. 'I think I'll go take my shower now.'

'Please do,' said Lex. 'Before the paint starts peeling off the walls.'

'My varnish is starting to bubble,' said Sidney.

'It's good to be home,' I said. And walked with dignity into the rear of the shop.

I locked the Mandrake Medallion and the teleport bracelet in the most heavily protected security boxes I had. As soon as the current mess was over, I'd find someone who could destroy the Medallion. Because too many people I knew would never feel safe as long as it was still around. The bracelet could stay in its box forever and a day, as far as I was concerned.

Polly was splashing happily in her shower cubicle, singing 'Too Drunk to Fuck' by the Dead Kennedys. I stripped off my sweat-soaked clothes and left them lying in a trail on the floor behind me as I headed for my cubicle. I ran the water as hot as I could stand and luxuriated in the pounding spray and billowing clouds of steam. It took half a bar of soap before I felt able to leave the cubicle and go looking for fresh clothes.

One of the advantages of always dressing in stark black and white is that I never have to waste time wondering what I'm going to wear next. I just open the wardrobe and grab the next set off the rack. I reclaimed the tools of the trade from my discarded clothes and settled them comfortably in my new pockets. Time to be Gideon Sable, master thief, one more time.

I'd rescued Polly. Now I had to find Annie.

Back in the main shop, Lex was talking to the stuffed bear. It wasn't saying anything in response, but it did appear to be listening respectfully. Lex studied me critically.

'You look more like yourself. How bad did it get on the island?'

'Pretty bad,' I said. 'It got a lot closer to the wire with Polly than I was comfortable with.'

'What about DeChance?' said Lex.

'I was ready to kill him,' I said steadily. 'But in the end, I ran into some people with a better claim. So I let them have him.'

'You are sure DeChance is dead?' said Lex.

'By now, he's resting in pieces.'

Lex just nodded. Sally came back in, arm in arm with Polly. The tall Indian girl was smiling happily and gleaming with the air of the freshly scrubbed, though her long dark hair was still damp. She was wearing black motorcycle leathers, knee-high boots and a black silk scarf at her throat. Her favourite look. She posed before us like some glorious pagan goddess, and I felt like applauding.

'Thank you, Gideon,' she said. 'You went a long way to save me.'

'Any time,' I said.

'Polly has been telling me all about her adventures,' Sally said proudly. 'Our little girl is all grown up!'

Polly walked up to me, kissed me on the forehead and then pushed me away.

'Thank you for rescuing me. Don't ever do that again. I have my reputation to consider.'

'Of course,' I said. 'What was I thinking?'

'Hey! Has no one got a good word to say to me?' Sidney said loudly. 'I helped!'

Polly smiled at the standing mirror. 'Then I owe you too. What do you give the mirror who has nothing? Tell you what . . . How about I give you some advance warning the next time I'm going to take a shower?'

'Oh, I spy on everyone in their showers,' Sidney said airily.

We all looked at him.

'It can't come as a complete surprise to you that I am a dedicated voyeur,' said the mirror. 'How do you think I ended up like this in the first place?'

'Oh, darling,' said Sally. 'If I'd known you were watching, I'd have put on a show.'

Lex scowled at the mirror. 'I can feel seven years of bad luck hovering on the horizon.'

'Moving on,' I said quickly.

Polly frowned. 'Sally told me about Annie being kidnapped. I can track like you wouldn't believe, but if there isn't a trail . . .'

'I have something in mind,' I said.

'You have a plan,' said Lex. 'Imagine our surprise.'

'I still remember how freaked out I felt when I was kidnapped from that flat in Paris,' said Sally. 'No idea what was going on or what might happen to me. But I never doubted you guys would come and rescue me. So I just concentrated on messing with my captors' heads and playing the situation to my advantage. We must have faith that Annie can do the same. She's stronger than you think.'

I didn't say anything. Annie was many things, and many people, but I wouldn't have said strong was one of them. Not when I thought of all the other personas rattling around inside her head, so she could hide from the strain of being herself.

Polly looked at me expectantly. 'How are we going to find Annie?'

'I usually rely on Sidney to find people,' I said. 'But since he can't help . . .'

'There's nothing I can do!' said the mirror.

'It's all right, Sidney,' I said. 'We understand.'

'It's not all right!' the mirror said bitterly. 'The one time you really need me, and I'm letting you down! I have a sub-routine doing nothing but searching the world for traces of Annie, but the kidnapper must be concealing her behind shields operating on a level I've never encountered before. But I'm damned if I'll be beaten! I will never stop trying to find her.'

'We know that, Sidney,' I said.

'I care about her too,' the mirror said quietly.

'Of course you do,' I said. 'You're part of the crew. That makes you family, as well.'

The mirror started to say something, but he couldn't. His glass misted over. Sally hurried over to stand before him.

'Oh, Sidney, sweetie, are you crying?'

'I wasn't always a mirror,' said Sidney. 'I was a person, once.'

'What happened, darling?' said Sally. 'Were you cursed?'

'No,' said Sidney. 'I asked for this.'

'Why?' I said.

'So I could do penance,' said Sidney. He cleared his throat, a disconcerting sound from something that didn't have a throat. 'We need to concentrate on what matters. What do we know about why Annie was kidnapped?'

Polly looked to me. 'The kidnapper needs you to steal Time's Arrow. Which means . . . Annie is just a means to an end.'

'This whole thing strikes me as personal,' Sally said firmly.

'A chance for the kidnapper to get what he wants and have his revenge on you at the same time. He has to be someone you know!'

'I had already worked that out,' I said. 'But I can't think of anyone that mad at me, who's still among the living. Lex has always been very thorough when it comes to cleaning up after us.'

'Even when you didn't approve,' said Lex. 'Because I always knew a day like this would arrive, eventually.'

Polly frowned. 'If he knows about you, Gideon, he must expect you to turn to us for help. So he must believe he's strong enough to stand against all of us. In which case . . . maybe we need to reach out to our friends: the special people with special skills, that the kidnapper won't be expecting.'

'If you know anyone who's better at finding people than me, you go right ahead and contact them!' said Sidney. 'I'm not proud. Well, I am, obviously, but . . .'

'If you can't see the kidnapper,' said Polly, 'maybe we need someone with better eyes.'

'Do I tell you how to do your job?' said Sidney. 'Do I lecture you on how to chase postmen or hump people's legs?'

'I do not chase postmen!' Polly said loudly.

'Hush, children,' said Sally. 'Grown-ups are talking. Gideon . . . you've made some pretty powerful friends in your time, some of whom still owe you favours. The Wild Card, Madam Osiris, Cleopatra Bones . . .'

'And there's always Sandra Ransom,' said Lex. 'God's little sister.'

I raised a hand to forestall what promised to be a long list of names and résumés.

'The kidnapper must be keeping a close eye on us. If I reach out to anyone powerful, he might kill Annie, rather than risk being caught.'

'So we're just going to do everything the kidnapper wants?' said Sally.

I smiled. 'Well, that's what we want him to think. But while he's watching us apparently doing what he wants, we will actually be doing something else. I have a plan. In fact, I have plans within plans, like a Russian doll. So many of them that he'll never be sure what's coming next or what's really going on. Until it's far too late.'

Lex nodded solemnly. 'I've always enjoyed listening to the way you think.'

Sally clapped her hands delightedly. 'Yay, team! The crew is back!'

Polly grinned wolfishly, and Sidney sang 'Happy Days Are Here Again' until we threatened to throw things at him if he didn't stop.

'All right,' said Lex. 'What do we do first?'

'What we do best,' I said. 'Steal something.'

They all looked at me until it became clear I'd said all I was going to.

'What about your plan?' said Sally. 'And the plans within plans?'

'I'll tell you what you need to know, when you need to know it,' I said.

Polly bristled. 'What's the matter? Don't you trust your own crew?'

'Of course,' I said carefully. 'But the kidnapper must have been planning this for some time. He could have bugged this place and be listening to every word we're saying.'

'No way in Hell!' Sidney said loudly. 'I'd know!'

'Would you?' I said. 'You didn't see who took Annie, and you can't see past the kidnapper's protections.'

'Someone is going to pay for undermining my confidence,' the mirror said darkly.

'What are you going to do?' Polly said sweetly. 'Fall on them?'

Sidney sighed, a low, mournful sound like the wind moaning in a chimney. 'No one takes you seriously when you're just a talking mirror. If I was giving you some big prophecy, or pontificating about the One True Ring, you'd be all attention and arguing over merchandising rights.'

'Anyway!' I said loudly, glaring everyone into silence if not submission. 'My plans are staying where they're secure: inside my head.'

'OK . . .' said Polly, in her best *I am changing the subject for the good of all* tone of voice. 'What kind of a place is the Midnight

Museum? I've heard about it – because everyone has – but what's it for?'

'The Midnight Museum is the world's most secure repository for some of the rarest and most amazing items ever gathered together under one roof,' I said. 'Everything thieves like us dream about, and treasures beyond the hopes of the most rabid collectors . . . But only Members of the Midnight Club get to see them.'

'What kind of things are we talking about?' said Lex. 'Valuable, historical, mythical?'

'I can't say for sure,' I said carefully. 'But you don't build a reputation like the Midnight Museum's on anything but the most incredible exhibits.'

'Why haven't we gone after this place before?' Lex said bluntly.

'Because the Midnight Club has defences that could eat us alive,' I said. 'And that is not a metaphor.'

'But we are still going in?' said Polly.

'Of course,' I said. 'We have to.'

'So the Club Members . . . just keep these things to look at?' said Sally. 'They don't even get to play with them? Where's the fun in that?'

'You never were an aesthete,' said Lex.

'Darling, I couldn't even spell it,' said Sally.

Lex looked at me sharply. 'We used to be all about taking down bastards like these and making them pay for their sins. Why don't we just clear out the Midnight Museum while we're there – take the lot, and teach the selfish little shits a lesson they'll never forget?'

I was already shaking my head. 'The Club Members include some seriously dangerous people. They might overlook losing one item, which they might not even realize is missing for some time, rather than appear vulnerable. But if we make this a personal insult, they'll never stop coming after us. No, Lex, stick to Time's Arrow.'

'But who are these people?' Polly said stubbornly. 'You must have some idea.'

'The high and the mighty, the low and the devious,' I said. 'The best and the scariest in their field.'

'Why are you being so careful not to mention any names?' said Lex.

'Because the first rule of the Midnight Club is that they don't talk about the Club,' I said. 'I've heard lots of names mentioned, but those are the ones I believe least. Real Members don't boast for fear of being black-balled with extreme prejudice. Anyone could be a Member.'

'Including the kidnapper?' said Polly.

'That would explain how he knows about Time's Arrow,' I said. 'He'd also know enough about the Club's security to be sure he'd need a master thief to go after it.'

Lex nodded. 'Where do we start, Gideon?'

'Lean in close, my best beloveds,' I said. 'And prepared to be amazed.'

We all drew up chairs and sat down facing each other. The chairs appeared out of nowhere, as required, but no one said anything. It's always been that kind of shop. Even Sidney trundled closer on his squeaky casters, to make sure he wasn't left out.

'We're going to use a stalking horse, to get inside the Midnight Museum,' I said quietly. 'Sally will approach the Club Curator, one Malcolm Greely, and apply for Membership. He's a dried-up old fossil, but he knows his business, so we're not even going to try to fool him. Sally will present him with something so special he'll even be ready to admit a small-time thief like Switch It Sally to get his hands on it. Her reputation will ensure they won't see her as a serious threat.'

Sally started to object, then thought about it and nodded stiffly. Lex patted her hand comfortingly.

'They just don't know you like we do.'

'Or they'd never let you within a mile of the Club, for fear you'd switch the gold fillings out of their teeth,' said Polly.

Sally beamed at her. 'How well you know me.'

'The item I have in mind will definitely get you Membership in the Midnight Club,' I said. 'And that will allow you to study the Club's security from the inside. You are going to find us a back door, Sally.'

Lex leaned forward. 'Hold it. Doesn't that mean the Club Members will put the blame on Sally, once they realize Time's Arrow is gone?'

'No,' I said patiently. 'Because they'd know that would mean taking on you, as well.'

'Damned right,' said Lex. 'I'd make the whole Club extinct if they so much as looked at Sally the wrong way.'

'He is such a sweetie,' Sally said proudly.

Polly frowned at me. 'Are you going to give Sally something from your shop?'

'I don't have anything special enough to guarantee Club Membership,' I said. 'So we are going to have to flim-flam them. Razzle-dazzle the bastards, till they won't know which way is up.' I looked steadily at Lex. 'Everyone knows your story. How you damned yourself when you murdered two angels with the Iscariot Device and stole their halos.'

'I can't offer you the Device,' said Lex. 'That's long gone. And I would never put a weapon like that in their hands anyway.'

'I had something else in mind,' I said. 'Sally is going to say she stole one of your halos while you were sleeping, and wants to present it to the Club in return for Membership, and its protection from you.'

They all sat up straight in their chairs.

'But . . . I would never do anything like that!' said Sally.

'They don't know that,' I said. 'They think you're still the cheap little thief you used to be, before you married Lex.'

Sally pouted. 'I was never that bad. And I was certainly never cheap!'

'There is a problem with this ingenious plan, Gideon,' said Lex. 'My halos won't come off. God knows I've tried.'

I shook my head patiently. 'We're not going to offer the Club one of your halos, Lex. Razzle-dazzle, remember? I know where we can get another halo.'

'So Sally can run a game on the Curator!' said Polly.

'That is so cool!' said Sally. 'I always wanted to be a glamorous secret agent, working undercover and running rings round the bad guys. What do you want me to do? Seduce the Curator into spilling the beans about all the secret ways in and out of the Museum? I could do that!' She shot me a smouldering glance, then remembered where she was and smiled quickly at Lex. 'Of course, I'd be thinking about you the whole time, darling.'

'I should hope so,' said Lex.

I gave Sally my best stern look. 'No need to be so obvious, Sally. You can't afford to do anything that would seem suspicious.

Given your reputation, Club security will be all over you like stink on cheese. Just stroll around the Club and take a polite interest in everything, as any new Member would. And then, once your experienced eyes have found a gap in their defences, quietly get word to us, so we can just stroll in and help ourselves.'

Sally pouted. 'I don't get to seduce anyone? I can remember when your plans were fun . . .'

'They were never that fun,' said Lex. He looked at me steadily. 'Where are you going to get your hands on another angel's halo?'

'From an impeccable source.' I nodded to the standing mirror. 'Sidney, where is Ethel Makepeace?'

'That's more like it!' Sidney said cheerfully. 'Finally, I get a chance to do something useful! You just sit tight, and I will track her down in two shakes of a lamb's tail.' He paused. 'Do lambs actually have tails? I've never looked . . . Never mind! Sidney the talking mirror is on the job!'

'Try being on the job quietly,' I said. 'We still have things to discuss.'

'Quietly it is, boss.'

'Are we seriously talking about conning someone who used to be an angel?' said Polly. 'The word *smiting* comes to mind, and not in a good way.'

'We're not going to con Ethel,' I said. 'I'm sure she'll be only too happy to help us, once I've explained things.'

'I don't know, Gideon,' Sally said dubiously. 'Do we want to risk getting an angel mad at us? I am not spending the rest of my life as a pillar of salt!'

'Have a little faith,' I said.

'Can Sidney really locate an ex-angel?' said Polly. 'Won't she have her own shields?'

'She doesn't believe in them,' Sidney said quickly, happy for a chance to show off his extensive knowledge of the hidden world. 'Ethel wants everyone to know where she is. So people who need help can always find her, and to make it clear to all the powers and forces of this world that she isn't afraid of anyone.'

'That is what I'm counting on,' I said.

'The last time we talked with Ethel, she made it clear she didn't want anything to do with our world of crime and intrigue,' said Lex.

'But we're the good guys!' said Sally. 'Sort of.'

'We are not going to run a game on her,' I said. 'We will be entirely upfront and appeal to her better nature.'

'And if that doesn't work?' said Lex.

'Then we run a game on her,' I said. 'I'm sure she'll forgive us, eventually.'

'I think I want to hide behind something,' said Polly.

'But you're a werewolf!' I said.

'And I'd like to stay that way, and not end up as someone's hearth rug.'

Lex stared at me. 'This is your ingenious plan? Piss off someone who used to be an actual Messenger of God? Really not a good idea, Gideon! Angels are what God uses when he wants a city destroyed, or the first-born of a generation slaughtered! Do you think you can talk someone like that into just giving up their halo?'

'It's not like she's using it for anything,' I said. 'I'm sure she'll understand. She knows us.'

Sally shook her head glumly. 'You say that like it's a good thing.'

'I thought you said we couldn't afford to contact any powerful people?' said Polly.

'But Ethel isn't people,' I said. 'Technically speaking. So hopefully she'll be under – or possibly even over – the kidnapper's radar. But even if he does spot us going to see her, he won't be able to hear what we're saying, because . . . well – *angel!* He'll probably just assume we're there looking for advice. It's a calculated risk, all right?'

'We are talking about an angel who defied God's will, to become human,' said Lex. 'Because she'd had enough of being ordered around. I honestly don't see how we could talk her into doing anything she doesn't want to.'

'I thought I'd just ask politely,' I said. 'Isn't that what you did when you went to her for help?'

'You might remember, that didn't work out too well,' said Lex.

'She does want to help people,' I said. 'You were just a tougher problem than most.'

Lex shook his head stubbornly.

'When you told us about meeting her,' Polly said slowly, 'you said she didn't have her wings any more. What makes you think she'll still have her halo?'

'She'd never give that up,' said Lex. 'It's the source of her power.'

'Exactly!' said Sally. 'It would be like a retired gunslinger giving up their guns.'

'Liking this plan less and less all the time,' growled Polly. 'My hackles are standing on end, and I have a lot of hackles.'

'We'll be fine, as long as we're polite and respectful,' I said. 'If that doesn't work . . . Leave it to me. I'll fast-talk her and tie her in mental knots.'

'There is no way Ethel will give up her halo,' said Lex.

'Why would she want to hang on to it?' I said.

'I don't know! Maybe to protect her from people like us!' Lex said loudly.

Sally patted his hand comfortingly. 'Breathe, dear . . .'

'You can always stay here, Lex,' I said. 'If you want.'

He stared at me. 'I can't believe you said that. You really think I'd let you walk into danger on your own?'

'I'm sorry, Lex,' I said. 'I don't know what I was thinking.'

I was thinking I always knew which buttons to push to get him to do what I wanted, but I didn't say that. There was a lot going through my head that I didn't feel like sharing with the crew.

'This is what being around angels does to people,' said Lex. 'Because they're so much bigger than us, we tend to lose sight of what's important. If things should start going wrong, you're going to need me. If only to hide behind.'

I turned to the standing mirror. 'Any luck, Sidney?'

'Found her!' the mirror said loudly. 'Wasn't that difficult. Just the weight of her existence puts a strain on the world. She could probably break the whole material plane just by walking up and down in it.'

'Wouldn't doubt it for a moment,' I said patiently. 'But where is she, right now?'

'In her local tea room,' said Sidney. 'Just down the road from where she lives.'

'What's she doing in a tea room?' said Sally.

'Having tea,' said Sidney. 'With a few friends. A few rather disturbing friends.' The mirror cleared the throat it didn't have in an upset sort of way. 'They do seem to be a rather . . . unusual bunch, Gideon.'

'Define unusual,' I said.

'People who have renounced any allegiance to Heaven or Hell,' said Sidney. 'People who have gone their own way, and want everyone else to know it.'

'What would they want with Ethel?' said Lex, frowning.

'It appears to be a self-help and support group,' said Sidney. 'With Ethel in the chair.'

'This might not be the best time to bother the angel,' Polly said tentatively. 'It sounds like these people have their own problems.'

'I don't care if she's talking to a bunch of part-time Apostles or Succubi Anonymous,' I said. 'The sooner we get things moving, the sooner we can get Annie back. Don't let these supernatural types impress you. The weirder they are, the easier it is to run rings around them, because they can't believe mere humans could be smart enough to out-think them.'

'Oh God, he's getting confident again,' said Sally. 'That always worries me.'

'He runs rings around us easily enough,' said Lex. He looked at me. 'Or perhaps you thought we didn't notice?'

'Good to know you're paying attention,' I said.

Sally shook her head. 'Annie had better appreciate what we're putting ourselves through to rescue her.'

'It's game time, people!' I said. 'I want to see cheerful smiles and positive attitudes from all of you. We won't fool Ethel for one moment, but she'll appreciate the effort.'

I got to my feet, and one by one the others did too. The chairs quietly disappeared.

'Where do they go when we're not using them?' said Polly.

'Into storage,' I said. 'They're very tidy.'

'OK!' Sidney said importantly. 'Everyone form a line in front of me – no pushing, no shoving. And please don't mention to Ethel that I had anything to do with this. In fact, the moment you're gone, I am packing my bags and going on a long holiday.'

'You stay right where you are,' I said sternly. 'If I have to yell, I want you ready to yank us right out of there.'

'On it, boss,' the mirror said sourly.

'Calm down, Sidney,' said Sally. 'If you're very good, when we get back, I'll give your frame a good rub with the beeswax polish. You know how much you like that.'

His glass steamed over.

'Try to act like a professional, Sidney,' I said.

His glass cleared to show a pleasant little tea room. It was all very cosy, in a touristy sort of way, with tables covered in gleaming white cloths, and people sipping tea with their little fingers elegantly extended.

'Go!' said Sidney. 'Go now!'

I strode into the glass, with the others so close behind they were almost treading on my heels. And just like that, we were standing in the tea room.

Bright sunlight streamed through the windows, bathing everything in a golden glow. The air was heavy with the scent of freshly baked pastries. None of the tea-room patrons seemed particularly surprised by our sudden appearance. If Ethel was a regular customer, they were probably used to such things. A young woman in a traditional black-and-white maid's outfit came hurrying forward and planted herself right in front of us.

'Sorry,' she said, in a voice that suggested she wasn't at all. 'We're booked up, for a private function. Not a table to be had. You'll just have to come back some other time. Or not. See if I care.'

I showed the Maid my most charming smile. 'We're here to see Ethel Makepeace. And knowing her, she's almost certainly expecting us.'

The Maid sniffed loudly. 'She's busy. Try again tomorrow. Who knows, you might get lucky. Though I wouldn't put money on it.'

Lex regarded her coldly. 'I am the Damned.'

'And I'm saved,' said the Maid. 'Got it in writing and everything.' She looked him over critically. 'Did you choose that outfit, or did you lose a bet?'

Sally grinned. 'I like this one.'

Polly growled at the Maid, who glared right back at her.

'And keep your doggie on a leash, or I'll do it for you.'

Polly drew herself up to her full height, her eyes flashing. 'Oh, you did not just go there . . .'

The Maid was suddenly holding two really large guns. Sally moved quickly to put herself in front of Polly and smiled dazzlingly at the Maid.

'Nice shooters, darling. But I've already swapped your silver bullets for some cork plugs I just happened to have with me.'

The Maid pulled the triggers anyway. Nothing happened.

'How very distrustful of you,' said Sally. 'Now, go tell Ethel we're here, or I will show you a similar trick involving all your fillings and a bunch of chilli peppers.'

Ethel's voice hailed us from the back of the room. She sounded warm and friendly, like your favourite aunt after she's had a gin or two.

'Bring them over, Deirdre. They wouldn't be bothering me unless it was important, because they know what I'd do to them if it wasn't. I haven't had a good smite in ages.'

The guns disappeared from the Maid's hands. She gave us all a hard look, turned on her heel and led us through the closely packed tables to the back of the room. None of the other customers so much as glanced at us. Even when Polly growled at a man who didn't pull his chair in fast enough. The Maid delivered us to Ethel's table and gave her a hard look.

'You want them? They're all yours. Try to keep a lid on things; I have my licence to think about. You want some more ginger cake?'

'Not right now, Deirdre.'

The Maid strode off, her stiff back radiating disapproval.

'Hello, Ethel,' I said.

'What is it this time?' said the ex-angel.

'Don't you know?' I said.

'I try very hard not to,' said Ethel. 'It gets in the way of being ordinary.'

'Annie has been kidnapped,' I said.

Ethel sighed. 'If you will insist on leading such interesting lives, you shouldn't be surprised when interesting things happen to you. Still, you have chosen an opportune moment to drop by. My friends here may be able to help you. Or possibly vice versa. It's a funny old world, though I don't always approve of the punchline.'

The grey-haired little old lady sitting next to Ethel nodded at me amiably. She was wearing a baggy tweed suit, pearls and bifocals. Her pleasant face was deeply lined, as much from experience as age, and her smile came and went so quickly it was hard to be sure whether it had ever been there.

'I'm Jessica Montefiore,' she said, in a voice decades younger than her face. 'I was on track to be named the first official living saint, but I declined the honour. The Church just wanted me to sit around and parrot the party line, while I felt it was more important to get out into the world and help people.'

The man sitting beside her coughed delicately to draw our attention and then studied us with twinkling eyes. Tall and slender and handsome enough to get by, he had shoulder-length wavy hair and was dressed to the height of seventies fashion – the decade that taste forgot. His yellow silk shirt had collar points that came halfway down his chest, while his flared jeans were so electric-blue they were practically fluorescent. He wore a golden medallion on a chunky chain, and tinted pince-nez perched on the end of his nose. A peach-coloured cravat added the final touch.

'I am the Dandy Devil,' he said, in a voice so refined it sounded like he was speaking a second language. 'The only sinner ever to escape from Hell, and stay out.'

'What did you do?' said Sally. 'Dazzle the guards at the gate?'

'Something like that,' said the Dandy Devil.

'Could you be more explicit?' said Lex. 'I might find it useful, some day.'

'Sorry,' said the Dandy Devil. 'I might want to go back, some day.'

'Why would you want to do that?' said Polly. She sounded honestly curious.

The Dandy Devil smiled. 'It's all about the company. One does pine for one's own kind.'

The final figure at the table looked like an accountant on his dinner break. He wore a neat suit without style or character and had the kind of face you forget the moment you stop looking at it. Except for the two small horns on his forehead and a faint but definite halo round his brow. He smiled at me diffidently.

'My name is Peter Bell, and I believe that, in the end, Good and Evil balance out. Because you can't have a coin with only one side. Thus, I refute Heaven and Hell. On the grounds that they are not destinations, but merely two ends of the same spectrum. I maintain the Balance by making sure that every good thing I do is balanced by something equally bad. Of course, sometimes the pendulum swings back and forth so much that I am forced to greater and greater efforts. Hence the horns and the halo.'

'Yes, he's weird,' Ethel said briskly. 'But he means well. My three friends came to me to learn how to avoid being forced to conform to other people's beliefs, and I have taken them under my wing.'

'You're ready to defy Heaven and Hell?' I said.

'That is how I ended up here,' said Ethel. 'Do help yourself to some tea; there's plenty in the pot.'

I nodded to my crew, and we all dragged chairs over to the table and sat down.

'I'll be mother!' Sally said grandly, and she poured tea for all of us into delicate china cups I was sure hadn't been there a moment before.

The ex-angel pushed a plate of assorted biscuits towards us. 'Help yourselves; that's what they're for.'

Polly grabbed the biggest chocolate biscuit on the plate, crammed the whole thing into her mouth and chewed noisily. Lex stared thoughtfully at Ethel's friends.

'You know who I am,' he said. It wasn't a question.

'Of course we know,' said Jessica. 'You give everyone in our line of business bad dreams.'

'Lex Talon the Damned,' said the Dandy Devil. 'Scariest agent for the Good that the Good ever had.'

'Angel-killer,' said Peter Bell.

Lex stared him down. 'There was more to it than that.'

I wanted desperately to talk to Ethel about Annie, but I made myself sit quietly. Because Ethel said these people might be able to help. The Dandy Devil peered at Lex over his pince-nez.

'Your reputation strides ahead of you, Lex. Blowing a trumpet and banging a big drum. I don't know whether to applaud or hide under the table.'

'I'm not here for any of you,' said Lex.

'But just by being here, you put all of us in danger,' said Jessica.

'The entire supernatural community keeps an eye on you, to see what you'll do next,' said the Dandy Devil.

'They do?' said Lex.

'Of course,' said Ethel. 'In case you decide to do it to them.'

'And if they're watching you,' said Peter, 'that means they're watching us. We have no interest in their tedious little wars. We just want to be left alone, to get on with our small human lives.'

'And we really don't want anything to do with someone who chooses to call himself the Damned,' said Jessica. She shot a quick look at the Dandy Devil. 'Present company excepted.'

'It's the smell of sulphur, isn't it?' the Dandy Devil said sadly. 'You wouldn't believe how much aftershave I get through.'

'Don't worry about Lex,' said Ethel. 'He's just here to make sure I don't do anything upsetting to his friend Gideon. I won't let Lex do anything to hurt you.'

'How could you stop him?' the Dandy Devil said reasonably. 'He's already murdered two angels.'

'I don't do that any more,' said Lex.

'Well, that's a relief,' said Peter.

The Dandy Devil smiled suddenly. 'Be fair, Peter. Haven't you ever wanted to kill an angel? They can be such arrogant little pricks.'

Peter considered the question seriously. 'If I did, I'd have to kill a demon as well. To balance things out.'

The Dandy Devil stirred uncomfortably in his chair and turned his attention to his teacup. Since everyone seemed to have run out of things to say, I nodded to Ethel.

'Can we talk about Annie now?'

'In a minute,' said Ethel. 'We have to deal with something else first. By the pricking of my thumbs . . .'

The shafts of sunlight falling through the windows suddenly cut off, as though someone had cancelled summer. Shadows gathered among the tables, like predators on the prowl. I sat up straight as I caught the scent of spilled blood, sulphur and soured milk. Heavy unhurried footsteps were approaching, from a direction I could sense but not name. *Something wicked this way comes . . .*

Everyone else abandoned their tables and headed at speed for the rear exit, held open by the Maid. All of us except Ethel rose to our feet, to face what was coming. Lex, Sally and Polly stood shoulder to shoulder to shoulder, ready to take on whatever turned up. Ethel's three friends looked resigned but determined. Ethel remained seated, calmly sipping her tea. I braced myself. Whatever was coming, it was going to regret showing up now. Because they were getting in the way of rescuing Annie.

Mark Stone suddenly appeared before us. The Hound of Hell. Tall and lean and expensively dressed, devilishly handsome and wearing a pair of very dark sunglasses. He struck a pose, to make it clear he was the most important person in the room, and then pulled his sunglasses down his nose so we could all see his eyes were on fire. They burned fiercely, with leaping crimson flames.

'All the better to see you with,' he said. He laughed softly as he pushed the sunglasses back into place. 'The old jokes are always the best.'

And then the Maid appeared out of nowhere, to stand between him and us. Mark's eyebrows appeared briefly over his sunglasses.

'What the hell are you doing in my tea room?' said the Maid.

He smiled at her easily. 'I am Mark Stone. Hell's bounty hunter in the world of men. When someone goes missing from Hell, or doesn't turn up there when they should – and yes, both those things have been known to happen – I get sent to drag them down to where they belong.'

'No one here fits that description,' said the Maid. 'So you have no business being here.'

'I am on Hell's business,' said Mark. 'Which means there's always going to be work for me in this world.'

The really large guns reappeared in the Maid's hands. 'You'll have to get past me first.'

Mark looked down his nose at the guns. 'Wormwood bullets, blessed and cursed. Someone's been doing their homework. Why are you so keen to get involved? Oh . . . You think you're protecting Ethel! How sweet, and how very human. She doesn't need protecting, little person, though she likes people to think she does. It helps her feel more ordinary.'

'She didn't ask me,' said the Maid. 'I volunteered.'

'And that's the oldest trick of all,' said Mark.

'It's all right, Deirdre,' Ethel said calmly. 'I'm in no danger from Mark. We're old friends, in a manner of speaking. Go and look after the customers, and I'll handle this.'

Mark nodded to the Maid. 'Be seeing you, Deirdre. So be good, for goodness' sake . . .'

The Maid snarled at him, spun on her heel and headed for the rear exit.

'She's right,' I said to Mark. 'Nothing that's happening here is Hell's business. But you do sometimes work for British Security, for reasons that defy rational explanation. Is that why you're here?'

'I work with them because I like to keep busy,' Mark said cheerfully. 'But I'm not here for you, Gideon. I hope you get Annie back safely. Before you ask: no, I can't help. I'm working.'

'The last time we met, we were able to come to an agreement,' I said.

He didn't quite wince, but for a moment the flames from his eyes rose above his sunglasses.

'And I'm still getting yelled at because of it. So, not this time, Gideon. I am here for these three individuals, who should have realized that if you're not a friend, you're the enemy. And that puts them on my list.'

'Not going to happen,' I said. 'Ethel says they can help me find Annie.'

Lex fixed Mark with his cold gaze. 'You really think you can stand against me, when I armour myself with Heaven and Hell?'

'Right!' said Sally. 'Piss off, law man.'

'Growl,' said Polly.

And just like that, Mark wasn't smiling any more. 'Nothing can stand against me when I walk Hell's path, because what is done in Hell's sight has Hell's strength.'

I showed him my most confident smile. 'I beat you before you even turned up, Mark. Because I am the man with the plan. I have Polly the werewolf, to bring you down.'

'Love to,' growled Polly.

'I have the Damned in his armour, to hold you in place.'

'With Heaven and Hell's strength,' said Lex.

'And Switch It Sally to fight dirty,' I said.

'Like you wouldn't believe,' said Sally.

Before Mark could say anything, Jessica Montefiore, the Dandy Devil and Peter Bell stepped forward, placing themselves directly before the Hound from Hell.

'Thanks for your support, Gideon,' said Jessica. 'But we can fight our own battles.'

'Not against me, you can't,' said Mark.

Jessica back-handed him across the face so hard his sunglasses went flying across the room. And while Mark was distracted, the Dandy Devil booted him hard in the nuts. Mark dropped to his knees. Peter Bell knelt beside him.

'Jessica stands for Heaven, the Dandy Devil stands for Hell, and I serve the Balance. What are you in the face of that? Especially when we've learned such very direct tactics from living as ordinary people. Now go home, or we'll all take turns pissing in your eyes till the flames go out.'

Ethel raised her voice. 'Thank you, my dears, but I think I can take it from here.'

She put down her teacup, got to her feet and came over to stand before Mark. She studied him for a moment and then put out a hand and helped him to his feet.

'Never underestimate ordinary people,' she said. 'They're the biggest bastards of all.'

'No argument from me,' said Mark, making himself stand upright.

'Well, now,' said Ethel. 'It's been a while, hasn't it? How are things?'

'Oh, you know,' said Mark. 'Hell is still crowded, Heaven is still snotty, and you can never find a parking space when you need one.'

'Keeping busy?' said Ethel.

'Like you wouldn't believe. You?'

'I am retired,' Ethel said firmly. 'It's very restful. You should try it.'

'Not as long as I'm sworn to Hell's service,' said Mark.

'You're only bound to that job because you believe you are,' said Ethel.

'Well, you would say that, wouldn't you?' said Mark.

They laughed quietly together. Ethel handed him his sunglasses, and he put them back on.

'Just go, Mark,' said Ethel. 'These three are under my protection.'

'And hasn't that set off alarm bells in certain quarters?' said Mark. 'But I'm afraid you gave up your authority in such matters when you stepped down from being an angel.'

'I decide what is and isn't my business,' said Ethel. 'That's sort of the point.'

Mark looked at her steadily. 'This has been ordered where all the things that matter are decided. They're going down, Ethel. All the way down.'

'We won't let you take them,' I said. 'It just isn't right.'

Mark looked at me with a terrible patience. 'You don't understand what's happening here, Gideon. All three of these people died, quite recently. Their fates have been decided and determined. They don't get to argue with that! They have to go to the place provided for them.' He turned to Ethel. 'The only way you could save them is to use your angel's power, and the moment you do that, your time as a human is over. Heaven only indulged you in this little gap-year holiday in the hope you would learn something useful from the experience. But the moment you interfere in the way things are, Heaven will send someone to take you back.'

'Someone like you?' I said.

'Basically, yes,' said Mark.

Ethel nodded to me. 'Unfortunately, he's quite right. Angels are great ones for rules. But I like to think I've started a quiet revolution, and these are my first foot soldiers. So, Gideon . . . I'm going to ask you and your crew for a favour. Hold Mark's attention, while I spirit these three away and hide them where Heaven and Hell will never find them. In return, you can ask me for anything.'

'Deal,' I said.

Mark looked at me sharply. 'Don't do this, Gideon. You don't know what you're getting into. You can't fight the natural order of things.'

'You mean the law?' I said. 'Locking people in cages, for not being what someone else thinks they should be? To Hell with that.'

'That's what we're all about,' said Sally.

'Lone wolves, and proud of it,' said Polly.

'What they said,' said Lex.

I felt a sudden absence beside me, and when I turned to look, Ethel and the others had disappeared. Leaving me and my crew to face the Hound of Hell. I looked at him, and we both shrugged in a *What can you do?* sort of way.

'Hello,' said Mark. 'I must be going.'

I yelled to Lex. 'Armour up and grab him! We have to hold him here, to buy Ethel time!'

The armour surged over Lex as he moved forward. Absolute darkness and absolute light swept across him in a moment, and the power of Heaven and Hell beat on the air like giant wings. Polly disappeared under a thick pelt of black fur, as she erupted into a great humanoid wolf, half bursting out of her leathers. Sally searched frantically in her pockets for something useful, and I took out my time pen.

'What happened to you, Mark?' I said. 'The last time we met, I would have sworn you were trying to be one of the good guys.'

He shrugged. 'It's the job. Sometimes I just have to do what I'm told. And anyway, by aiding and abetting three fugitives from divine justice, technically that makes you the bad guys.'

'I will decide what is good and bad,' I said. 'Because I don't trust the powers that be to get it right.'

Mark smiled. 'That's how a lot of people end up in Hell.'

'You really think you can take us?' said the Damned. His voice was cold and inhuman behind his featureless armoured mask.

'Of course,' said Mark. 'Because I am the Hound of Hell, and all the power of the Pit is mine to call on.'

He gestured sharply at the Damned, and just like that, the dark side of Lex's armour was driven back into the bracelet on his wrist. The light half couldn't remain on its own, so it also retreated, leaving Lex standing alone, with nothing but two glowing bands at his wrists. He launched himself at Mark anyway, putting all his strength into a blow that should have taken the Hound's head right off. Mark swayed lightly on his feet, and the blow sailed harmlessly past his head. Lex stumbled on, caught off balance, and Mark clubbed him to the ground with a single blow. Sally screamed with outrage and thrust a hand at Mark.

'I will swap out your heart for a tea cake!'

And then she cried out in pain and collapsed moaning to the floor.

'Sorry,' said Mark, and he almost sounded like he meant it. 'But I'm protected. And feedback is a bitch, isn't it?'

Werewolf Polly leapt for his throat, fangs bared, but Mark held her in mid-air with a gesture. She hung there, struggling helplessly, while he looked her over, and then he slapped her away with a backhand so vicious it sent her flying across the tea room to crash into the empty tables. She disappeared under the wreckage and didn't move again.

That just left me. Alone and without my crew, facing a power from the Pit. Everything had happened so quickly that I didn't have time to get involved, but when Mark turned his burning gaze on me, I was ready. I hit the button on my pen, and Time crashed to a halt. The sunlight descended into a crimson glow of infra-red, and I was surrounded by all the silence in the world. I advanced quickly on Mark, racking my brain for some way to bring him down before I ran out of air. He snapped out of his frozen pose and snatched the pen from my hand. He hit the button, and Time slammed back into motion. The pleasant tea-room light returned, and Mark smiled easily at me.

'I'm afraid you've been using the time pen just a little bit too often, and its original owners finally noticed. They wanted it back, and you know I'm always open to a little extra work on the side.'

He tucked the pen away in an inside pocket, and my heart lurched painfully. It was like losing an old friend.

'Who are the original owners?' I said. Just to be saying something.

He shook his head kindly. 'You don't want to know. Not if you like sleeping at night. Just be grateful they understand it was stolen by the original Gideon Sable, not you.' He looked at Lex and Sally, lying sprawled at his feet, and then at Polly, half buried under the tables, and finally he nodded to me. 'Goodbye, Gideon. It's been fun, but I really must be going. And it's not like there's anyone here who can stop me.'

I showed him my best confident smile. 'That's what you think.'

Mark frowned. 'You really believe your other little toys will make any difference?'

'I could always call on Sandra Ransom for help,' I said. 'You remember, God's little sister?'

Mark laughed, apparently genuinely amused. 'Is she still running that con? She isn't even God's answering machine.'

'Then who is she, really?' I said.

Mark put a finger to his lips. 'Hush. You never know who might be listening.'

'Let's make a deal,' I said briskly. 'You know how good I can be, when it comes to putting together agreements where we both come out on top.'

Mark shook his head. 'I should punch you out right now, before you talk us into even more trouble. I just know I'm going to regret this, but . . . Give it your best shot, Gideon.'

'I need Ethel to give me her halo, so I can rescue Annie,' I said. 'If she agrees – and I'm pretty sure I can talk her into it, because, after all, that's what I do – that will strip Ethel of most of her power. Which means she will no longer be able to interfere with the way things are, and upset your lords and masters. Isn't that what you want? And you'd still have to get past me. The man with the plan. Are you sure you know everything I've got in my pockets? You allow Ethel time to get her people to safety, and I will declaw the angel. Then we all come out ahead.'

Mark laughed softly. 'I love the way your mind works.'

'Do we have a deal?'

'Of course. You knew that before I even arrived.' He looked at me over his sunglasses for a moment, to show off his burning eyes. 'Nice doing business with you, Gideon.'

He turned and walked away, disappearing in a direction that made no sense at all to human eyes. The atmosphere in the tea room eased, and I relaxed a little. I knew that if Mark would just let me start talking, I had him. Because I'm not just the man with the plan; I'm also always the smartest man in the room. I looked around as Lex heaved himself to his feet, shaking his head like a boxer who'd just taken a solid blow. Sally groaned and sat up, and Lex helped her to her feet. Sally took in the empty tea room and scowled at me.

'You let him get away?'

'Yes,' I said. 'Aren't you grateful?'

And then we all looked round as a whole bunch of broken tables went flying through the air and something wild emerged from beneath them. The werewolf growled fiercely and then shrank back into Polly as she realized the threat was gone. Her stretched and torn leathers hung loosely around her.

'I'm fine!' she said loudly. 'Since I'm not even catching a sniff of the Hound from Hell, I'm guessing Gideon talked at him till he ran away. God knows I feel like doing that sometimes.' She zipped up the front of her leather jacket. 'I'll say this for the Hound: he's got one hell of a backhand.'

Lex looked at me accusingly. 'Did you make a deal with Mark, to save our lives?'

'No,' I said. 'I knew you wouldn't want that. I made a deal to save Annie.'

And then we all jumped just a little as Ethel appeared before us. She took in the tea room's wreckage and sighed quietly.

'Someone's going to have to pay to put this right, and it isn't going to be me. I'll just have to give the owners another winning lottery number.' She nodded briskly to me. 'You bought me enough time that I was able to hide the refugees so completely that even Heaven and Hell will have a hard time finding them. Now . . . I know what you want: to get Annie back.'

'Of course you do,' I said.

'I used to know everything,' said Ethel. 'Now I only know what I need to know, when I need to know it.'

'Do you know who has Annie?'

'I'm sorry, Gideon. There's nothing I can tell you.' Ethel looked at me for a long moment. 'Does it have to be my halo? My last link to who I used to be?'

'It's in a good cause,' I said.

'I have so many enemies,' said Ethel. 'My chosen situation upset a lot of people, and some things that couldn't pass for people if you nailed a people mask to their face. I caused a lot of ripples in the way things are, when I gave up being ineffable to be human. Some people just don't like change; they wouldn't recognize the potential for true freedom if you showed them the door and booted them through it. Would you leave me helpless in the face of my enemies, Gideon?'

'I won't tell if you won't,' I said. 'The whole point of my plan is that the Midnight Club will think it's one of Lex's halos. And you did say I could ask you for anything . . .'

'And I will always wonder if you set this up,' said Ethel.

I nodded modestly. 'It does sound like something I'd do.'

'Take the halo,' said Ethel. 'It's too much of a temptation for me, anyway. For a moment there, I was actually ready to use my power on Mark, and that would never do. I am human now. Only human. One day at a time . . .'

She walked back to her table, still standing miraculously upright, and picked up a battered old handbag. She took out a brightly shining bracelet, considered it for a moment and then came back and handed it to me.

'This isn't what my halo usually looks like; I reconfigured it so that it looks like the Damned's.' She stared coldly at Sally. 'And don't try posing with it in front of the bathroom mirror. You wouldn't like what you'd see.'

'The thought never even crossed my mind,' said Sally, not entirely convincingly.

I hefted the halo in my hand. It felt heavy and solid and very real.

'Try to bring it back in one piece, Gideon,' said Ethel. 'It does have great sentimental value.'

'Sidney!' I said. 'Front and centre, right now!'

The standing mirror appeared in front of me. 'What's been happening? What did I miss? I couldn't see anything because that damned angel put a whole new bunch of shields in place . . . and she's standing right behind me, isn't she?'

'Hello, Sidney,' said Ethel.

The mirror swivelled round on its squeaky castors to face her. Ethel's reflection didn't appear in his glass. Perhaps because even Sidney wasn't capable of reflecting what was actually there.

'How much longer do I have to stay like this?' said Sidney.

'That's up to you, dear,' Ethel said kindly. 'It always was.'

'Take us home, Sidney,' I said.

FIVE

The Con Is On

I t should have been instantaneous.

When we stepped into the mirror in the tea room, we should have stepped out into my shop without a moment having passed. But all the lights had been turned off, leaving everything masked in gloom and shadows, and a quick glance at the window confirmed that although we'd left the tea room in bright sunlight, outside it was night. I turned to the mirror, which took one look at my face and backed away.

'Sidney! What the hell just happened?'

'I don't know!' he said. 'Something went wrong! It's not my fault!'

'Have you brought us back to the night we left?' I said, forcing my voice into a more normal tone because it didn't help the crew to hear me losing control. 'Or have you taken us forward, to the night of the next day?'

'We're in the early hours of the morning after,' said Sidney. 'But I didn't choose this! Someone messed with my coordinates!'

'So the kidnapper has had to hold on to Annie for longer than he expected,' I said tightly. 'Without hearing anything from us and unable to make contact. Which means she could be in real danger.'

'You know I'd never do anything to put Annie at risk!' said Sidney. 'No one is supposed to be able to interfere with my Space/Time coordinates. It's like someone reached inside my head and rearranged my thoughts.'

'Maybe it was the kidnapper,' said Sally.

I rounded on her, and she actually fell back a step. I clamped down hard on my emotions and did my best to speak calmly.

'Why would he want to do that?'

'Why would he do anything?' Polly said quickly. 'Since we

have no idea who he is, we have no way of knowing what his actions might be.'

Sometimes the reasonable answer really isn't what you want to hear.

'This could be an attack,' said Lex. 'By someone who doesn't want us going after Time's Arrow.'

He glanced at Sally, and they moved quickly to stand back to back, so they could cover the whole shop. Polly took on her wolf form, bursting through her black leathers so quickly she split some of the seams. She tilted her shaggy head back and sniffed at the air.

'I'm not picking up any recent visitors,' she said.

'Sidney?' I said. 'Is there anyone else in the shop?'

'Not unless they're out in the stacks,' the mirror said immediately. 'You know what it's like, back there.'

I hit all the switches, and it was like turning on the bedroom light after you've woken from a nightmare. Everything seemed to snap into sharp focus. But this time the light brought no comfort, because it allowed me to see what had been done to my shop while I was gone.

Someone had trashed the place. All the shelves had been broken or torn away from the walls. The glass display cases had been smashed and the contents scattered. The main counter had been reduced to firewood. As though someone had been searching for something and didn't care who knew it. I turned to the front door, ready to demand an explanation from the stuffed bear I'd left on guard, but he wasn't there. He'd been torn to pieces and left lying all over the floor. The ragged edges suggested brute force, rather than a weapon, though it was hard to think of anyone who could overcome the bear so easily. The floor was patterned with sawdust and loose stuffing.

It took me a while to spot the torn-off head, lying wedged up against the wall. I knelt down and turned it round to face me. The jaws were frozen in mid-snarl, but after a moment the eyes came alive and knew me. When the bear finally spoke, its voice was just a shadow of his normal testy growl. The sound of something hurt.

'I'm so sorry, Gideon.'

'So you should be,' I said quietly, smoothing his rumpled fur. 'What happened here?'

'There was nothing I could do,' said the bear. 'He didn't break through the outer protections or walk through the front door. He was just suddenly here, laughing. He tore me to pieces with his bare hands and then ran riot in the shop. Just for the fun of it. He never stopped laughing.'

'Hush,' I said. 'It's only things. I can always get more things. After I've put you back together.'

'You're going to need a lot of thread, for the stitches,' said the bear. 'Maybe you'd better send out for a stapler.'

After everything that had happened, he was still trying to make me laugh. I forced a smile for him.

'I thought I'd go with superglue, this time.'

'I let you down,' said the bear.

'It's been that kind of a day,' I said. 'None of us are at our best. Can you tell me who did this?'

The bear didn't answer. The light had faded from his eyes. I hardened my heart and gave the head a good shake.

'Come on, Yogi! You can hibernate later! I need to know who did this!'

The eyes focused on me again. 'It wasn't anyone I recognized. And he didn't stop laughing long enough to introduce himself. When he ran out of things to break, he disappeared out the back. I could hear him smashing things there too. He sounded like he was having a really good time doing it.'

'Could he still be there?' I said.

'Why would I go anywhere,' said a voice behind me, 'when we have so much to talk about?'

I took my time putting the bear's head down and only then stood up and turned to look. Lex and Sally were already standing side by side to face the newcomer, their hands clenched into fists. Wolf Polly moved in beside them, a savage challenge rumbling in her throat. I gestured sharply for all of them to stay where they were and then nodded calmly to the new arrival.

'Hello, Mark. I know I invited you to stop by whenever you had a moment, but I didn't know you liked to play so rough.'

Mark Stone smiled cheerfully back at me, striking his usual arrogant pose before the entrance to the rear of my shop.

'I am Hell's agent, after all. I have to leave a certain amount of chaos in my wake. It's expected of me.'

'Next time,' I said, 'take a moment to clean up after yourself.'

'And ruin my reputation?' He looked happily around him. 'I have been busy, haven't I? Since I couldn't find what I came here for, I had to do something to keep myself amused until you got back. And you know how much fun it is, breaking things. Some of them screamed very prettily.'

I took a moment to be glad the wee-winged current junkies had disappeared earlier. I could just see Mark grinning broadly as he tore their wings off. I struck my own casual pose, as though we just happened to be passing the time. I knew he was trying to bait me, and I was damned if I'd give him the satisfaction.

'Maybe I should keep a box of breakables handy, for when you feel like dropping by,' I said. 'I'm told popping bubble wrap can be very soothing.' A sudden insight hit me. 'You interfered with Sidney's transfer.'

'Of course,' said Mark. 'So I could get here first and have a good look round.'

I glanced at my crew. For all the anger in their faces, they were still holding their positions, because they trusted me to know what I was doing. I had to hold them back; I wasn't sure any of us were a match for the Hound from Hell. That's why I always made time to play games with Mark's mind and keep him off balance: I knew what would happen if we went head to head. I took a step forward, quite casually, making sure my voice sounded calm and reasonable and not at all upset.

'I thought we had a deal?' I said. 'That we'd agreed on a live-and-let-live scenario, because that was in both our best interests?'

'Your deals only ever benefit you,' said Mark. He was still smiling, but suddenly there was no humour in his voice. 'I let you think you'd out-manoeuvred me, so you'd stop seeing me as a threat. You think you're so smart . . . But you didn't see this coming, did you?'

I thought of how much his little game had cost me, and of how much extra danger Annie might be in, and decided I'd had enough of the verbal sparring.

'What do you want, Mark? Isn't there some bus-load of blind orphans you could be setting fire to, or some puppies that need kicking?'

'I'll get around to them,' said Mark. 'Ethel said she was going to hide her three new friends somewhere no one could find them, and it only took one look at you to remind me of those very secure rooms Old Harry set up at the rear of this shop. Where privacy is guaranteed by shields so powerful even Heaven and Hell can't listen in on what's said inside them.

'So I played the good-natured but not-too-bright young fellow, who really didn't mind being thrown off the scent, just so I could check out the back of your shop. I had a great time overturning all those shelves and watching them topple like so many dominos. I thought I'd never stop laughing.

'Oh, don't look so hurt, Gideon. I'm the Hound of Hell, servant to the Houses of Pain! I was never going to be the good companion you wanted. But . . . you could still be helpful. Because despite all my hard work, I still couldn't locate your secure rooms. Of course, if their shields really are as strong as they're supposed to be, I wouldn't be able to detect them, would I? And that makes me even more determined to take a look inside and say *Peek-a-boo!* to Ethel's little friends. I shall enjoy the looks on their faces, as I drag them down to where they belong.'

He cocked his head to one side, like an inquisitive bird. Behind his sunglasses, the flames from his burning eyes flared up briefly.

'Tell me how to find the rooms, Gideon, and I'll forget how upset I am. And then we can be good chums again! But if you don't tell me what I need to know, I'll do to your crew what I did to that stupid bear.'

'I've spent my life fighting Hell and all its agents,' said Lex. 'And I'm still here.'

'Not now, Lex!' I said, never taking my eyes off Mark. I took another step forward to hold the Hound's attention, careful to keep my face open and transparent.

'No one can get to the secure rooms until I say the proper activating Words. Old Harry saw to that.'

The sudden menace radiating from Mark made me want to back away, but I didn't.

'Say the Words, Gideon,' said Mark, smiling like a shark. 'And then you can show me the way.'

I smiled right back at him. 'Go to Hell.'

Mark took off his sunglasses and tucked them into his breast pocket, so I could see the flames leaping from his burning eyes.

'Look what my masters did to me, Gideon. Have you any idea how much this hurts? All so I could see more clearly, to track down Hell's runaways. Don't fight me, Gideon. Or I'll do terrible things to your little friends.'

'Why do you serve such awful masters, Mark?' I said steadily. 'You must know they're not worthy of you.'

'Oh, stop being so disappointed in me,' he said harshly. 'It's not like we were ever really friends – just two toilers in the same muddy fields who occasionally had goals in common.' Almost despite himself, his voice softened. 'Don't think too badly of me, Gideon. I'm just someone who made a really bad deal, because all the alternatives were worse. I just want to pay off my debts, so I can go home again.'

For a moment, I thought I saw genuine remorse in Mark's face, but I made myself harden my heart. If I gave Mark what he wanted, he wouldn't have any reason to go on being reasonable. I took another step forward and stared unflinchingly into his burning gaze.

'You made yourself the enemy, Mark. So whatever happens next is down to you.'

'Ah, well,' Mark said easily. 'I had to try.' He showed me his old arrogant smile. 'It's not like you have a choice. Remember how easily I put down your crew, back in the tea room? You've made a good name for yourself, Gideon, operating in your own little world . . . But you're playing with the big boys now. So take me to where I need to be, or watch helplessly as your friends scream their lives away.'

'Listen to me, Mark,' I said. 'You know I have no reason to lie to you.'

'Everybody lies,' said Mark. 'It's what people do.'

'The three can't be here,' I said. 'In the secure rooms, or anywhere on the premises. Because I haven't had a chance to give anybody access.'

'But then . . . you would say that, wouldn't you?' said Mark. 'Tell you what, how about a show of faith on your part? Hand over the halo Ethel gave you, and then I'll take you seriously.'

I glanced back at my crew. Lex and Polly were getting ready

to throw themselves at Mark, but I caught their gaze and shook
my head firmly. I turned back to Mark and produced Ethel's halo
from my jacket pocket. He laughed softly.

'Pretty little thing, isn't it?'

'You can't give him that, Gideon!' Sally said loudly. 'He'll
kill us all the moment he's got what he wants!'

'One more word out of you,' Mark said pleasantly, 'and I will
turn you inside out and leave you that way.'

Lex put himself in front of Sally. 'You even look at my family
in a way I don't like, and I will punch your heart out. Assuming
you still have one.'

Mark laughed softly. 'I do love it when the bad guy thinks he
can wipe out a lifetime's sins just by making a heroic gesture.
Who do you think you're fooling, Lex? After everything you've
done, after all the people you've killed, do you honestly believe
playing the good husband and father will make the slightest
difference to what's waiting for you?'

'I didn't become an agent for the Good to save my soul,' said
Lex. 'I'm damned. I know that. I do it to show my contempt for
Hell. You should try it sometime. It's very invigorating.'

Mark looked at me. 'If I ripped his jaw off, do you think that
would be enough to stop him talking?'

Polly growled loudly: a harsh animal sound. My crew were
starting to look as though they didn't trust me to know what I
was doing. I held up the glowing bracelet, and Mark put out a
hand to take it. And I lightly tossed the halo to Lex. He snatched
it out of mid-air, and I smiled easily at him.

'Two halos gave you your armour,' I said. 'I wonder what
adding Ethel's halo will do to the mix? Two parts Heaven to one
part Hell should produce something even a Hound from Hell
would have trouble dealing with.'

'You bastard, Gideon,' said Mark. And then he smiled broadly.
'Now, that was sneaky. I'm actually impressed.'

Lex pressed Ethel's halo against his heart and summoned his
armour. It surged over him in a moment, but this time there were
no dark and light halves. Instead, his armour shone brightly from
head to toe, leaving only the occasional shadow to drift across
his chest like passing clouds. The light was painfully bright, and
the armour's presence filled the room like the will of God: clear

and uncompromising. Mark flinched away from it – just for a moment, before he regained control, but we all saw it and knew what it meant. Mark drew himself up to say something threatening, but I just talked right over him.

'When there were two equally matched halos, from Above and Below, you could force the dark half back into its bracelet, and the light half couldn't stand on its own. But now there are two Heavenly halos, I'm betting you just lost any control you had over the armour.'

Mark glared furiously at the Damned, but nothing happened. Mark's face went blank, as he struggled to come up with a new plan. But a man with his power had never felt the need for strategy. I nodded to the Damned.

'Go get him, Lex. Show him what we do to people who mess up our lives.'

The Damned surged forward and slammed into the Hound like a runaway train. Mark stood his ground, refusing to be driven back, and the two of them lashed out, throwing terrible punches backed by inhuman strength. Sally and Polly looked to me, but I shook my head. Sidney had already flattened himself against a wall.

We all stayed well back, as two forces of nature went to war.

Mark and the Damned lurched back and forth, smashing through anything still standing that got in their way, their punches strong enough to make holes in the world. I would have flinched at so much more destruction, but I was too caught up in willing the Damned on. Because if he failed, the odds were, we were all dead. Mark drove his fist into the Damned's face, but not even Hell's strength could put a dent in the new armour. The Damned hammered his fist into Mark's side, and we all heard ribs break and shatter. Mark staggered backwards, blood flying from his mouth. The Damned kicked his legs out from under him, and Mark crashed to the floor. He rolled to one side just in time to avoid the armoured foot that came slamming down to crush his skull. He spat a mouthful of bloody defiance at his opponent, forced himself up on to his feet again and threw punch after punch with inhuman speed. But even his most vicious blows just glanced harmlessly away from the Damned's armour. Mark fell back and circled the Damned. Blood spilled down his chin as he grinned steadily at his opponent.

Polly started forward, but Sally grabbed the wolf's hairy arm with both hands.

'You can't help him!' she said harshly. 'There's nothing human happening in that fight. Leave your father to finish the job. He knows what he's doing.'

Blow by terrible blow, the Damned drove Mark back. His armoured fists reduced Mark's face to a bloody pulp, and the Hound's breath rasped harshly through a broken nose and ruined mouth. And then the Damned broke Mark's left shoulder with a single blow, leaving the Hound's arm hanging uselessly at his side. Mark retreated, desperately trying to defend himself with his one good hand. The Damned went after him pitilessly.

Sally looked to me. 'Can Lex kill him?'

'No,' I said. 'I'm pretty sure Mark can put right any amount of damage if Lex gets tired and slows down.'

'So what do we do?' said Polly.

'There must be something!' said Sally.

'There's always something,' I said. I looked at the standing mirror, pressed against the wall. 'Get over here, Sidney.'

'Don't want to.'

'Don't make me come and get you.'

The mirror edged reluctantly forward. 'What can I do that the Damned can't?'

'Get ready,' I said. 'And when I give you the word, send Mark where I tell you.'

'I suppose you know what you're doing,' said the mirror. 'Actually, I don't, but I'm ready to grasp at any straw. Where could I send the Hound that he won't be able to come back from? And you know he'll come back mad.'

'Not from where I have in mind,' I said. 'Lex! Finish this!'

The Damned's armoured fists rose and fell, bludgeoning the Hound again and again, until Mark was left kneeling helplessly, unable even to raise a hand to defend himself. His head hung down and he coughed raggedly, spattering the floor with blood. The Damned drew back a fist, to drive it into the back of Mark's skull and out through his face.

'Hold it, Lex!' I said. 'You can't finish him that way. Mark Stone died long ago. He only got out of Hell by making a deal to be their bounty hunter.'

The Damned slowly drew back his hand. 'I could still make him scream,' he said, his voice inhumanly cold behind his armoured mask. 'Show him what happens to people who threaten my family.'

'But that's what he'd do,' I said. 'We're supposed to be better than him.'

The Damned didn't say anything, but he did take a step back. Mark didn't look up. He was still bracing himself on his one good arm, staring at the floor. And though the flames still leapt from his eyes, blood dripped steadily from his ruined face. When he spoke, he sounded broken and lost, like a child who'd been punished and didn't know why.

'I only wanted to walk the Earth again. I want to go home.'

I felt sorry for him, but I still remembered what he'd done, and what he'd threatened to do.

'There's only one place you belong, Mark. And that's where I'm sending you.' I looked to Sidney. 'Open a gateway to Hell.'

'No!' Sidney said loudly. 'You can't ask me to do that! The energies would destroy me!'

'If you don't do this,' I said, 'Mark will recover and kill us all. Please, Sidney. You're the only one who can save us.'

'That's the nicest thing you've ever said to me, you bastard,' said the mirror. 'Get everyone out of the way. And whatever happens, don't look in my glass.'

I pulled Sally and Polly back, and then I yelled to the Damned.

'Get ready, Lex. Wait for your cue. Sidney, put yourself right in front of Mark.'

The mirror trundled forward, his wooden frame shaking. Mark slowly raised his bloody face and then stopped, mesmerized by what he saw in the mirror's reflection. I hauled Sally and Polly in behind the mirror. The one place where we should be safe. The Damned stood looming over the kneeling Hound. I raised my voice.

'Do it, Sidney! Do it now!'

A terrible light blasted out of Sidney's glass. Even tucked away behind the standing mirror, the heat was almost unbearable. The Damned in his armour just stood there and took it. Mark screamed like a child at what he saw. Sidney wailed miserably as his wooden frame caught on fire, burning with flames the same colour as Mark's eyes. I yelled to the Damned.

'Do it, Lex! Send him home!'

The Damned grabbed Mark with both hands and threw him into the mirror. Mark's scream cut off abruptly as Sidney closed the gateway. The heat was suddenly gone, and the light was sane and normal. Sidney's screams became whimpers. His frame was still burning. I pulled off my jacket and wrapped it round the top of the mirror's frame, smothering the flames. Polly ripped off her jacket and used it to beat out the rest of the fire with her wolf strength.

'Good man, Sidney,' I said. 'Good man.'

He didn't say anything.

Finally, I took my jacket away and stepped back, and Polly did the same. Smoke rose from the scorched and blackened mirror frame. I moved around to the front. The glass was undamaged and showed only my reflection. I didn't like what I saw in my face. Lex stood beside me, no longer in his armour. He put out a hand to pat the top of the mirror and then thought better of it. He didn't want to hurt Sidney. I nodded to Sally and Polly.

'Look after Sidney.'

'How?' said Sally. 'What can we do?'

'Comfort him,' I said. 'I have to check what damage Mark did at the back of the shop.'

'We just sent a man to Hell,' said Polly, back in her human form and pulling her charred jacket about her. 'Did we do the right thing?'

'We did what we had to,' I said. 'And anyway, Mark's masters will let him out again, eventually. Once they're done punishing him for failing. They need their Hound.'

Lex lowered his voice. 'Do you think the three might be in the secure rooms?'

'They can't be,' I said. 'I tried to tell Mark that. But if he did as much damage back there as the bear seemed to think, all kinds of dangerous things could have got loose. They have to be put back. You'd better come with me.'

Lex nodded. He was still holding Ethel's halo. He looked at the shining bracelet for a long moment.

'That felt . . . different. As though I wasn't the only one inside the armour. Do you want the halo back, Gideon? Ethel did give it to you.'

'You hang on to it for now,' I said. 'You're less likely to be tempted by its power. Just . . . keep it safe . . . until we need it.'

Lex shrugged and stuffed the bracelet into his pocket. I headed for the back of the shop and on into the great maze of tall shelves that stretched off into the distance. To my surprise, everything appeared intact and undamaged.

'Could Mark have been putting on a show?' said Lex. 'To mess with you?'

'He's not that subtle,' I said. 'More likely, the stacks here put themselves back together. Looks like I won't be needing you for protection, after all, Lex. You'd better stay here and guard the entrance.'

Lex raised an eyebrow at that. 'Are you expecting visitors?'

'After Mark got in so easily, I don't feel like taking anything for granted,' I said. 'If anyone turns up that you don't recognize, feel free to knock them down and sit on them till I get back.'

Lex nodded slowly. 'Is there anything you can do to help Sidney? He was very brave.'

'Yes,' I said. 'He was. I'll think of something.'

'Of course you will,' said Lex.

I wished I had his confidence, but I couldn't say that, of course. So I just set off into the stacks.

I walked steadily down the main aisle, heading deep into the shelves that rose around me like a great forest. I inherited the shop from Old Harry, when he had to leave in something of a hurry, and many of its secrets still eluded me. Including just how far back the shop went, in defiance of all the usual rules of space and distance. I still wasn't clear on whether or not there were things living in this forest. From time to time, I thought about putting down traps, but I had a suspicion something might object and start setting traps for me. So I didn't. Live and let live, if you know what's good for you.

I finally reached my special security boxes. Where I keep the tools of my trade that I never discuss with anyone. Because a magician's trick only works if no one knows how it's done. Ever since Mark took my time pen, I'd been feeling a bit vulnerable. It was time to replace the pen with something else. I had been wondering why Mark didn't use the pen to defend himself from the Damned, but presumably he'd already returned the pen to its owners. They had sounded rather impatient.

I stopped before a particular shelf, checked the numbers on the boxes and unlocked one. I took out a chased silver ring in the shape of the snake Ouroboros, forever swallowing its own tail. A short-range teleporter, the ring could move any small object from one place to another. I hadn't used it in some time, because I had the time pen. And Switch It Sally. But now I had a specific use in mind, and the comforting thought that no one would ever suspect me of using it. Because I had Switch It Sally.

I slipped the ring on my finger, and a thought struck me. I opened another security box and took out a handful of portable doors. The small black blobs always came in handy when I felt the need for a sudden and unexpected exit. I slipped them into my pocket and then paused, to make sure I hadn't forgotten anything. I didn't see any point in checking out the secure rooms. If all else failed, the rows of stacks would have conspired to make sure no intruder could reach them by constantly changing the route. Legend has it that there are still some unauthorized visitors from Old Harry's time wandering endlessly through the stacks, trapped in a maze with no exit. Just another reason not to put down traps.

The journey back seemed to take a lot less time than the way in, but that's the shop for you. I picked up Lex along the way. He didn't ask any questions about what I'd been up to, which was just as well, because I had no intention of telling him.

When we walked back into the main shop, smoke was still curling from Sidney's scorched wooden frame. He was crying quietly, as much from shock as pain, and his glass showed nothing at all. No one can look at Hell without being damaged by the experience. I'd known that when I ordered Sidney to open the gateway. It had to be done, to save us all. But knowing that didn't make me feel any less guilty.

Sally and Polly were taking it in turns to murmur comfortingly to the mirror. Sally looked up angrily as I went over to join them.

'You have to do something! It's your fault he's like this!'

'I never thought he could be hurt,' said Polly. 'I never really thought of him as a person. Isn't that awful?'

'Of course we'll help him,' I said. 'He's family.' I turned to Lex. 'The halos you took from the dead angels made your armour, but Ethel's halo was freely given. I'm thinking it might still have a few miracles left in it.'

Lex looked at me. 'You think I can heal the mirror?'

'I think the halo can,' I said. 'If you ask it nicely. Technically, it is still part of Ethel.'

Lex took the bracelet out of his pocket and held it out before the mirror.

'Please, Ethel. Help him.'

And just like that, the wooden frame was spotless and undamaged. Sidney cried out with relief.

'I'm back! I feel great! Let all the worlds tremble and beware: Sidney the Wonder Mirror, the All-Seeing Eye, is back on the job!'

Lex smiled at me briefly. 'He's back.'

'Of course,' I said. 'An angel's halo can heal souls as well as bodies.'

Sally and Polly took it in turns to hug the mirror. And I felt the pressure on my conscience ease, just a little.

Lex looked at the bracelet in his hand. 'I'm not used to doing good things.'

'Do you think you could manage one more?' I said, gesturing at the bits and pieces of what had once been my bear, lying scattered across the floor. Lex addressed the bracelet again.

'Ethel, one more time, if you please. He was a good bear.'

The separate pieces rolled across the floor, connected with each other and put the bear back together. He scrambled on to his feet and stood proudly in his usual spot by the front door. He flexed his clawed hands and snarled happily. I went over to the bear and hugged him.

'Best of bears . . .'

The bear stood very still, caught off guard, and then hugged me gently back, careful of his great strength. The moment I let go, he did too.

'Thank you,' said the bear. 'But let us never talk of this again. I have a reputation to think of.'

'Understood,' I said. 'Don't ever make it necessary again.'

'That is the plan,' said the bear.

He turned to face the front door and took up his watchful stance again.

'Nice one, Yogi,' I said.

He didn't wince, but he looked as if he wanted to. I went back to join my crew, who looked at me expectantly. Fortunately, I had a plan.

'Now we've taken out the trash and repaired the damage, it's time to get to work,' I said. 'First . . . Sally, there's a change in your role. Mark's messing around with time has put us seriously behind schedule, so . . . you will still take the halo to the Midnight Club and present it to the Curator, Malcolm Greely, in return for Club Membership. You will still identify the halo as belonging to the Damned, which you stole while he was sleeping. Pile on the arrogance and pride, and play up your small-time thief background, and Malcolm will eat it up with spoons. But . . . instead of just wandering around the Club, looking for a gap in their defences, your job now is to hold Malcolm's attention while the rest of us make our own way in.'

Sally clapped her hands happily. 'I get to seduce someone, after all!'

Lex growled ominously. 'What kind of a man is this Malcolm Greely?'

'A dried-up old stick, who has given his life to collecting rare items,' I said reassuringly.

'I love a challenge,' Sally said happily.

'Just keep the man talking,' I said. 'Anything more than that would probably kill him.'

'Relax, darling,' said Sally, showing me her best demure smile. 'I know how far to go, and when to back off.'

'That has not always been my experience,' said Lex.

I turned to Sidney. 'Now that you're feeling so much better, is there any chance you could transport us into the Club?'

'There's no way I can get you inside,' the mirror said flatly. 'Their shields are just too much.'

'But you just opened a gateway to Hell!' said Polly.

'The gates to Hell are always open,' said Sidney.

'I believe I've worked out how to get us inside the Midnight Club,' I said. 'Lex, normally you use your two halos to cover yourself in armour. I think we can use Ethel's halo to cover and

contain all of us, and then Sally can just carry the bracelet right
into the Club, past all their protections.'

Everyone looked at me, lost for words. Even Sidney managed
to project a sense of *Are you freaking kidding?*

'Really?' he said finally.

'I think Ethel's halo has a few more miracles left in it,' I said.

'I'm having trouble getting my head around this,' said Sally.
'And given some of the tricks we've pulled on previous heists,
that's saying something.'

'Once you hand the bracelet over to Malcolm,' I said, 'he'll
want it examined by his best experts. It will take him some time
to assemble a team, so he'll have the bracelet placed in the
Museum, because that's where the Club's shields are strongest.
Your job is to keep Malcolm talking, Sally, while we emerge
from the halo and go to work.'

'Just like that?' said Polly.

'Pretty much,' I said.

'What about the Museum's internal security?' said Lex.

'The Club's defences should be more interested in looking
out, not in,' I said.

'That word *should* worries me,' said Lex.

'Once we've got our hands on Time's Arrow,' Polly said slowly,
'how are we going to get away?'

'I will slap a portable door against the nearest wall and create
a new exit,' I said. 'The protections against such things should
be a lot weaker on the inside.'

'There's that word again,' said Lex.

'Once we're out, I will peel off the portable door, and there
will be no trace it was ever there,' I said. 'Don't worry so much,
Lex. It'll give you wrinkles. Sally, allow us a reasonable time
and leave when you're ready. No one will connect you with the
stolen item, because you will have been in plain sight all along,
with Malcolm Greely.'

'Cool!' Sally said happily. 'You wait and see; I'll have him
eating out of my hand. Or anything else he fancies.'

'How long will it take us, to get to the Midnight Museum?'
said Lex.

'It's not far,' I said. 'Just two streets down from here, on the
left. You can't miss it.'

'Of course,' said Polly. 'Old Soho is where everything worth stealing turns up.'

'Well,' I said. 'That goes without saying.'

'It'll all end in tears,' Sidney said darkly.

I turned to Sally. 'Just walk in the front door. If anyone gives you any trouble, say Old Harry sent you.'

Lex produced a sudden snort of suppressed laughter, and we all looked at him. Laughter wasn't something we normally associated with the Damned. He smiled briefly.

'Of course Harry would have influence with the Midnight Club. It wouldn't surprise me if he was a Member.'

'It wouldn't surprise me if he founded the place,' I said. 'The point is, dropping his name will make sure Sally's offer is taken seriously.'

Sally tossed her head and gave us her most devilish smile. 'Well, I should hope so, darlings. I do have a reputation, after all.'

'Of course you do,' I said. 'But they'll let you in, anyway.'

Sally looked at Lex. 'You hit him; you're nearer.'

'Once you're inside,' I said quickly, 'all you have to do is show Malcolm Greely the bracelet and you'll have his full attention.'

Sally frowned. 'What if he asks why I didn't steal the other bracelet as well?'

I hung on to my patience with both hands. 'Just say you were planning to, but Lex started to wake up, and you panicked and got the hell out of there. They'll believe that. It will also help to explain why you're so keen to swap the halo for Club Membership: so you can claim their protection if the Damned comes after you.'

'Could they really protect her from me?' said Lex. He sounded honestly curious.

'Some of the Members could eat you on toast,' I said flatly. 'We are talking seriously dangerous people, which is why we don't want any of them to know we were involved in stealing Time's Arrow.'

Polly looked dubiously at the small bracelet Lex was holding. 'You really think we can fit inside that?'

Lex cleared his throat. 'I have been communing with the halo.'

Sally looked at him sharply. 'It's been speaking to you?'

'There's a voice inside my head saying it's the halo, so I hope that's what it is,' said Lex. 'The halo says it's happy to cooperate; it wants to be helpful. And yes, the experience was just as spooky as it sounds.'

He took a firm hold of the halo with both hands and pulled steadily. The glowing metal stretched like taffy and expanded into a great silver sphere. The top opened like a flower, and a series of dimples appeared in the glowing exterior, to provide a stairway.

'OK . . .' said Polly. 'If this thing turns into a giant pumpkin drawn by four liveried horses, I am out of here. I'm not wearing glass slippers for anyone.'

'That was last year's model,' I said. 'We're going to rob the prince, not dance with him.'

I climbed the sphere and dropped inside. The gently glowing interior was surprisingly roomy, though I couldn't help noticing I cast no reflection in the walls. Lex and Polly quickly joined me. I was about to ask the halo to provide some steps on the inner wall when they just appeared in front of me. I hoped the halo was merely anticipating my needs, and not actually looking inside my head. I climbed the wall and peered out of the opening.

'Sidney, would you come over here, please?'

The mirror trundled forward on its squeaky castors. 'You're leaving me behind again, aren't you? I never get to go anywhere.'

'You will this time,' I said. 'Lex, can you come up here a moment?'

He appeared beside me. I leaned out of the opening and took a firm grip on the mirror.

'Lex, help me get Sidney inside.'

Between us, we hauled the mirror up the side of the sphere.

'What? What?' said the mirror. 'Put me down! Help! Sidney's being shanghaied!'

We soon got him inside the silver sphere. The moment we let go, he tried to back away from us, but there was nowhere to go.

'I don't want to end up as an exhibit in the Midnight Museum!' he wailed.

'Trust me, that's not going to happen,' I said. 'You're not that special.'

'Why do I have to go along?' Sidney said sulkily.

'It's part of the plan,' I said. 'Come on . . . You're always saying I never take you on missions.'

'I meant somewhere nice!'

'You'll love it,' I said briskly. 'It'll broaden your horizons.'

'I am having a really bad day,' said the mirror.

I turned to Lex. 'Since you're the one who's established a close personal relationship with the halo, please ask it to close itself and return to normal size.'

Lex nodded to the nearest wall. 'Please do what the nice man said.'

I had to raise an eyebrow. 'You're being very polite.'

'There's a reason for that,' said Lex.

The opening irised shut. We were now standing inside a silver sphere, whose curving walls radiated a calm and soothing light. I turned to Sidney.

'You will be our means of keeping an eye on what's happening outside.'

'You didn't have to abduct me! You could have asked.'

'You might have said no.'

'Bully!' hissed the mirror.

'Show us Sally,' I said.

She appeared in the mirror's glass, staring at the small shining bracelet in her hands.

'Hello, Sally!' I said. 'Can you hear me?'

'Yes!' she said, not quite jumping out of her skin. 'Is that you, Gideon, yelling at me from out of nowhere?'

'Out of the halo, actually,' I said. 'Just think of it as a novelty phone.'

She stared suspiciously at the bracelet. 'Lex, sweetie? Are you all right in there?'

'I'm fine,' said Lex. 'I can see you clearly in the mirror. Please don't drop us.'

'We're all fine,' I said, just a bit pointedly. 'Now let's get this show on the road. Sally, tuck the halo away somewhere safe about your person and go straight to the Midnight Club. Don't try too hard to sell the con. Let them think they're talking you into it. That'll make them feel like they're in charge.'

Sally sniffed loudly. 'I have done this before, you know.'

Her image disappeared from the glass. It wasn't replaced by our reflections. Possibly because Sidney couldn't be bothered.

'We're moving,' he said. 'If that helps.'

'You could sound more enthusiastic,' I said.

'Don't want to be here,' said the mirror. 'Don't feel safe. Want to go home and watch my soaps.'

I sighed. 'I wonder if it's too late to swap you for a speaking clock.'

Polly grinned. 'It's like listening to an old married couple.'

'It shouldn't take Sally long to get to the Midnight Club,' said Lex. 'Unless she gets distracted along the way, which is always a possibility.'

There was a pause as we considered that.

'What else is there in the Midnight Club, apart from the Museum?' said Polly.

'I'm afraid we're back in the land of gossip and rumour,' I said. 'There's supposed to be an Armoury, with an excellent collection of rare and legendary weapons; a Library, with many weird and exotic volumes; a Restaurant, offering dishes made from extinct species; and an all-sexes Sauna, offering holistic massages, soul cleansing and chakra realignment.'

Polly grinned. 'Oh, we have got to check that out. I am just in the mood for some professional pampering.'

'Business first,' I said.

She sniffed loudly. 'You're no fun any more.'

'Lots of people have been telling me that,' I said. 'The moment we're out of the halo, use your tracking skills to locate Time's Arrow. We don't want to hang around any longer than we have to. And Lex, whatever happens, do not put on your armour. That would set off every alarm in the place, and every Club Member on the premises would come running.'

Lex smiled briefly. 'Let them come. I love a challenge.'

'Bring them on!' Polly said happily. 'Fun time, after all!'

I shook my head. 'I am surrounded by children. We're not doing this to enjoy ourselves. Annie is depending on us.'

'I hadn't forgotten,' said Lex.

'We're just trying to make the best of a bad situation,' said Polly.

'What if something goes wrong with the plan?' said Lex.

'I have backups in place, just in case.'

'Like what?' said Lex.

'It's a surprise,' I said.

'I hate surprises,' said Sidney.

'Hush,' I said. 'Or I'll wipe your glass down with a dirty handkerchief.'

'I must have done something really bad in a past existence,' said the mirror. 'Oh, wait, I did, didn't I? That's how I ended up like this.'

After that, we just stood around and waited.

'Are we there yet?' said Lex.

'Ask the halo,' I said.

Lex nodded to the wall before him. 'Excuse me, has Sally reached the Midnight Club?'

Ethel's voice answered him. 'We're almost there, dear. Not long now.'

Lex looked at me. 'Now you know why I'm being so polite. The halo is still connected to Ethel, and I don't think we want to upset her.'

'So . . . we're inside an angel?' said Polly.

'Everybody watch their language,' said Sidney.

'Sally has just walked into the Club lobby,' said Ethel's voice.

'Show us what's happening, Sidney,' I said.

'On it, boss.'

The glass showed a typical lobby from an old-fashioned gentleman's club. Parquet floor, walls with boring paintings and glowering portraits, sturdy Victorian fittings and furnishings. The kind of smug, respectable setting that always makes my fingers itch to rob someone blind. And there was Switch It Sally, standing tall and proud as though she belonged there, chatting cheerfully away with the Club Curator, Malcolm Greely.

A tall, slender figure in an ill-fitting Edwardian outfit, he had swept-back grey hair over a long, gaunt face. The thin mouth looked as though it wouldn't know what to do with a smile if it happened, and his icy blue eyes were sharp and focused. Sally hit Malcolm with her most dazzling smile, and I was surprised to see his mouth twitch in response.

'Well, how about that,' I said. 'I always thought Malcolm only lived for his work, but perhaps that was only because no one ever got around to making him a better offer.'

'You know the man?' said Lex.

'We move in the same circles,' I said. 'We're always bumping into each other in pursuit of the good stuff.'

'So you're friendly rivals?' said Polly.

'Rivals, anyway,' I said. 'We were at the same auction not long ago, trying to out-bid each other over the long-lost sword, Ex Caliburn. That was when Malcolm informed me that under no possible circumstances would I ever be admitted to the Midnight Club, no matter what item I presented, because they could never trust me. I took it as a compliment. When he finally out-bid me, I sneaked round the back and stole the sword before he could collect it. I later swapped it for a pookah's paw, but that's another story.'

We crowded together before the mirror, watching fascinated as Sally flirted up a storm with Malcom Greely. To my astonishment, a new spark appeared in Malcolm's eye, and he actually started to smile. Sally leaned in close and tap-tapped her fingers on his chest, grinning mischievously.

'I never knew she was such a good actress,' said Polly. She sounded a little embarrassed.

'Sally was a first-class con artist in her day,' I said. 'When she turned on the charm, she could make a bishop kick a hole in a stained-glass window. Though it does help when the mark wants to be conned. Look at Malcolm go; I never knew he had it in him.'

Sally was so close to Malcolm now she was practically thrusting her bosoms in his face, to his clear delight. But then something seemed to remind him of his professional duties, and he made himself step back.

'What exactly have you brought me, Ms . . .?'

'Oh please, darling, call me Sally.'

'Very well, Ms Sally it is. And you must call me Malcolm.'

'Delighted!' said Sally. Her fingers stirred briefly with his bow tie, and his breathing deepened. Sally smiled brightly as she produced Ethel's halo from her cleavage.

Lex sighed. 'Only Sally would hide an angel's halo between her breasts. I knew there was a good reason why I married that woman.'

Sally handed over the halo with a flourish, and the silver bracelet seemed to shine supernaturally bright. But that was nothing compared to the light in Malcolm's eyes, as he realized what he was looking at.

'Is this what I think it is, Ms Sally?'

'An angel's halo,' Sally said proudly. 'Cut off the head of a murdered angel, by Lex Talon, the Damned. Dear Lex wasn't very subtle in those days.'

'How on earth did you acquire this?' said Malcolm, turning the halo over and over in his hands.

Sally fed him the agreed story, and Malcolm nodded in all the right places, but his attention was fixed on the treasure he was holding.

'So . . . is this halo from Above or Below?'

'I don't know,' said Sally. 'Does it matter?'

'I suppose not,' said Malcolm. 'This is beyond my area of expertise. I'll have it taken to the Museum, while I put the word out for the right people to come and examine it.' He looked up from the bracelet and smiled quickly at Sally. 'That will take a while, but I see no reason to concern yourself, Ms Sally. You have quite definitely earned your Club Membership.'

Sally smiled at him dazzlingly and then stretched languorously, taking her time.

'You do want it, don't you, darling?'

'More than anything,' he said, almost shyly. 'Acquiring a piece like this will be the pinnacle of my career. You have made my day, Ms Sally. But I'm afraid you cannot leave the Club until the halo's status has been determined. Standard procedure, I'm afraid. You know how it is.' He hesitated, and I could see him gathering his courage with both hands. 'Perhaps you would care to keep me company in the Club bar, until the word comes through? And then afterwards . . . I could show you round the Museum, if you like. I have such wonders to show you.'

Sally laughed throatily, holding his gaze with hers. 'I'm sure you do, darling.'

Malcolm extended his arm in a most gentlemanly fashion, and Sally slipped her arm through his and pressed it against her side.

'I've always had a thing for older men, Malcolm.'

'You've made this a very happy day for me, Ms Sally. I'm not used to feeling happy.'

'Buy me several drinks, sweetie, and I'll show you how happy you can be.'

They laughed together and walked out of the lobby. I gestured to Sidney, and he shut the scene down.

'I almost feel sorry for Malcolm,' I said. 'He never stood a chance.'

Lex was frowning. 'Sally was acting. He wasn't. Is what we're doing . . . just a bit cruel?'

'We're doing this to save Annie,' I said. 'I'll find a way to make it up to Malcolm, afterwards.'

'I never saw Sally like that before,' said Polly. 'Like a wolf closing in on a sheep.'

Sidney laughed raucously. 'Oh, come on! This is Switch It Sally we're talking about! The queen of double-dealing and back-stabbing!'

'She's my wife now,' Lex said coldly.

'And my stepmother,' said Polly.

'I'll shut up now, shall I?' said Sidney.

'Sally is doing her job,' I said. I raised my voice to address the silver wall before me. 'Has the bracelet been delivered to the Museum yet?'

'My halo has been given a place of honour,' said Ethel's voice. 'The Curator's people have left, so you now have the Museum all to yourselves.'

'Is that really you, Ethel?' I said.

'This is a recording,' said Ethel's voice. 'I'm afraid Ethel isn't here right now because she has more important things on her mind, like remembering where she put her reading glasses. So stop wasting time and get on with it.'

'Open the halo, please,' said Lex.

The silver sphere blossomed like a flower, and I led the way up the indented steps and out into the Museum. Lex came after me, with Sidney balanced effortlessly on one shoulder, while the mirror complained bitterly about the lack of dignity involved. Polly brought up the rear, almost climbing over Lex and Sidney in her eagerness.

The long, pleasantly lit gallery was packed full of glass display cases, signposted exhibitions and dioramas, and all manner of things standing upright in wall niches. The greatest treasures of the hidden world, locked away for the private delectation of the privileged few.

I put on my sunglasses and checked the Museum for hidden protections, and was astonished to find there weren't any. I spent some time looking back and forth, convinced I must be missing something, but finally I accepted what I was seeing and put away the sunglasses.

'The coast is clear,' I said. 'Apparently, the Club has so much faith in its outer defences that it didn't see the need for any in here. I can only assume no one ever told them the story of the Trojan Horse.'

'What about guards?' said Lex. 'There must be regular patrols.'

'They won't enter the Museum without orders,' I said confidently. 'The Club Members don't care to share their treasures with the common crowd.' I tore my eyes away from the marvellous displays and looked sternly at Lex. 'But whatever happens, don't put on your armour. We need the Club to believe that halo came from you. It might prove a tad difficult to convince them of that, with the Damned in his armour standing right in front of them.'

Lex nodded reluctantly. I turned to Polly.

'All right, you're up. Point us the way to Time's Arrow.'

'I can't use my tracking instincts unless I go full wolf,' she said. 'Won't that set off the alarms?'

'They're used to weirder things than you in this place,' I said. 'There's so much industrial-strength strangeness being generated by these exhibits that a werewolf won't even be a blip on the radar.'

Polly growled deep in her throat, and the wolf erupted out of the human body that contained it. Her torn and stretched leathers still somehow stayed in place, though a few zips blew off like shrapnel. Polly tilted back her shaggy head to sniff the air and then set off purposefully down one particular aisle. Lex and I hurried after her, with Sidney trundling manfully along behind. His squeaky castors were the loudest sound in the Museum.

'It does you good to get out now and again, and see the sights,' he said chattily.

'Not feeling so shanghaied any more?' said Lex.

'You even try putting me over your shoulder again and I will show everyone nude photos of you as a baby,' said the mirror.

'Keep the noise down, Sidney,' I said. 'Unless you want to end up permanently displayed here as a Bad Example.'

'Why do you always have to look on the dark side of things?' said Sidney.

'Experience,' I said.

'You didn't expect your plan to go this well, did you?' said Polly.

'Not really, no,' I said, peering cautiously around me. 'First rule of the con: no plan survives contact with the enemy.'

'The sheer amount of Really Good Shit they have here is incredible!' said Sidney. 'I'm seeing things that haven't appeared in the underground auctions for generations. I'll tell you this for free, Gideon: this Museum knocks your little shop into a cocked hat and then pees all over it. There are things here I've only ever heard about. The Song of Solomon in a bottle! A mummy from the Tombs of Mars! The Captain's Log from the *Marie Celeste*, complete with blood-stains on the cover!'

'That isn't actually blood,' I said.

'What is it, then?'

'You don't want to know,' I said kindly.

'Yes, I do,' said Sidney, wistfully. 'I really do . . . Oooh! Oooh! A haunted coat-hanger from C.S. Lewis's wardrobe!'

Lex looked at me. 'The flotsam and jetsam of the hidden world. Are things like this really so important?'

'They're rare,' I said. 'That makes them collectable and therefore valuable. I know people who would sell their soul, or yours, to get their hands on some of the exhibits in this Museum.'

Lex shook his head. 'People are weird.'

And then Polly stopped so abruptly that Lex and I almost walked over her. She looked quickly around, growling under her breath. I moved cautiously in beside her.

'What is it, Polly?'

'Something smells bad,' she said quietly.

'Define bad.'

'Dangerous,' said Polly. 'Threatening. I feel like I just walked into the big cats' enclosure in the zoo.'

'There aren't any live specimens in the Museum,' I said.

Polly shrugged quickly. 'All I know is my instincts are screaming at me to get the hell out of here.'

'Keep moving,' I said.

'Did you really think they'd leave their precious Museum unguarded?' Polly said fiercely. 'Something is watching us! I can feel it.'

And then all our heads snapped round, as Sidney started making loud retching noises.

'Sidney!' I said. 'Not now!'

'It's not me!' said the mirror.

He broke off into loud choking noises as two huge, clawed hands burst out of his glass and clamped on to both sides of the frame. Vicious claws gouged deep into the wood as the hands tightened their hold and then hauled the rest of the body through. A huge humanoid feline creature covered in thick striped fur rose before the mirror. It had a tiger's head, with great snarling jaws and fierce green eyes. It growled slowly: a deep, threatening sound that reverberated in my bones. The big cat scent hung heavily on the air: blood and sweat and musk.

Polly crouched down low, so tense her muscles stood out like cables. She was growling too, a harsh rumble of hate and aggression. The claws on her feet dug into the wooden floor as she braced herself for the leap that would put her at the tiger's throat.

I said her name, but she didn't hear me. I shot Lex a warning look, but he only had eyes for the tiger. At least he hadn't summoned his armour. I turned my attention back to the tiger figure as it towered over us, eight feet of lean muscle and jungle savagery. But I could still see a human intelligence in the slit-pupiled eyes – and human hatred.

Sidney made loud spitting noises. 'I am getting really tired of having my defences overridden! I've got fur all over me! I'm going to be coughing up hairballs for weeks . . .'

'Do you have any idea what this is?' I said.

'Big horrible scary cat thing,' said Sidney. 'But I'll tell you this: it's come a long way to be here. I was getting glimpses of some kind of jungle . . .'

The tiger lashed out, and the mirror went flying backwards to slam into a row of display cases. It crashed to the floor, half buried in the debris, and didn't move again. Lex tensed.

'No armour!' I said urgently. 'We're lucky that thing hasn't already triggered every alarm in the place.'

And then I broke off, as the tiger addressed us in a low growling voice. 'I'm suppressing the alarms because I don't want to be interrupted. We have unfinished business to take care of.'

'Really?' I said, keeping my voice carefully calm and unimpressed. 'What did you have in mind?'

'Revenge,' said the tiger. 'Did you really think you could destroy my business, release all my captives, put my life in danger and not pay for your sins, Gideon Sable?'

Lex looked at me. 'I should have known this would turn out to be your fault. You know this thing?'

'The face isn't familiar,' I said. 'But I recognize the attitude. Hello, DeChance.'

The tiger's shape blurred, and suddenly DeChance was standing before us. He was still wearing his Great White Hunter's outfit, but now it was tattered and torn and soaked in his own dried blood. He smiled coldly at me.

'You thought I could be brought down by the animals I hunt?'

I shrugged, doing my best to appear casual. 'When did you become a weretiger, DeChance?'

'I always have an extra ace up my sleeve,' he said. 'And it does add a little extra excitement to the hunt when you can bring your prey down with your own claws and teeth.'

Lex glared at me. 'You promised me this bastard was dead!'

'He should be!' I said. 'The things I put on his trail should have been more than enough to do the job.'

DeChance laughed at me. 'I know my island and its jungle better than anyone. All the hidden traps and secret weapon caches . . . More than enough to hold the animals at bay until I could get off the island. They're probably still searching the jungle for me. Let them have it, until I return in triumph to hunt them down.'

'Talks a lot, doesn't he?' said Lex.

'Like you wouldn't believe,' I said. I nodded to DeChance. 'So you ran away from your own island. Driven off by the very creatures you used to hunt. Do you know where you are now?'

'Of course,' said DeChance. 'I've been a Member of the

Midnight Club for years. It took me a while to track you down, Gideon, but I never let anything get between me and what I want. Not even my own Club's security. And now, I will do to you what those animals did to me; only I will finish the job. And when your friends and loved ones see what's left of your body, they'll never stop vomiting.'

'If I rip his head off,' said Polly, 'do you think that would be enough to stop him talking?'

'Worth a try,' said Lex.

'I've always wanted to kill a weretiger,' said Polly. 'And this time, DeChance, there's no Medallion to protect you.'

She launched herself at the tiger, teeth and claws leading the way, and the impact sent DeChance crashing back through several display cases. The tiger threw off the wolf and sent her flying through the air. Polly hit the ground hard, ducked and rolled, and was quickly back on her feet. The two weres surged forward again, straining for each other's throats, and slammed into each other like crashing trains. Jungle hate blazed in their eyes. Claws tore into flesh, and blood spurted, but neither of them gave an inch.

The wounds they made healed almost as fast as they inflicted them. Polly ducked under a flailing arm and sank her fangs into DeChance's throat, worrying his flesh as blood jetted from the severed arteries. DeChance thrust his clawed hands deep into her sides and tore out handfuls of ribs. Both weres fell back, snarling loudly as their injuries repaired themselves.

'I could stop him, with my armour,' said Lex.

'Could you?' I said. 'Your armour is many things, but silver isn't one of them.'

'I could tear him in two,' said Lex. 'Let's see him repair that.'

'We can't let anyone in the Club know the Damned was here!'

'Then think of something!' said Lex. 'I won't lose my daughter!'

I thought quickly. 'Sidney! Front and centre, right now!'

The mirror scooted forward. 'What do you need, boss? Because short of hitting the tiger over the head with me, I don't see what I can contribute.'

'If we force the tiger through your glass, could you send him back to the island?' I said.

'Not a hope,' said the mirror. 'You saw it for yourself; he can override my coordinates.'

'Can you see the layout of this Club?' I said.

'Oh, sure!' said Sidney. 'Now I'm inside their shields, I can see everything.'

'Can you locate the Armoury?'

'Easey peasy,' said the mirror. 'It's just a few corridors away.'

'Then open a way to the Armoury, Sidney. We are going through.'

I glanced back at Polly and DeChance, who were circling each other watchfully.

'Keep him occupied till we get back, Polly! Lex, with me.'

'Always,' said Lex.

Lex and I dived into the scene in the glass.

The Armoury turned out to be a great hall with a high cross-timbered ceiling, its walls covered with swords and axes with famous names, murder wands and aboriginal pointing bones, cursed guns and blessed rifles. Suits of medieval armour stood to attention at regular intervals.

I looked quickly round until I spotted one particular sword, leaning casually against a wall. I moved over to stand before it. The sword was taller than me, with a blade wide enough to punch a hole through a charging rhino. When I lifted the sword, it was so heavy I needed both hands just to lever it off the floor.

And then the silence of the Armoury was broken by the sound of heavy footsteps. A suit of medieval armour was heading straight for us, its boots slamming down hard enough to break the floor-boards. A brutal killing machine, cast in steel. Sidney was already backing away at speed. Lex stepped forward to block the suit's way.

'I know,' he said, not looking back. 'Don't use my armour.'

'Give it hell, Lex,' I said.

Lex strode steadily forward. The suit of armour lashed out with a spiked fist. Lex swayed to one side and the blow sailed harmlessly past his head. Lex grabbed the steel arm with both hands and ripped it off the shoulder. There was no blood. There was nothing inside the steel arm, though the spiked glove still flexed. Lew threw the arm the length of the Armoury, and then punched the steel helm right off. There was nobody inside the suit. Lex tore it to pieces, scattering them far and wide.

'Lex!' I said. 'Time to go!'

'Sounds like a plan,' he said.

I turned to the mirror. 'Back to the Museum!'

'On it, boss.'

The tiger's claws opened dreadful wounds in the wolf's hide, tearing through her leathers as though they were nothing. Polly howled horribly. Her claws ripped through the tiger's throat, but the wounds healed even as her claws burst out the other side. The tiger punched the wolf so hard in the chest that I heard the breastbone break, and Polly dropped to one knee. The tiger grabbed the wolf's head with both hands and took a good hold, getting ready to tear it off.

'DeChance!' I yelled. 'Your fight isn't with her; it's with me!'

The tiger threw the wolf away and turned to face me. He padded unhurriedly toward me, and it took all the strength and leverage I had to keep the sword pointing at him. I waited till the tiger was in range and then thrust the sword forward. The tiger evaded the blow easily and threw himself at me. But I stood my ground and held the sword steady, and the impact of the tiger's lunge impaled him on the long blade. It punched right through the tiger's heart and out of his back, slicing through flesh and muscle and bone as though they were nothing but mist.

The tiger grabbed the sword blade with its great clawed hands. The edges lacerated his palms as he pulled himself along the blade, inch by inch, desperate to get his hands on me. I stood my ground and shoved the sword further through the tiger, and the light went out of his eyes. He dropped to his knees, the great head lolling forward as though it had grown unbearably heavy. Human hands dropped away from the sword – and just like that, there was no tiger. Nothing but a dead man transfixed on a sword. I pulled the long blade out of DeChance, and he toppled forward on to his face and lay still.

So many victims of the hunt, avenged at last.

'I don't understand,' said Lex. 'That blade isn't even silver . . .'

'Remember how I stole the sword Ex Caliburn?' I said. 'I swapped it back to Malcolm in return for a pookah's paw. So he wouldn't lose face for failing to acquire the sword. And because I really needed a pookah's paw. Given that Ex Caliburn was created to destroy dragons . . .'

Lex nodded slowly. 'Hand me the sword, Gideon.'

I passed it to him. Lex hefted the long blade as though it weighed nothing at all, and then walked over to DeChance's body and cut the head off.

'Just in case,' he said. He booted the severed head the length of the hall. 'That's for hurting my daughter, you son of a bitch.'

He handed the sword back to me and went to check on Polly. She was back in her human form, sitting with her back pressed against a wall. She smiled tiredly at Lex, grasped his extended hand and allowed him to pull her to her feet.

'Thanks, Dad.'

'No problem.'

I turned to Sidney. 'Armoury, please.'

'You got it, boss.'

He showed me the great hall, and I threw the sword through. Sidney made the view go away.

'I would have liked to take the sword with me,' I said. 'But they would have noticed that was missing in a moment.'

Lex offered Polly his arm, but she shook her head. 'I'm fine, Dad; don't fuss. I would have had him in a few more moments.'

'Of course you would,' said Lex.

'Now DeChance is dead, he's not suppressing the alarms any more,' I said. 'We need to grab Time's Arrow and get the hell out of here. Where is it, Polly?'

'Right there,' she said, pointing.

We stood together before the display case. Sidney crowded in behind us, peering over our shoulders and complaining he couldn't see anything. Time's Arrow turned out to be just an ordinary-looking arrow.

'That's it?' said Lex.

I checked the descriptive panel on the front of the case. 'Apparently. Why do these things never come with an instruction manual?'

'Maybe you need a bow, as well?' said Polly.

'No,' I said firmly. 'I would have heard.'

Lex raised a hand to smash the glass lid, but I stopped him.
'That really would set off the alarms.'

Polly gestured at the display cases she and the tiger had smashed in their brawl.

'What about them?'

'That was accidental,' I said. 'This would be deliberate. Alarms can tell.'

'Then open the case with your skeleton key,' said Lex.

'Security would be ready for something that obvious,' I said. 'Which is why I brought something new.'

I raised my hand to show them the Ouroboros ring. I concentrated on the activating words, and Time's Arrow disappeared from the case and reappeared in my hand.

'Nice one,' said Lex.

'I thought so,' I said.

I stuck the Arrow through the back of my belt, moved over to the nearest wall and took out one of my portable doors. I slapped the black blob against the wall, and it slid down to the floor. I looked at it for a moment and then tried again. Same result. I tried all the blobs in my pocket, and not one of them worked.

'Come on, Gideon,' said Lex. 'This is no time for anxiety issues.'

'They're not working,' I said numbly. 'Club security must have come up against portable doors before.' I gathered up the fallen blobs, stuffed them back in my pocket and thought hard. The others looked at me expectantly. I turned to Sidney. 'DeChance found a way into the Club through you, so he must have opened up a tunnel through the Club's defences. Is it still there?'

'It was,' said Sidney. 'But something just closed it. Boss, I think we're in trouble.'

Alarms suddenly filled the air, harsh and strident, coming from every direction at once.

'They know we're here,' said Polly.

'And we've nowhere to go,' I said.

'You should have hung on to the sword,' said Lex.

We moved to stand closer together, as a great many people came running to see what was happening.

SIX

All Kinds of Endings

I looked at Lex. 'And we were so close to getting away with it.'

'It was a good plan,' said Lex.

'If it had been a good plan, it would have worked.' I turned to Sidney. 'Any chance you can get us out of here?'

'We can't leave without Sally!' Lex said immediately. 'Not now the Club knows something is wrong.'

'She'll be perfectly safe,' I said. 'She has Malcolm for her alibi.'

'I won't leave without her,' Lex said flatly.

'We can't stay here!' I said.

Sidney rolled forward and forced his wooden frame between us.

'Things have come to a pretty pass if I'm having to be the voice of reason,' he said sharply. 'Can I just point out that what sounds like an entire army of security guards is heading straight for us, to express their extreme displeasure at our being here?'

'What he said,' said Polly. 'Only with perhaps a little less hysteria.'

'You are so judgemental,' said Sidney.

'Let them come,' said Lex. 'Security guards don't bother me,'

'But there are bound to be Club Members on the premises,' I said. 'And some of them, we really don't want to meet.'

That was when three Members of the Midnight Club came striding into the Museum, at the head of a great many security guards carrying heavy-duty tasers and electric cattle prods. Presumably, because they didn't want to risk any stray bullets damaging the exhibits. The Club Members slammed to a halt, and I was pleased to see real concern on their faces as they recognized Lex Talon. I knew them all, from various past associations and a few ill-judged partnerships. The criminal history of Old Soho can be a very complicated affair.

The Constant Cutie, also known as the Velvet Vampire, was a compact blonde bombshell in a half-unbuttoned blouse, leather mini skirt, fishnet stockings and white plastic stilettos. Cutie always believed in dressing to impress. Taste didn't get a look in. She specialized in the long con, during which she would drain her victim's wealth, health and eventually their lives. Not an actual vampire, but more a hard-hearted predator with some really nasty tricks up her sleeve.

Standing beside her was a tall, aristocratic fellow dressed in khakis. Ronnie Appleyard, the Genteel Graverobber. An archaeologist and necromancer, he could raise the voices of the dead to tell him where best to dig. There wasn't a tomb, mausoleum or old-time resting place he hadn't plundered and left littered with the dead of those who tried to stop him.

Finally, there was Ken Kelley, the Dream Thief. Ken could look into people's heads while they dreamed, steal the amazing things he found there and give them shape and form in the material world. And then he'd sell them to collectors who only thought they'd seen everything. The Dream Thief's victims had an unfortunate tendency to die, go crazy or just never wake up, but it had never been reported that he gave a damn. A round little man of more than middle age, with a bald head and a smiling face, Ken wore the best suit Savile Row could provide, badly.

Well, I thought, *at least the more powerful Club Members aren't around today. That's something.*

It also helped that I couldn't stand any of them. I only target people who deserve it, and I always make a point of being sure no innocent bystanders are harmed. Because I'd been one, more often than I cared to remember. I smiled broadly at the Constant Cutie, the Genteel Graverobber and the Dream Thief, happy that whatever happened, they had it coming to them.

The security guards were going to be a problem. They had the look of professional thugs, just waiting to be let off the leash so they could get to work with the tasers and cattle prods. Interestingly, though, they weren't paying any special attention to Lex. Which suggested they didn't know who and what he was. Because no one sane would look that composed, facing the Damned.

And then the guards suddenly parted, falling back as two larger specimens escorted their prisoner to the front. They were holding Sally's arms so tightly it had to hurt, but she wouldn't lower herself to show it. Thunderclouds formed in Lex's face, and he started to move forward.

'They're just trying to bait you into starting something,' I said quietly. 'And we're not ready yet.'

'Get ready,' said Lex, not taking his eyes off Sally.

The alarms suddenly shut down, and a hush fell over the Museum. As though the curtain had just gone up and the play was about to start. But the guards stayed where they were, and the Club Members remained silent, and I had to wonder what was holding them back. Clearly, I was missing something. So, when in doubt, muddy the waters and throw in a crocodile. I took a step forward and showed everyone my most charming smile.

'You know, there is a perfectly reasonable explanation for our being here . . .'

'Don't waste your time, darling,' said Sally, ignoring her guards with magnificent disdain. 'You've been under constant surveillance ever since you appeared inside the Museum.'

'Well,' I said, 'that's just cheating. How did they get you?'

Sally started to shrug, but the guards' hold didn't allow for that much movement.

'Really not my fault! I was having a perfectly lovely time enjoying drinkies in the Club bar with Malcolm, who can be surprisingly good company when you get a few drinks inside him, but the moment the alarms went off, these two steroid-abuse cases appeared out of nowhere, grabbed me here and there, and just hauled me away! Malcolm did go to bat for me, the sweetie, but they wouldn't listen. I put it down to bad toilet training.'

She broke off as the guards' hands clamped down hard. The crowd was parting again, to let someone important through. And when I saw who it was, I knew why the Cutie, the Graverobber and the Demon Thief had been so willing to wait. Strolling through the guards as though he had all the time in the world, and looking inordinately pleased with himself, was the Midnight Man himself: Johnny Occult. Founder of the Midnight Club and holder of its most disturbing secrets, Johnny was one of the most feared powers in Old Soho. I bowed courteously, but he didn't bow back. He came to a halt at the front of his guards, and the three Club Members moved in behind him.

Well dressed and smartly turned out, Johnny could have been a businessman or an investment banker . . . something important in the City. Until you looked him in the face and saw the ice in his eyes and the devil in his smile. He was tall, fashionably slender and darkly handsome, with the easy confidence of a man who was always going to be the most dangerous presence in the room.

Some said Johnny Occult could drive you crazy with a look or kill you with a word. That he could rip the soul right out of you and wolf it down like a party snack. I only had to glance at the three Club Members to see they believed every word. And these were people with reputations for being seriously dangerous in their own right. Johnny's smile widened a little, like a shark contemplating lunch.

The self-proclaimed King of Old Soho for more than a century didn't need to introduce himself. There were all kinds of theories as to who and what he really was. The only thing everyone agreed on was that after all the terrible things he'd done, he couldn't possibly be human. Unfortunately for Johnny Occult, my various crimes and cons had brought me into contact with real powers and dominations. Everyone from Old Harry to Sandra Ransom to Ethel who used to be an angel, and they told me many things. Johnny was just a minor-league chancer who'd stumbled into the heist of a lifetime and played it for all it was worth.

Somehow, he'd got his hands on some appallingly powerful objects being guarded by agents from Heaven and Hell, and he used them to set up the Midnight Club and build his murky reputation as the Midnight Man. As long as he stayed in the shadows of those sacred and profane items, he was untouchable by any agent from Above or Below, and that made him a man of power and influence. A spider spinning his webs of power, in the depths of a Club he could never leave.

'Gideon Sable,' said Johnny, in a light, pleasant voice, as though we'd just bumped into each other in passing. 'I knew you'd drop by for a visit, eventually. How could you resist?'

'Hello, Johnny,' I said, just as casually. 'You didn't have to go to all this fuss, just for me. Or is there a problem? If we've chosen a bad time to drop by, we can always come back some other time.'

And just like that, Johnny wasn't smiling any more. Because he couldn't stand the thought that someone wasn't taking him seriously.

'You should never have come here,' he said coldly. 'No one takes what's mine. You know . . . I think you and your fellow lowlifes would make a splendid addition to my collection. A diorama, perhaps, stuffed and mounted, still alive and endlessly suffering. As a terrible warning to all.'

'No!' a voice said suddenly from the back of the guards. 'Not Sally!'

Everyone turned to look, as the Museum's Curator forced his way through the crowd, using his bony elbows on any guard who didn't get out of his way fast enough. And they were so startled that they let him do it. Even the three Club Members fell back to give him room. Malcolm finally came to a halt, breathing heavily, as much from his passions as his exertions. He stood face to face with Johnny, scowling fiercely, and Johnny looked calmly back, a little amused if anything.

'My dear Curator, most trusted advisor and protector of all my treasures,' he murmured. 'What could possibly have stirred you from your dusty old office?'

'This is my Museum!' Malcolm said loudly. 'I decide what is worthy to be displayed here. And I am certainly not going to allow anything as vulgar as a diorama of Thieves in Aspic! I've spent decades fitting everything together, to get the ambience just right. I suppose a case might be made for setting them up in the lobby, but not Sally! I will not stand for her being harmed.'

'Well, colour me surprised,' said Johnny. 'Who knew the old man had so much fire in him?'

Malcolm stirred uneasily. Now that he was standing before the Midnight Man himself, he could feel the authority draining out of him. He turned his scowl on the guards holding Sally.

'Let go of her! Right now!'

The guards looked to Johnny, who nodded briefly. They released their hold, and Sally ran straight past Malcolm to throw herself into Lex's arms. They held each other tightly, murmuring words of comfort. Malcolm watched it all and said nothing, but I saw something die in his eyes. He slumped for a moment, as though he'd been hit, and then he squared his shoulders and lifted his chin and turned back to face Johnny. Just a dogged dry stick of a man, surprised late in life to discover there was something he cared more about than his precious Museum. He looked Johnny square in the eye, and his voice was perfectly calm.

'I ask for Switch It Sally to be spared. She's just a small-time thief and not worthy of this Club's condemnation.' He carefully didn't glance at Sally, keeping his gaze fixed on Johnny, who stared unblinkingly back. Malcolm cleared his throat and moved quickly on to his next argument. 'Sally has just presented the Midnight Club with its biggest bequest in years: one of Lex Talon's halos!'

There was a sudden interested murmuring among the Club Members. They all looked a lot happier now they thought they wouldn't have to take on the Damned in his armour. Johnny looked from Malcolm to Lex and back again, but his expression didn't change at all.

'At least, now we know what the Damned is doing here,' he said lightly. 'But . . . if Sally betrayed the trust of the man she's supposed to care for, she'd betray anyone. I really must question your judgement in this matter, Curator.' Malcolm started to say something, but Johnny just kept talking. 'She used you, so her friends could sneak in. I don't even know why you're still defending her; you just saw her run back to her sugar daddy like a dog to its vomit.' He turned his cold gaze on Sally, and she glared right back at him. Johny smiled unpleasantly. 'Did you really believe a nobody like you could become a Member of this Club? A sneak thief and small-time con artist, whose only reputation comes from being brave enough to sleep with the Damned? You're not fit to clean our toilets.'

Sally waited a moment, to be sure he was done, and then raised a single eyebrow.

'Well, really, darling. I always heard the Midnight Man was a gentleman. Not an arsehole with delusions of grandeur.'

She turned to Lex, and they solemnly high-fived each other.

Johnny turned his glare on Malcolm. 'You see, you stupid old man? She doesn't give a damn about you!'

'You think I didn't know that?' said Malcolm. There was something in his quiet dignity that made us all pay attention. Malcolm looked steadily at Johnny Occult. 'I ask for Sally's freedom anyway, because she matters to me even if I don't matter to her. I have been Curator of this Museum for many years, and I believe I have earned the right to a personal favour.'

Johnny sighed. 'Is there anything more irritating than a functionary who forgets his place? You're fired. Get out of my sight.'

Malcolm swayed on his feet. All the colour dropped out of his face, as though he'd been hit.

'After all my years of service? I gave my life to making this Museum a thing of beauty and joy forever!'

'Just because I let you play with my toys doesn't mean they belong to you,' said Johnny. 'Now, will you please just shut up and go away? I have thieves to punish.'

'No!' Malcolm said loudly. 'Listen to me!'

A gun appeared in Johnny's hand. He fired it quite casually, and Malcolm's chest exploded in a shower of blood. The impact sent him stumbling backwards, and Sally leapt forward to catch him. His weight sent both of them crashing to the floor. Sally held Malcolm to her tightly, as though she could prevent his life from leaving him.

'Why, Malcolm?' she said. 'Why would you put everything on the line for me?'

He managed a small smile for her. 'For the pleasure of your company. For a moment of kindness . . .'

And then he died.

Sally held on to him for a moment, and then gently put the body to one side. She extended a hand to Lex, and he helped her to her feet. The three Club Members stirred uneasily at what they saw in Sally's face, and even Johnny looked at her thoughtfully.

Sally looked steadily at Lex, and when she spoke, her voice was very low.

'He was a nice old stick, but he never meant anything to me.'

'I know that,' said Lex.

'So did he,' said Sally. 'That's what makes it so sad.'

'You made him happy for a while.'

Sally turned the full force of her glare on Johnny. 'What kind

of a life did you make for Malcolm, that someone like me could
be the best thing that ever happened to him?'

'Sentiment?' said Johnny. 'From a slut who sleeps with the
Damned? Whoever would have thought it . . .'

Sally tensed, and Lex looked ready to back her up, so I stepped
quickly forward to draw everyone's attention back to me.

'There's no need for raised voices. There's still room for the
quiet voice of reason . . .'

'No, there isn't,' Johnny said flatly. 'Save your speeches; I
know better than to strike a deal with the infamous Gideon Sable.'
He turned to the Constant Cutie. 'Time for you to show you're
worthy of your Membership, my dear.'

She nodded quickly and moved forward to stand in front of
me. Every movement was carefully considered, for maximum
impact. She tossed her head artlessly, letting her blonde hair fall
to her shoulders in careful disarray, and showed me her very best
smile. It was all something to see, but if you knew what to look
for, you could tell Cutie's charm was just a weapon, and nothing
more. She nodded casually to me, and I nodded easily in return.

'Hello, Daphne,' I said. 'It's been a while, hasn't it?'

Her smile snapped off. 'I've told you before: don't call me
that! I haven't been that person in ages. I am the Constant Cutie,
the Velvet Vampire, destroyer of men and delighter in their
ruin . . . and don't you ever forget it! I have moved up in the
world.'

'That's a matter of opinion,' I said. 'Don't waste your time
trying to impress me, Daphne; I knew you when. But it is nice
to catch up. How are things?'

She giggled suddenly. 'Oh, you know – the usual. Breaking
hearts and taking fools for everything they've got. You?'

'Much the same,' I said. 'But I only go after people who
deserve it.'

Cutie pouted playfully. 'Where's the fun in that?'

'Are you really ready to throw me to the jackals?' I said.

'Of course, lover,' said Cutie. 'It's what I do.'

Lex cleared his throat, and we both turned to look at him. He
sniffed loudly.

'You know this . . . person, Gideon?'

'A long time ago,' I said. 'We were different people then.'

'You might have been,' said Cutie. 'But I always knew there was a Velvet Vampire inside me, just waiting for her chance.'

'That's a shame,' I said. 'I liked Daphne. She was fun.'

'Sorry, lover,' said Cutie. 'But you're going down. I worked hard to get my Club Membership.'

'No you didn't,' I said. 'You stole a Demon Lord's heart. I saw it in a display case.'

She shrugged prettily. 'And afterwards, he cried and he cried and he cried. It was so embarrassing . . . Still, memories like that can warm my heart at night.'

'You have a heart?' I said politely.

Her eyes flashed. 'Now, that was just mean! How could I enjoy breaking hearts if I didn't have one?'

'And you love every moment of it,' I said.

Her smile came back. 'Bet your sweet arse, lover.'

She suddenly seemed to remember that Johnny was waiting. She reached into her cleavage and brought out a simple plastic clicker in the shape of a small green frog. She handed it to Johnny.

'It took me a while to decide on the best item, but this should do the trick. You wouldn't believe what I had to go through to get my hands on it . . .'

'And I don't care,' said Johnny.

Cutie shrugged and stepped back into the crowd. She did waggle her fingers at me in a goodbye.

'Old flame?' said Lex, doing his best to avoid sounding judgemental and not even coming close.

'Old mistake,' I said.

'Been there, done that, dug the grave,' said Lex.

Johnny cleared his throat to draw everyone's attention back to him. He held up the plastic clicker.

'The ultimate on/off switch – this little fellow works on anything, including your precious armour, Lex. Which has to be a lot weaker, now you're down to just the one halo.'

He waited expectantly for a response, but Lex just stared calmly back at him. Johnny shrugged.

'First, we strip you of your armour, and then we get to have some fun with you. For as long as you last. And once I have both bracelets in my possession, no force from Heaven or Hell will ever be able to stand against me.'

He hit the clicker, and its sharp decisive sound echoed loudly on the quiet. Everyone looked at Lex's wrists, waiting for a bracelet to fall away, but nothing happened. Johnny gave the clicker a hard shake and then tried it again. Still nothing. Lex smiled slightly.

'People keep coming to me with some strange object they've stolen or cobbled together, expecting it to work miracles. But my armour is powered by Heaven and Hell, and nothing in the world can stand against that.'

Johnny looked to the three Club Members, but they were already backing away. Johnny took a moment to scowl at them before turning his gaze back to Lex. He frowned, thinking hard, and then his eyes widened. His head snapped round, and he stared unbelievingly at Sally.

'You cheated me! The Damned still has both his halos!'

Sally showed him her most dazzling smile.

'Suck my dick, loser.'

A dark murmur moved among the guards as they realized they were going to have to take on the Damned in his armour, after all. They hefted their tasers and electric cattle prods but didn't seem to have the same confidence in them. Johnny threw the clicker away, and it skidded across the floor. He took a deep breath to steady himself and then smiled at Lex.

'Even your armour is no match for some of the exhibits in my Museum. No one steals from me and gets away with it.'

I nodded to Lex. 'I'm getting tired of this. Show this arrogant little turd how wrong he is.'

'Love to,' said Lex.

He armoured up, and everyone fell back as blindingly bright armour covered the Damned from head to foot. Black clouds sailed across his blazing chest, like passing dark thoughts. Some of the nearer exhibits disappeared from their display cases. Other cases went blank, as though trying to hide their contents. One spontaneously combusted. And a mummy from the Martian Tombs emerged from its wall niche, knelt before the Damned and bowed its horned head to him . . . before crumbling into a pile of dust that blew away on an unfelt breeze. Sally looked at the Damned.

'What was that about?'

'Beats the hell out of me,' said the Damned.

The Cutie, the Graverobber and the Dream Thief backed even further away, huddling together like frightened children. Only Johnny Occult stood his ground.

'Get the crew out of here, Gideon,' the Damned said quietly. 'I'll hold them off and join you later.'

'Lex,' I said carefully, 'I'm not sure even you can beat odds this bad.'

'Have a little faith,' said the Damned.

'I'm not going anywhere until I've made that snotty little creep pay for what he did to Malcolm!' said Sally.

The Damned turned his blank face to her. 'Don't even think of going up against the Midnight Man. He's protected. And anyway, killing is what I do, not you.'

'Oh, sweetie,' said Sally. 'You've always been so wonderfully short-sighted regarding certain areas in my spotted past. And I love you for it.'

'I wanted to protect you from my world,' said the Damned.

'I don't need protecting,' said Sally. 'And I am not leaving you to fight all these guards on your own.'

'Damn right!' said Polly. 'The whole point of the crew is that we're stronger together than we ever were apart.'

'Because the crew is family,' I said. 'One for all, and all the blood and horror in the world for our enemies.'

'Go crew!' said Polly.

'You are all bat-shit crazy!' said Sidney. 'Fortunately, so am I.'

He rolled forward to face the guards, and his voice rang out, harsh and assured. 'I just opened a gateway to Hell itself! Stand down or I'll do it again. Right here, right now!'

'If there's one thing I loathe, it's an uppity appliance,' said Johnny. 'With my Club's shields in place, you are prohibited from making contact with anywhere.'

'Ah . . .' said Sidney. 'I was sort of hoping you didn't know that. Ah, well, it was worth a try. Forget I said anything.'

He glided quickly backwards to join the rest of us. Sally patted him fondly on his wooden frame.

'Nice threat, darling. Very convincing.'

'Right up to the point where it didn't work,' I said.

'I'm new to this!' said Sidney. 'If you have a plan to get us out of here, now would be a really good time to set it in motion.'

'I'm working on it,' I said.

'Work faster,' said the mirror.

'Will you all just stop talking!' said Johnny. His face was flushed, and his voice was harsh. It had been a long time since anyone had dared defy him. 'There's nowhere you can go and nothing you can do. Accept your fate gracefully, so the rest of us can get on with our lives.'

'Not what we do,' I said. 'Lex, I am right out of plans. Let's just hit the problem and see what breaks.'

'Sounds like a plan to me,' said the Damned.

He plunged into the guards, and the whole crowd scattered like so many panicked birds. He was quickly in and among them, striking guards down with his armoured fists and trampling them underfoot. Bones broke and shattered, and blood flew on the air. Guards shot at him with their tasers, but the barbs couldn't penetrate the armour and fell harmlessly away. Other guards stabbed at the Damned again and again with their cattle prods. Showers of sparks rose up or skittered across his armour, but still the Damned strode on, untouched and unmoved, a remorseless killing machine insulated from the world and everything in it. The guards broke and ran.

Polly erupted into a terrifying lupine form still somehow contained inside her stretched and torn leathers. She howled like it was a full moon and the killing madness was upon her, and slammed into the guards like a runaway train. She went to work on them with fangs and claws, and no one could stand against her or even slow her down. Several tasers hit her at once, and all her fur stood on end and crackled with sparks, but the pain just made her angrier. She tore out throats, ripped open bellies and stormed on through the guards, dragging dangling taser cords behind her. She easily dodged the thrusting cattle prods, and the guards hit each other instead. Polly laughed silently as bodies fell convulsing to the floor. She was in full wolf mode, savage and primal, and faced with people who'd threatened her family, she saw no reason to hold back.

Johnny yelled at the three Club Members to do something, but none of them wanted anything to do with a maddened werewolf.

They backed away even further, and Johnny went with them, though he was the only one who looked like he was making a tactical retreat and not just running away. Polly tore through the guards, leaving blood and bodies and horrified screams in her wake.

Switch It Sally searched her pockets for the small useful objects she always carried with her, so she could do appalling things with them. I searched my own pockets, though the few tools of the trade I had left weren't going to be much help. The compass, the skeleton key and the short-range teleport ring all had their uses, but not against such overwhelming odds. For every guard the Damned and the werewolf tore apart, it seemed a dozen more came running to take their place. Johnny must have called in every warm body in the Club.

Sidney moved in beside me. 'You'd better hide behind me, boss. It's getting ugly out there.'

I nodded and stepped behind the standing mirror, peering past his wooden frame at the surging mayhem.

'I'm a thief, not a killer,' I said. 'It's usually my job to try to prevent things getting this bad.'

'We're in the Midnight Club, boss,' said the mirror. 'It was always going to get this bad. Now stay back behind me. I hate cleaning blood off my frame.'

'Thanks, Sidney,' I said. 'I always knew you'd come in handy for something.'

'Could I get it in writing?' said the mirror. 'Only I might need a reference after this mess is over.'

The Damned picked up guards and threw them like missiles. Blood streamed down his shining armour as he smashed in skulls, stove in ribs and kicked guards so hard they went flying through the air. The only reason the guards still came at him was because they were more scared of Johnny than they were of the Damned. After all, the Damned was just trying to kill them. The Midnight Man had done far worse things than that.

Polly raged on, while desperate guards fought to drag her down with their bare hands; they'd tried everything else and none of it had worked. She darted in and out, never still for a moment, teeth and claws leading the way. Tasers shot past her to light up other guards, and the cattle prods didn't even come close. Blood spurted in showers as the wolf did horrible things to anyone who got in her way and defied the guards to do anything about them.

I watched it all from behind Sidney, trying desperately to think of something I could do. I'd tried to teach Lex and Polly there were better ways than bloodshed and slaughter, but now that they were facing the Midnight Man and all his guards, there was no other way.

Some of the guards noticed Switch It Sally standing alone and saw her as something they could use as leverage against the Damned. Half a dozen headed for Sally, and she met them with a dazzling smile as she swapped out their arteries for lengths of string. They collapsed screaming, clutching at their violated chests. Apart from one, who ducked and dodged as he closed in on her. Sally waited till he was almost on top of her, and then switched his eyes for two ping pong balls. The guard screamed horribly and staggered past her, blood streaming down his cheeks from where his eyes used to be.

I looked quickly round the Museum, but didn't see anything I could use as a weapon. Short of picking up a display case and hitting a guard over the head with it. Johnny Occult was standing inhumanly still in the midst of the mayhem, untouched by any of the awful things going on around him. He raised his voice to address the three Club Members, huddled together on the outskirts of the fighting and hoping not to be noticed.

'Get stuck in, or I'll revoke your Club Memberships! And given all the awful things you've done, none of you would survive ten minutes without the Club's protection. You have access to the Club Armoury! Help yourselves to anything you fancy!'

Cutie, the Graverobber and the Dream Thief frowned hard, concentrating, and weapons appeared out of nowhere to fill their hands. I yelled to the Damned and the werewolf. They both looked round, and I gestured for them to fall back and join me. They came hurrying back, and the surviving guards were happy to see them go.

Cutie had two slender daggers in her hands. Poison streamed down grooves in the blades, to hiss and spit as it ate into the floor. The Borgia Blades. The Graverobber had a long-barrelled pistol with a stylized dragon etched into the steel. The Wyrm Gunne fired really incendiary bullets. And a very familiar long sword appeared in the Dream Thief's hands. I frowned. I wasn't having that. I stepped out from behind Sidney and thrust out my hand. Ex Caliburn ripped itself out of the Dream Thief's grasp and sailed through the air to nestle into my hand. The blade felt weightless and perfectly poised. I smiled cheerfully at the dumb-founded Dream Thief.

'It likes me,' I shouted. 'And it really doesn't like you.'

The Dream Thief snarled and concentrated again, and a huge axe slapped into his hand. It was just as big as Ex Caliburn, and the axe head glowed with malevolent forces. The Dream Thief gestured to me to come to him.

'Don't fall for that, Gideon,' said the Damned. 'You're a thief, not a killer.'

'This whole mess is down to me,' I said. 'I have to do something.'

I headed straight for the Dream Thief. The guards looked at my face, and at what I was holding, and hurried to get out of my way. I was still mad as hell over what had happened to Malcolm. I might not have liked the man much, but it was my plan that put him in danger. I couldn't get to Johnny to make him pay, and there were too many guards for me to deal with, but the Dream Thief was right in front of me, and just the awful things he'd done that I knew about made him a really good start.

I swung Ex Caliburn with both hands and drove the Dream Thief back, blow by blow and step by step. Flurries of sparks flew on the air as the heavy blades slammed into each other. It was all the Dream Thief could do to keep a hold on his axe. Like me, he was a thief, not a killer, and he didn't have the cold rage that was driving me. Finally, my blade sheared right through the axe head and buried itself in the Dream Thief's shoulder. The impact drove him to his knees, and he cried out miserably when I yanked the blade out. I brought Ex Caliburn crashing down with all my strength, and it sliced all the way down through the Dream Thief's skull until it ground to a halt in the teeth of the lower jaw. I pulled the sword free, and the Dream Thief fell forward and didn't move again.

I looked around for another target and found the Damned had returned to the fight to back me up. He was surrounded by guards thrusting their cattle prods at him, filling the air with showers of sparks. He struck out with his armoured hands, but there were too many of them for him to make any real impression. Like a lion threatened by a pack of jackals. The Graverobber targeted the Damned with his incendiary bullets, but they shattered harmlessly against the shining armour. The Graverobber shot the Damned right in his blank face, but he didn't even flinch.

The Graverobber saw Polly racing forward to help and turned the Wyrm Gunne on her. He shot her in the chest as she reared up, and her fur burst into flames, but still the burning wolf charged on, barging guards out of her way and setting them on fire. She leapt for the Graverobber's throat like a blazing comet. She tore the man's throat out before he could fire again, and they crashed to the floor together, but only Polly got up. She rolled quickly back and forth on the floor to smother her flames, then crouched there with steam rising from her scorched hide, snarling at anyone who got too close while she regathered her strength. And that was when Cutie slipped silently in behind Polly and stabbed her in the back. There must have been some silver in the blade because it sank all the way into the hilt. Polly cried out and spun round, but Cutie was already gone, taking the knife with her, and leaving a bloody wound in Polly's back that refused to heal.

The werewolf swayed from side to side, head hanging down, and Cutie came at her from another blind side. She raised the Borgia Blade, but Polly turned back into her human form, and the blade swept through the air where the larger body had been. Cutie stumbled forward, caught off balance. Polly started to go after her but collapsed as her legs gave out. Blood was streaming down her back from the wound that wouldn't close. She turned back into her wolf form, but that just stretched the wound open, and by the time she could see through the pain, Cutie had disappeared among the guards.

There hadn't been time for me to help the Damned or the wolf, but now Johnny Occult was right in front of me. He fired his gun at me, but I blocked the bullets with Ex Caliburn's blade, the long sword leaping lightly to where it needed to be. Johnny kept firing till he ran out of bullets and then threw the gun away. He fell back, to hide among his guards. I cut a bloody path through the guards with Ex Caliburn, littering the way with corpses, but by the time I got there, Johnny was gone. When I turned to look, he was standing behind Sally with a knife pressed against her throat.

'Your gift won't work on me, Switch It Sally,' Johnny said loudly. 'I'm protected! I'll kill you if you even try.'

'Fair enough,' said Sally, holding very still.

Johnny looked quickly around him. Cutie was the only Club Member still standing. The Damned was half buried under guards, who'd been reduced to piling on top of him in the hope they could drag him down by sheer weight of numbers. The werewolf was crouched on all fours, barely moving, and I was too far away to reach any of them. Johnny raised his voice.

'Everyone stand down! Lex, I have Sally!'

Everyone stopped fighting. The Damned shook the last of the guards off him and turned to see the knife at Sally's throat. Johnny smiled at him.

'Lose the armour, Lex. Or watch her die. It's up to you.'

'I'm sorry, Lex!' said Sally. 'I never saw the sneaky bastard coming!'

'Shut up!' said Johnny. 'Dear God, your voice grates.'

The Damned studied them both. He knew he could never get to the Midnight Man before Sally paid the price. She saw the Damned hesitate and called out again.

'Lex! Don't you dare! Get the little shit!'

Johnny pressed the knife against her throat, and her skin parted under the keen edge. A thin runnel of blood coursed down her neck. Sally stopped talking. The Damned's armour disappeared back into the bracelets at his wrists, and he stood revealed to the world, alone and unprotected in the midst of his enemies. I was relieved to see he wasn't holding Ethel's halo, so we still had an ace in the hole. Johnny peered at Lex over Sally's shoulder and laughed softly.

'She always was your Achilles heel. Don't feel bad; everyone has one. Well, everyone but me, obviously. Now, take off your bracelets and drop them on the floor. The halos will make fine additions to my Museum.'

'I can't,' Lex said steadily. 'They don't come off.'

Johnny raised an eyebrow. 'You wouldn't lie to me, would you, Lex? Not with my knife pressing against Sally's throat?'

'I wouldn't lower myself,' said Lex.

Johnny shrugged. 'There's no need to be rude. It doesn't matter; I can always have the guards hold you down and cut off your hands, and then take the bracelets off your wrists. And you'll let me do it, because if you don't, I'll give Sally to the guards and let them play with her. For as long as she lasts . . .'

'Don't hurt her,' said Lex. 'I'm not going anywhere.'

Johnny nodded to Cutie as she emerged from the guards. 'You're all I have left? The quality of Club Members isn't what it used to be. All right, lose one of those knives and summon a gun.'

The knife in her right hand was immediately replaced by a pistol.

'Well, don't just stand there!' said Johnny. 'Point it at Lex! I want to see how many holes you can put in him before he finally falls!'

Cutie aimed her gun at Lex. Her hand was perfectly steady. Lex saw Polly brace herself for one last desperate leap, took in the blood coursing down her side, and knew she'd never make it.

'Stand down, Polly,' he said. 'We have to protect Sally.'

Polly nodded reluctantly. I pointed Ex Caliburn at Johnny, and he nodded appreciatively.

'Nice sword.'

'I thought so,' I said. I shot a quick glance at Sidney. 'Stand firm. We'll get through this.'

Sidney moved in beside me. 'Whatever happens, it's been an honour, boss.'

Cutie moved in beside Johnny, covering all of us with her gun. She was smiling, and it wasn't a nice smile.

'Let me shoot them all, Johnny,' she said, in a spoilt-little-girl voice. 'I want to shoot them all. No one humiliates me and gets away with it!'

'You always did make bad choices when it came to the men in your life,' I said. 'Daphne.'

'Stop calling me that!' said Cutie. 'I could always recognize a man on the way up, and that was never you. Just stand there and let me shoot you, Gideon, and I promise I'll make it quick and clean.'

I didn't believe her, and she could see I didn't. Which made her smile even more.

'Bloodthirsty little thing, isn't she?' said Johnny. 'I knew there was a good reason why I let her hang around.'

'You see?' I said to Cutie. 'You're not his girl or his partner. You're his pet.'

'Shut up!' said Cutie. 'Why do you always have to spoil everything?'

She aimed her gun at my groin, and her aim was perfectly steady. I deliberately turned away to look at Lex and Sally, Polly and Sidney. 'Sorry, crew. I always knew that, in the end, we'd go out like Butch and Sundance.'

'Don't shoot Gideon just yet, Cutie,' said Johnny. 'We need to start with the most dangerous one. Shoot Lex.'

'Love to,' said Cutie.

She shot him in the chest. The impact sent him staggering backwards, blood coursing down, but he didn't fall. Cutie snarled and fired again and again, and finally Lex did fall, because without his armour he was just a man. He went down on one knee, breathing harshly. He tried to raise his head for one last look at Sally but didn't have the strength. He fell forward and lay still. Cutie giggled happily and blew imaginary smoke from the barrel of her gun.

Sally back-elbowed Johnny in the ribs, and his hand jerked the knife away from her throat. Sally ran forward to bend over Lex, and Cutie shot her in the back. Sally collapsed across Lex's body, twitched a few times and then stopped moving. Polly got ready to leap, and I raised Ex Caliburn. Cutie raised her gun, hesitated over who to go for first and then shot at me.

And that was when Ethel Makepeace appeared out of nowhere, hanging overhead on outstretched wings made of light. The bullet from Cutie's gun stopped in mid-air and dropped to tinkle harmlessly on the floor.

Everyone stood very still, staring at Ethel. She smiled easily around her and gestured lightly at Lex's body. The glowing bracelets disappeared from the dead man's wrists and reappeared in Ethel's waiting hands. The third bracelet edged out of Lex's pocket and then shot through the air to form a glowing halo around Ethel's head.

Cutie started to aim her gun at the angel and then turned and ran out of the Museum. All the surviving guards followed her, desperate to escape the judgemental gaze of the angel. That just left Johnny Occult, glaring resentfully at the angel as she descended unhurriedly to stand before him.

'Hello, Johnny,' said Ethel. 'It's been a while.'

'Not long enough,' said Johnny.

'You stay right where you are,' said Ethel. 'I'll get to you in a moment.'

Polly was back in her human form, kneeling beside the bodies of her parents. I moved in beside her.

'There's nothing you can do,' I said, as gently as I could. 'They're gone.'

'I know that,' said Polly. 'I've smelt enough death in my time. Just . . . give me a moment.'

'As long as you need,' I said. I turned to Ethel. 'You couldn't have got here a few minutes earlier?'

'No,' said Ethel. 'The items Johnny stole from Heaven and Hell protected him from outside interference. That's how he survived so long. But the death of Lex Talon the angel-killer, and the ending of his link with the halos, was momentous enough to shatter the shields. So I could finally get in here.' She looked at the bracelets in her hands, and they faded away. 'I'll see they're returned to their original owners.'

'The original owners are dead,' I said. 'Lex shot them with the Iscariot Device the moment they took on material form.'

'You can't kill an angel,' said Ethel. 'Only the bodies they appear in.'

I stared at her. 'So Lex went through all that guilt for nothing?'

'The guilt was real because the crime was real,' said Ethel. 'But you know as well as I do, his real guilt came from killing Hammer's personal assistant, Anathea.' She looked sternly at Lex and Sally, together in death as they had been in life. 'All right! That's enough lying around. Up on your feet! There are things that need doing!'

The spirits of Lex and Sally appeared, standing over their own bodies. It was hard to tell which of them looked the most surprised. They clung to each other tightly.

'I thought I'd lost you!' said Sally.

'Never,' said Lex.

Polly scrambled to her feet, and her father and mother opened their arms to embrace her.

'Yes, well, that's all very sweet,' said Ethel. 'But there are things we need to discuss.'

Lex and Sally let go of Polly, and Lex gently pushed her away, as though moving her out of the line of fire. He nodded to the angel.

'It's time to go, isn't it?'

'Yes, dear,' said Ethel.

Lex looked at Sally. She was still holding his hand. Gently but firmly, Lex pulled his hand out of hers.

'You can't go where I'm going. Where I've always known I was going.'

Sally shook her head stubbornly. 'You're not going anywhere without me. Because if you're not with me, that would be hell anyway.'

'Some people are so slow on the uptake,' said the angel Ethel. 'Sometimes they need a little push to get them headed in the right direction.'

She snapped her fingers, and a tall, elegant blonde appeared out of nowhere to stand facing Lex. He stared at her.

'*Anathea?*'

Fredric Hammer's personal assistant, dead for so many years, walked up to Lex, holding his gaze unflinchingly.

'Kneel.'

Lex knelt before her, and she leaned forward and kissed him on the forehead.

'You're forgiven,' she said. 'So get over yourself.'

She smiled briefly and disappeared. Lex rose slowly to his feet. Sally took him by the hand again, and he held on tightly. Ethel smiled approvingly.

'How could you be damned, Lex, when you have so much love in you?' She shook her head. 'Life is actually very simple; it's people who insist on complicating things. Now, come along, dears.'

Sally looked thoughtfully at Lex. 'So that was Anathea. She was very pretty.'

'I thought so,' said Lex.

'Tell you what,' said Sally. 'I'll forgive you for her if you forgive me for Malcolm.'

'Sounds like a plan to me,' said Lex.

'Time to be going, dears,' said Ethel. 'Your adventures are just beginning.'

She snapped her fingers, and just like that, the spirits of Lex Talon and Switch It Sally were no longer there.

'As goodbyes go, that wasn't too bad,' said Polly. She started to stretch languorously and then stopped. 'Hey! My wound has healed!'

'You're welcome, dear,' said Ethel. She nodded to me. 'My time on Earth is over. Being human was fun, but I miss my duty.' She smiled suddenly. 'I almost forgot! A few last tasks, before I go.'

She moved over to the standing mirror, wrapping her wings around her like a shining cloak. Sidney looked as if he wanted to back away, but he held his ground. Ethel thrust one arm deep into the glass and pulled out an entirely ordinary-looking young man with a very surprised look on his face. Ethel let go of his hand and smiled at him cheerfully.

'Welcome back, Sidney. You've punished yourself long enough. All your sins are forgiven.'

Sidney bowed to her. 'Who am I to argue with an angel?'

'Precisely!' said Ethel.

Sidney turned to me and smiled shyly. 'We haven't actually met before. I'm Sidney. The original. The one and only.'

'Never doubted it for a moment,' I said. 'Get over here.'

He moved over to stand before me, and I hugged him. Just for a moment, and then I let him go.

'Welcome home, Sidney.'

'Good to be back, boss. I can still be useful!'

'Good to know,' I said.

Ethel turned unhurriedly to study Johnny Occult, still standing where she'd left him. Probably because he knew there was nowhere he could go that she couldn't find him. He stared defiantly back at her.

'You've been hiding for a long time, Johnny,' said the angel. 'Concealed and protected by the sacred and profane items you stole. However, it is not for me to pass judgement. I am leaving this world. But . . . I am leaving behind a few friends, who know all there is to know about moral judgements.'

She snapped her fingers, and three familiar faces appeared

beside her. Jessica Montefiore, the Dandy Devil and Peter Bell.

'Allow me to present the Saint, the Demon and the Balance,' Ethel said proudly. 'Together, they provide a whole new way of looking at things.' She smiled at me. 'You have your crew, and I have mine.'

'Where have you been hiding them?' I said.

'Under my wings,' said Ethel. She smiled at her crew and gestured grandly at Johnny. 'Allow me to present the Midnight Man, Johnny Occult. Not his real name. He stole things that matter from Heaven and Hell and used them to make himself a power on Earth. Hidden from all the agents that pursue, he thought he could get away with anything. But since he never dared leave his Club, he never really amounted to much. He still managed to hurt a lot of people, so I leave his fate in your hands.' She smiled briefly at Johnny. 'Who knows, dear, they might be merciful.'

'Don't I get to defend myself?' said Johnny.

She looked at him. 'It's a bit late for that, Johnny.'

He met her gaze with his best defiant glare. 'I'm supposed to accept judgement from this rabble? I never even heard of them!'

'They've heard of you,' said Ethel.

'The angel spent enough time living as a human to believe mortals should only be judged by mortals,' said Jessica.

'People who know all there is to know about sin, from both sides,' said the Dandy Devil.

'Who understand the need for balance,' said Peter.

'So,' said Jessica. 'For all the things you've done . . .'

'And all the things you planned to do . . .' said the Dandy Devil.

'It's time for you to go where you belong,' said Peter. 'Mark! He's all yours.'

And from out of the standing mirror stepped Mark Stone, the Hound of Hell. Entirely repaired and restored, cool and arrogant as ever, right down to the very dark sunglasses. He grinned about him, like a wolf in a good mood.

'It's good to be back! Johnny baby! I've been looking for you for such a long time . . .'

Johnny bolted for the exit. Mark gestured easily, and Johnny's feet shot out from under him. He crashed to the floor, fighting helplessly against some unseen force. Mark strolled over to him, reached down and grabbed him by the ankle. And then he dragged Johnny back to the standing mirror, ignoring the Midnight Man's screams and pleas for mercy. Mark stopped before the mirror and looked back at me. He smiled briefly and then pulled down his sunglasses to show the flames leaping up from his eyes.

'Be seeing you, Gideon . . .'

Hell's bounty hunter dragged his prey into the mirror, and the Midnight Man's screams cut off abruptly. The mirror burst into flames, and a few seconds later nothing remained of it but a small pile of ashes.

'I really should have kept up the insurance payments,' said Sidney. 'But I can't say I'll miss it.'

Jessica, the Dandy Devil and Peter bowed solemnly to me and my crew.

'Time to be going,' said Jessica.

'So much to do,' said the Dandy Devil.

'So be good, for goodness' sake,' said Peter.

Suddenly and silently and without any fuss, they were gone.

'Those were seriously scary people,' I said. 'If you think about it.'

'I'm trying very hard not to,' said Sidney.

I looked thoughtfully at Ethel. 'What items did Johnny steal that allowed him to stand off Heaven and Hell?'

'Like I'd tell you,' said Ethel. 'You'd only try to steal them.'

I nodded. 'This is true.'

'One last thing!' Ethel said brightly. 'It didn't seem fair that you should be left with such a depleted crew, Gideon. One rather battered werewolf and an ex-mirror. So I arranged for some replacements.'

She snapped her fingers, and standing before us were the gentleman adventurer Dominic Knight and the elf lady Evadne. He bowed courteously, and she waggled her long fingers artlessly.

'Hello again, Gideon,' said Dominic. 'Good to see you got away safely from the Babel Project.'

'But you're from another reality!' I said.

Dominic shrugged. 'When an angel says you're needed, you don't argue.'

'Quite,' said Evadne, in her smoky sultry voice. 'And it did sound like fun.'

I thought about the Dominic Knight I'd known. A good man who'd died in an accident that wasn't my fault but about which I still felt guilty. I smiled at him.

'Welcome to the crew.'

'We've had stranger,' said Polly.

'This is true,' said Sidney.

'Hello,' said Ethel. 'I must be going.'

And just like that, she was gone, and the world felt so much smaller without her.

Before any of us could say anything, we were interrupted by the sound of a great many feet heading our way. We all turned to look, and the Constant Cutie burst back into the Museum at the head of yet more guards, all of them heavily armed. Cutie glared at me, her face flushed with rage.

'You ruined the best deal I ever had! Messed up all my plans! And made me look like a fool in front of everyone!' She didn't even glance back at the guards. 'Kill them! Kill them all!'

Before the guards could even raise their weapons, Dominic Knight stepped forward and cleared his throat, with the practised authority that comes from being a gentleman adventurer. Everyone stopped to look at him. Dominic looked thoughtfully at Cutie and then turned to me.

'What an appalling person. Has she been bad?'

'Like you wouldn't believe,' I said.

'And the guards?'

'If they work here, it's a safe bet they all have innocent blood on their hands.'

Dominic nodded to Cutie and the guards in a regretful sort of way and then gestured at the elf lady beside him.

'Allow me to present Evadne, Queen of the Elves. Wherever she happens to be.'

Evadne smiled. It wasn't a nice smile. She raised her voice in a raucous call.

'*Hey, rube!*'

And from out of nowhere an endless sea of elves appeared, all flashing teeth and hungry eyes, to fall on Cutie and her guards. They all disappeared from sight under the swarming elves.

Dominic nodded to me. 'Time we were going.'

I led the way out of the Museum. 'This could be the start of a very disturbing friendship.'

'Best kind,' said Evadne.

I hefted the long sword, Ex Caliburn. 'At least I picked up something nice for the shop.'

'I am not polishing that,' said Sidney.

'You will if I tell you to,' said Polly.

'Well,' said Sidney. 'That goes without saying.'

From behind us came a terrible sound of feasting.

SEVEN

The Mastermind Behind It All

Any other time, that would have been the end of the story. A successful heist, someone else's treasure in my hands and a triumph over someone I really couldn't stand. I'd lost two good friends along the way, and I needed time to mourn them properly. I had new friends to welcome to the crew, and an old friend wasn't a mirror any more. But this story wouldn't be over until I found Annie and rescued her from her kidnapper.

I hefted the long sword Ex Caliburn and then thrust it awkwardly through my belt. Sidney raised an eyebrow.

'Are you going to use that to rescue Annie?'

'I don't believe in weapons,' I said. 'Mostly. But I think I'll take it with me. Just in case.'

It was Polly's turn to raise an eyebrow. 'Won't that attract attention?'

'On these streets?' I said. 'Old Soho has always been the kind of area where walking softly and carrying a really big weapon comes as standard.'

Sidney looked at Polly. 'He does have a point.'

'Yes,' said Polly. 'It's on the end of his sword.'

'Your sense of humour has really gone to the dogs,' Sidney said sadly.

'You want me to bite you?' said Polly.

Sidney waggled his eyebrows. 'Where did you have in mind?'

'Hush, children,' I said. 'Daddy has some thinking to do.'

I took Time's Arrow out of my belt. Just a dull wooden shaft and a flat steel head, with no indication as to how you made it work. An Arrow that could remake your past and change everyone else's history along the way really should come with an instruction manual. Dominic Knight moved in beside me and looked incuriously at the Arrow. I held it out for a better view, but he just shrugged, so I put the Arrow back in my belt.

'You do know what's been happening?' I said. 'And why this is so important to me?'

'Of course,' said Dominic. 'The angel was kind enough to brief both of us during the transition from our world to this. Downloaded the information directly into our minds. Very modern thinking, I thought – for an angel.'

Evadne sniffed loudly. 'She could have asked our permission first. Or at the very least warned us what was coming. I have brain cells that will never be the same again. Typical angel, always convinced she knows what's best.'

'To be fair,' said Dominic. 'That is pretty much the definition of an angel.'

Evadne growled, deep in her throat. 'The only person inside my head should be me. If I wanted visitors, I'd put out a sign.'

I thought I'd better change the subject. 'Do you have a Time's Arrow in your world?'

'Not to my knowledge,' said Dominic.

'Elves don't play with toys,' Evadne said loftily. 'We prefer to get our hands dirty. Or bloody, as the case may be.'

I thought of the ravenous elves descending on our enemies at the Museum and changed the subject again.

'Do you know my other self well in your world?'

'We've worked together, on occasion,' said Dominic. 'Good company, but a bit of a rogue.'

'Nasty piece of work,' said Evadne. 'Always getting you into trouble, Dom.' She glanced at me. 'You seem something of an improvement. So far.'

'Does he have an Annie?' I said.

'Not to my knowledge,' said Dominic.

I nodded. 'That would explain a lot.'

And then my phone rang. I stopped, and everyone else stopped with me. I took the phone out and looked at it for a long moment, letting it ring. Very few people knew my private number, and one of them was Annie. I put the phone cautiously to my ear.

'Who is this?'

A male voice answered: cool and flat and deliberately lacking in character.

'You know who this is. I have your Annie. She is perfectly safe, for the moment. Go back to your shop. I'm already inside, waiting for you. And come alone, or you'll never see Annie again.'

'Who is this?' I said.

But the phone had gone dead. I put it away and briefed the others. They all looked at me with the same expression on their face.

'You are not going back there on your own,' said Polly.

'It's a trap!' said Sidney.

'Of course it's a trap,' I said, careful to keep my voice calm and unconcerned. 'But the best way to deal with a trap is to walk into it knowing it's a trap.'

'We're going with you,' said Polly.

'No,' I said.

'You need backup, boss!' said Sidney.

'We'll keep well back and out of sight,' said Polly. 'He'll never know we're there.'

I shook my head. 'I can't risk anything going wrong, not now I'm so close to getting Annie back.'

'Wait a minute, wait a minute!' said Sidney, all but hopping on the spot as he struggled to work something out. 'We're missing something . . . How did the kidnapper know you have Time's Arrow? The kidnapper must be watching us!'

Polly looked around sharply. 'How? There's no one else on the street.'

'I don't know!' said Sidney. 'Maybe he's got a mirror like I used to be.'

'Or perhaps the kidnapper put someone on our trail, to observe from a distance,' said Dominic. 'There's never any shortage of bounty hunters, whatever world you're in.'

'No matter how many you kill,' said Evadne. 'Damned things are worse than cockroaches.'

We all looked up and down the street, but there were no lights at any of the windows, and nothing stirring in the shadows. Polly tilted back her head and sniffed hard at the air.

'I'm not picking up any recent scents . . . No passers-by, no traffic . . . which is odd. Old Soho never sleeps, if only because something might be sneaking up on it.'

'It's like everyone's been warned to stay inside,' said Sidney. 'So they won't have to see something they wouldn't want to be questioned about later.'

'To be fair,' I said, 'that does describe most of Old Soho, most of the time.'

'But there'd always be someone ready to peer past a curtain or lurk in an alleyway,' said Sidney. 'Looking for a chance to make some money on the side. Information is currency in these parts.'

I looked steadily at my crew. 'I have to do this alone.'

'Of course, boss,' said Sidney. 'We get it. You're the man with the plan.'

'I'll take everyone to this nightclub I know,' said Polly. 'I dance there sometimes. The Exploding Petunia.'

I had to smile. 'Is that retro sixties thing still happening?'

'Everything old is new again,' said Polly. 'And the sixties did turn out the best music to dance to. Besides, we need to hold a wake for Lex and Sally. See them off in style, with a great many drinks and some determined debauchery.'

'It's been a long time since I was in a nightclub,' said Sidney. 'Long time since I had a drink . . .' He drifted away on memories for a moment and then smiled at Dominic and Evadne. 'Come on – it'll be fun! We can explore the differences between our world and yours, and get totally shit-faced.'

'I'm always in favour of a few cocktails in a civilized setting,' said Dominic.

'Will there be sex and violence as well?' said Evadne.

'The night is young,' said Polly.

'It's been a long time for a lot of things . . .' Sidney said wistfully.

Polly grinned at him. 'Buy me enough drinks, and we'll see what happens.'

Sidney actually blushed. 'I'd like that. But I am a bit out of practice.'

'Practice makes perfect,' said Polly.

Sidney smiled. 'I am not worthy.'

'What's that got to do with anything?'

Dominic nodded solemnly and slipped his arm through Evadne's. 'It never stopped us.'

Evadne smiled. 'Mortals are such easy prey.'

Sidney looked at her. 'OK . . . Feeling just a bit disturbed now.'

I cleared my throat to bring their attention back to me and fixed Dominic and Evadne with a steady stare.

'I didn't ask Ethel to bring you here, but I do feel responsible. So if you decide you don't like this brave new world, I'll see you get back where you came from.'

Dominic raised an elegant eyebrow. 'You can do that?'

I thought about the Doppelganger Device in my pocket. 'I have my ways and means.'

'Nice to know some things haven't changed,' said Dominic. 'But, so far, I like it here.'

'I've been trying to get him to take a vacation for ages,' said Evadne.

'Then I'll be off,' I said. 'Things to meet, people to do. You know how it is.'

'Are you sure you'll be all right on your own?' said Polly.

'It's my shop,' I said. 'My territory.'

'Watch your back, boss,' said Sidney.

'Always,' I said.

I strode along the empty streets and my footsteps made a steady clatter on the pavements, like the ticking of an aggrieved clock. Only my pride kept me from breaking into a run, now the end was finally in sight. But if the kidnapper really was having me watched, I didn't want him thinking he had me under his thumb. And . . . I needed time to think. I was, after all, the man with the plan. And this time, I was going to need something really special if I was to out-think the man who'd been running rings around me.

My main worry was that he'd demand I hand over Time's Arrow before he let me see Annie. I couldn't do that. Once he had the Arrow, he no longer had any reason to keep her alive. I had to convince him I was ready to destroy the Arrow, rather than give it up for nothing, even if that put Annie at risk.

I couldn't understand why the kidnapper wanted to meet me in my shop. He must know that would give me the advantage. Perhaps he wanted me to feel over-confident, so I wouldn't try hard enough. I sighed. You can't out-think every possibility. All I needed was one big surprise to turn the tables. And my shop was full of surprises.

The long night was finally coming to an end. The sun was heaving itself wearily into the sky, and a great red glare outlined the rooftops, as though someone had set the horizon on fire. I hurried through the empty streets with Ex Caliburn bouncing lightly against my hip. I should have found the time to steal a proper belt and scabbard. But the long blade hardly seemed to weigh a thing, as though the sword had decided to adopt me.

I rounded the corner, and there was my shop waiting for me. I stopped a sensible distance away, so I could check out the scene. Still no one around, which was almost unheard of. The shop seemed perfectly quiet and undisturbed. I walked up to the door and tried the handle. It was locked. So I unlocked it, walked straight in and nodded to the stuffed grizzly bear I'd left on guard.

'Speak up, Yogi. Has anyone entered this shop since I left?'

'Not a living soul,' growled the bear.

'Is there anyone else in the shop?'

The bear shook his shaggy head. 'No. I'd know.'

That wasn't what I'd expected to hear. The kidnapper said he was waiting for me. Could there be some other way in that Old Harry never told me about?

'All right, Yogi,' I said. 'Stand guard. I'm going to check out the back of the shop. No one is to get through that door, until I tell you otherwise.'

'They shall not pass,' said the bear.

I looked quickly about me. There was still a lot of clearing up to be done in the shop itself, after Mark Stone's rampage: damaged shelves and furniture to be replaced. At the thought of all that work, the day's exhaustion hit me like a blow, trembling in my muscles and aching in my bones. I'd been on the move for so long, and now I was close to the end, it was like everything was catching up with me. But I couldn't afford to be tired or muddled in the head, not while Annie needed me. I straightened my aching back through an effort of will and shook my head hard to clear it.

I drew Ex Caliburn from my belt and leaned it against the nearest wall. The kidnapper would never let me anywhere near him with a weapon that powerful. I felt a wave of disappointment from the long sword and patted the crosspiece comfortingly. Another time . . . I patted my belt to make sure Time's Arrow was still there, and my phone rang. It was the same male voice.

'Now you're here, we can get down to business.'

'Where are you?' I said.

'Closer than you think,' said the voice. 'I've been holding Annie in one of your secure back rooms.'

And just like that, a whole bunch of things made sense. That was why no one could locate Annie. Why the bear had been so sure there was no one else in the shop. The secure rooms had shields so powerful not even Heaven or Hell could tell what was being discussed in them.

People paid a lot of money for rooms like that.

'We're in number seven,' said the voice. 'Bring me Time's Arrow, and we'll talk.'

'I'm not making any kind of deal until I see Annie,' I said flatly.

'Of course,' said the voice.

The phone went dead. I put it away and headed into the tall stacks. I strode quickly through the narrow passageways until I reached one particular shelf and my row of security boxes. The one place in the shop where the kidnapper wouldn't be able to see what was happening, because the shields surrounding those boxes were just as powerful as the back rooms.

I stared at one box I hadn't opened since I first placed the thing I was thinking of inside. I don't like weapons, but I always knew the day might come when I would need something really bad, to protect the people I cared about. I unlocked the box, lifted the lid and then very carefully reached inside and brought out the Iscariot Device.

The weapon was old, very old. The gun wore its history of bloodshed and slaughter like a comfortable patina. It had taken many forms down the centuries, but for now it was a gleaming steel revolver, with ivory-inlaid hand grips. It fired silver bullets, fashioned from the thirty pieces paid to Judas to betray the Christ. The Iscariot Device: the gun Lex used to kill two angels.

Afterwards, he put it in pawn with Old Harry, because that was the only place where it would be safe.

I hefted the gun, getting used to its more than natural weight, and then stuffed it in the back of my belt. The kidnapper would never know I had it, because the Device came with its own shields. The kidnapper undoubtedly had his own weapons, but whatever they were, they were nothing compared to the Iscariot Device. I walked on through the shelves, thinking, *Surprise!*

I reached the secure rooms a lot sooner than I expected. As though the stacks were trying to help me, by not playing their usual tricks. I stopped well short of the closed doors, but everything seemed quiet. For a moment, I wished I still had my time pen, to give me the advantage. But I was a professional, so I pushed the thought aside and headed for door number seven.

On any con, you work with what you've got.

I opened the door and pushed it all the way back. 'Hi, honey! I'm home!'

'Come in, Gideon,' said the male voice. 'We've been waiting for you.'

I strode into the room with my best confident swagger, as though I already knew everything that mattered and had a plan in place to deal with all of it. I was being Gideon Sable, master thief, because that was what the situation demanded. The only illumination came from a single hanging light bulb, and the room was only just big enough to contain a table, two very basic chairs and the two people waiting for me.

Annie Anybody was sitting at the far end of the table, and my breath caught in my throat to see her alive and well. She was wearing a simple white T-shirt over blue jeans, no makeup, her hair just a blonde buzzcut. Annie was being herself, and not one of her other personas. I had to wonder what psychological damage being just herself for so long might have done to her. She met my gaze and smiled at me reassuringly.

My first thought was *I'm missing something. And I've been missing it for some time.*

I tore my gaze away from Annie, to stare at the man standing next to her. He wasn't acting like a kidnapper. There was no sense of power over Annie and no sense of any danger. I was shocked to discover I knew the man, though I hadn't seen him in years. It was Sir Norman Powell: businessman and big noise in the City. I used the time pen to steal his most prized possession: a pookah's paw that guaranteed the owner good fortune . . . for as long as he held on to it. I needed it to begin my career as the new Gideon Sable, master thief. So I could bring down Fredric Hammer, the bastard who destroyed my life, and Annie's.

I studied Sir Norman carefully. He didn't seem to feel in any danger from me. The calm and casual way he was standing next to Annie sent my thoughts racing, as I tried to work out what was going on.

From what I remembered, Norman had been an iron-willed tyrant who ran his business as though slavery and oppression had never gone out of fashion. A colourless, heartless bastard, whose Savile Row suit was always going to have more style and character than the man who wore it. A terrible man, who deserved everything that happened to him. But after I robbed the man, I never thought to follow up and see what happened to him. Looking at Norman now, it was clear a lot had happened. His current suit looked as though it had come from a charity shop, and he looked older, tired, worn down and worn out.

He didn't feel like any kind of threat, and my instincts are usually pretty finely tuned when it comes to things like that. Which meant I was completely wrong about what was going on. Annie was in no danger and never had been. I'd been conned, led around by the nose right from the start. Annie must have seen the anger growing in my face because she gestured urgently for me to sit down.

'Please,' she said. 'We brought you here to tell you everything.'

I looked at the chair set out for me, opposite Annie. I sat down, took out Time's Arrow and placed it on the table before me. I kept one hand on it, so no one could take it from me. I didn't miss how Norman's eyes went straight to the Arrow, while Annie kept her gaze fixed on me. I could feel the Iscariot Device pressing against the small of my back.

'I know how you're feeling . . .' said Annie.

'You really don't,' I said. 'Talk to me. Because I'm starting to wonder if I've been played for a sucker.'

My voice must have been harsher than I intended, because Annie actually flinched for a moment.

'This was never about playing you for a fool,' she said. 'This was always about saving you from yourself. Tell him, Norman.'

Norman reluctantly tore his eyes away from Time's Arrow and then took a moment to clear his throat and prepare himself. He was a man with something important to say, and he wanted to be sure it came out clearly. His voice was low, haunted, not at all like the man I remembered.

'After you stole the pookah's paw,' he said steadily, 'I was ruined. Without it, my business collapsed. I lost everything. My homes, my possessions, my money . . . And my trophy wife, who was out the door and gone the moment things started going wrong.' He smiled briefly. 'I never liked her much anyway.

'My friends refused to have anything to do with me, in case failure was catching. My family stopped talking to me. I'd let them down by not being a success, like them. They acted as if I'd done it deliberately, to spite them.' He managed another small smile. 'I never liked them much, either. Though, to be fair, I never gave them much reason to like me.

'Once the good life was gone, I ended up on the streets. Because there was nowhere else that would have me. And for the first time, I made some real friends. I fell in with a group who used to hang out with the Ghost. An actual ghost, haunting that part of London. He stopped coming round, because he was working for you. And once they told me about you, I realized at last who'd robbed me of the paw.

'I became fascinated by your legend: the thief who stole from worse thieves. A modern-day Robin Hood, who stole from the rich and kept it, but wasn't averse to handing out a little justice along the way. And I was pleased to know I had helped to make your legend possible. Eventually, I heard about this shop, so I came here. You weren't in, so I talked to Annie. I told her I just wanted to say *Thank you*. And she said if I really wanted to show my appreciation, I could help her stage her own kidnapping.'

He stopped talking. Annie just sat there, staring at me. I stared back at her.

'You're the mastermind?' I said to her. 'You're responsible for everything I've been through? I've been going out of my mind! Why? Why all of this?'

'I needed you to give up being Gideon Sable if we were to have a life together,' she said calmly. 'You swore to me you'd retired from all that, but you still couldn't resist sneaking out at night, to run some heist or other. Did you think I wouldn't notice? I always believed you could give up being Gideon Sable, because you never were him, really. He's just an identity you stole.'

'I had to,' I said. 'It was the only way I could make us safe from Fredric Hammer. The only way I could win you back.'

'But we've been safe for ages,' said Annie. 'I want the man I used to know. The man I fell in love with originally. With him, I could be Annie all the time and never need to be anybody else. We had a good life together, running this shop, but you were addicted to being Gideon Sable. To the thrill of the heist. You didn't stop, because you couldn't. So I decided to force the issue. To put you in a situation where you couldn't afford to be Gideon Sable any longer. Now you've stolen Time's Arrow from the Midnight Club, you must know they'll never stop coming after you.'

I nodded slowly. She was right. Even with Johnny Occult dead – and three Club Members, and any number of guards – there were still a lot of people left who could point the finger at me. The Members couldn't afford to have word get out that I had burgled their precious Museum, in case that encouraged others to try their luck. Such a blow against their pride would have to be avenged, or they'd never feel safe again.

The most famous members of my crew, Lex and Sally, were dead. Polly had only been seen as a werewolf, and there was never any shortage of them on the scene. Sidney wasn't a mirror any more. Dominic Knight was supposed to be dead. And no one in this world knew Evadne, Queen of the Elves. The only one the Club Members knew about was me.

So the only way to survive . . . was to stop being Gideon Sable. I looked at Annie.

'Did you know Lex and Sally died in the Museum?'

'I saw it happen,' she said quietly. 'We've been watching you all along, on the shop's scrying mirrors. I don't know if I'll ever forgive myself for getting those two involved.'

'There was nothing you could have done. And it did work out well for them, in the end.'

'That's not the point.'

'I know.' I smiled suddenly. 'You used the scrying mirrors? I told you they were a good buy.'

Annie sighed. 'All right, so I was wrong, that time.'

I turned to Norman. 'Why did I have to steal Time's Arrow?'

'That was my price,' he said steadily. 'For helping Annie to help you. I had no right to insist on any conditions, but she indulged me. After I told her what I wanted it for.'

I sat back and looked at him thoughtfully. 'I did wonder why you would want such a thing.'

'Because I want to be someone else,' Norman said flatly. 'To have always been someone else. The life I lived was never one I wanted. My family forced me to take over one of the family businesses, even though I had no interest in it or aptitude for it. I made one bad decision after another, drove things into the ground . . . until I acquired the pookah's paw, quite by accident, and then everything changed. Suddenly, I could do no wrong, and the money kept pouring in . . .

'I became addicted to the good life, just as you were addicted to being Gideon Sable. And I became a monster, because I still wasn't happy. I hurt people, destroyed lives, because inside I was hurting all the time. Trapped in a life I never wanted.

'Time's Arrow will let me travel back into my past and undo all the bad decisions I made. Make all the suffering I caused never happen. Allow me to be the man I always wanted to be. A good man.'

And then he stopped and looked at me.

I thought about it. I'd come all this way to make sure Annie was safe, and she was. I'd wanted to punish the person responsible for kidnapping Annie, but that turned out to be her. I looked at Time's Arrow under my hand and then pushed it across the table toward Norman.

'Take it,' I said. 'It's yours.'

He picked it up, his face full of wonder. And hope, at last.

'Do you have any idea how to work that thing?' I said.

'You just need to want it enough,' he said. 'And I do.'

He disappeared. I stood up, and so did Annie. We moved

quickly round the table and fell into each other's arms, holding each other as if we'd never let go.

'If my quitting meant so much to you,' I said eventually, 'why didn't you just say so?'

'I did,' said Annie. 'But you wouldn't listen. So I had to find a way to get your attention. Fortunately, being around you for so long taught me the art of the con.'

'It's good to know I contributed something to our relationship,' I said.

'Are you ready?' said Annie. 'To give up being Gideon Sable?'

'Yes,' I said. 'I need you more than I ever needed to be him.'

We walked out of the secure room, arm in arm and leaning on each other. Something far back in the stacks started a round of applause, and we bowed regally.

'Let me take you to this nightclub I know,' I said. 'I want you to meet some old friends, and new ones.'

She smiled and nodded, and put her arm around my waist. And then raised an eyebrow.

'Is that a gun in the back of your belt?'

'Just something I need to drop off along the way,' I said. 'Hey! Did you see I picked up this amazing sword for the shop?'

'Yes!' said Annie. 'Ex Caliburn . . . Excalibur! Is it really King Arthur's sword?'

I shrugged. 'That's what Merlin told me.'

Together, we left the stacks behind us and walked back into the shop.

EIGHT

Afterwards

G ideon Sable and Annie Anybody disappeared. A different couple took over running the shop, who looked nothing like them.

A new Gideon Sable appeared on the scene: a middle-aged man, who looked as though he might have been a businessman in another life. A bright and cheerful soul, determined to rob the rich and do something useful with the money. His crew consisted of the gentleman adventurer Dominic Knight, who turned out not to be dead after all, the very scary elf lady Evadne, the exotic dancer and werewolf Polly Perkins and her husband Sidney, who knew all manner of things.

Some said there was a movement in the Vatican to declare Lex Talon a Saint. Which would no doubt have amused him greatly.